Wicked Widow

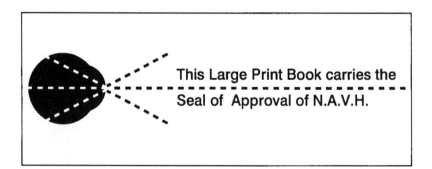

Wicked Widow

Amanda Quick

Thorndike Press • Thorndike, Maine

Large print ed.

3 1759 00131 1244

Published in 2000 by arrangement with Bantam Books, an imprint of the Bantam Dell Publishing Group, a division of Random House, Inc.

Thorndike Large Print Basic Series.

The text of this Large Print edition is unabridged. Other aspects of the book may vary from the original edition.

Set in 16 pt. Plantin by Rick Gundberg.

Printed in the United States on permanent paper.

Library of Congress Control Number: 00-090698
ISBN 0-7862-2596-3 (lg. print : hc : alk. paper)
ISBN 0-7862-2598-X (lg. print : sc : alk. paper)

FOR MARGARET GORDON,
a librarian's librarian,
with thanks

First Prologue

Nightmare . . .

The fire roared as it charged down the back stairs. The glow of the flames cast a hellish light in the hall. There was so little time left. She picked up the key that had fallen from her shaking fingers and tried once more to fit it into the lock of the bedchamber door.

The dead man lying in a pool of blood beside her laughed. She dropped the key again.

Second Prologue

Vengeance . . .

Artemis Hunt inserted the last of the three engraved watch fob seals into the third letter and placed it beside the other two on the desk. He studied the trio of letters in front of him for a long time. Each was addressed with a man's name.

The vengeance he had planned had been a long time in the making, but all of the elements were now in place. Posting the letters to the three men was the first step. It was designed to give them a taste of fear; to make them start looking over their shoulders on dark, fogbound nights. The second step involved an elaborate financial scheme that would ultimately ruin them.

It would have been a simple matter to kill the three. It was no less than they deserved, and with his unique skills he could have carried out the business readily enough. There would have been no great risk of getting caught. He was a master, after all.

But he wanted the three to suffer for what they had done. He wanted them to know first uneasiness and then outright fear. He would deprive them of their arrogance. He would rip away the sense of certainty and security they enjoyed by virtue of their positions in Society. In the end he would deprive them of the resources that enabled them to casually crush those who had been born into less fortunate circumstances than themselves.

Before it was over, they would have ample opportunity to confront the knowledge that they were utterly and completely destroyed in the eyes of the world. They would be forced to flee London, not only to hide from their creditors, but to escape the unrelenting scorn of Society. They would be barred from their clubs and excluded not only from the pleasures and privileges of their class, but from any prospect of repairing their fortunes through advantageous marriages.

In the end, perhaps, they would come to believe in ghosts.

It had been five years since Catherine's death. So much time had passed that the three debauched rakes who had been responsible must surely believe themselves safe. They had probably forgotten the events of that night.

The letters with the seals inside would

shatter their certainty that the past was as dead as the young woman they had destroyed.

He would allow them a few months to become accustomed to the notion of looking over their shoulders before he made his next move, Artemis thought. He would give them time to start to relax their vigilance. Then he would act.

He rose and went to the crystal decanter that sat on a nearby table. He poured himself a glass of brandy and made a silent toast to Catherine's memory.

"Soon," he promised the invisible phantom who haunted him. "I failed you in life, but I swear I will not fail you in death. You have waited long enough for your revenge. I shall give it to you. It is the only thing left that I can do for you. When it is finished, I pray that we will both be free."

He swallowed the brandy and put down the glass. He waited for a moment, but nothing changed.

The cold, empty sensation was still there inside, just as it had been for the past five years. He did not expect to ever know true happiness. Indeed, he was certain that such lightness of feeling was not possible for a man of his temperament. In any event, his training had taught him that joy was as illusory as all the other strong emotions. But he had hoped that launching his vengeance would bring him a sense of satisfaction; perhaps, ultimately, even some peace.

Instead he felt nothing except the unrelenting determination to see the thing through.

He began to suspect that he was doomed.

Nevertheless, he would finish what he had started with the three letters. He had no choice. They called him the Dream Merchant. He would show the three rakes who had murdered Catherine that he could sell nightmares.

Chapter One

They said she'd murdered her husband because she'd found him inconvenient. They said she'd set fire to the house to conceal her crime.

They said she might well be mad.

There was a standing wager in every betting book in every club in St. James Street. It offered a thousand pounds to any man who managed to spend a night with the Wicked Widow and lived to tell the tale.

They said many things about the lady. Artemis Hunt had heard the rumors because he made it a practice to stay informed. He had eyes and ears throughout London. A network of spies and informants brought him an endless tide of gossip, speculation, and snippets of fact.

Some of the flotsam that washed up on his desk was based on truth; some was only probable; some was blatantly false. Sorting through the lot required considerable time and effort. He did not waste either attempting to verify all of the information he received. Much of it he simply ignored because it did not affect his very private affairs.

Until tonight he'd had no reason to pay close attention to the gossip that swirled around Madeline Deveridge. Whether or not the lady had dispatched her husband to the next world had been of no particular concern to him. He had been occupied with other matters.

Until tonight he'd had no interest whatsoever in the Wicked Widow. But now, it seemed, she had developed an interest in him. Most would say that was an extraordinarily ill omen. He was amused to discover that he found it to be quite intriguing, one of the most interesting things to have happened to him in a long, long time. Which, he thought, only went to show how very narrow and circumscribed his life was these days.

He stood in the night-shrouded street and contemplated the small, elegant carriage that loomed in the fog. The vehicle's lamps glowed eerily in the mist that seethed and foamed around it. The curtains were drawn shut, concealing the interior of the cab. The horses stood quietly. The coachman was an indistinguishable mound on the box.

Artemis recalled the adage he had learned years ago from the monks of the Garden Temples who had instructed him in the ancient philosophy and the fighting arts of

14

Vanza. *Life offers an endless banquet of opportunities. Wisdom lies in knowing which ones to taste and which are poison.*

He heard the door of his club open and close behind him. Loud, drunken laughter echoed in the darkness. Absently he moved into the pool of deeper shadow created by a nearby doorway and watched two men stumble down the steps. They clambered into a waiting hackney and shouted directions to the coachman, demanding to be driven to one of the gaming hells in the stews. Boredom was the enemy of their sort. They would go to any lengths to defeat it.

Artemis waited until the old vehicle lumbered off down the street. Then he glanced again at the dark, ethereal little carriage in the mists. The problem with Vanza was that, for all its arcane learning and instructive philosophy, it did not make sufficient allowance for the very human factor of curiosity.

Or at least, it did not make allowance for *his* curiosity.

Artemis made his decision. He moved out of the doorway and walked through the drifting fog to the Wicked Widow's carriage. The stirring of anticipation within him was the only warning he got that he might come to regret his choice. He decided to ignore it.

15

The coachman shifted and tensed as he drew near.

"Can I help ye, sir?"

The words were properly respectful, but Artemis caught the edge beneath the surface. It told him that the man, hunched beneath a many-caped greatcoat and a hat pulled low over his ears, served as guard as well as coachman.

"My name is Hunt. Artemis Hunt. I believe I have an appointment with the lady."

"So yer the one, eh?" The man did not relax. If anything, his tension seemed to increase. "Get in, if ye please, sir. She's expectin' ye."

Artemis raised his brows at the peremptory orders, but he said nothing. Instead he reached for the handle and opened the carriage door.

Warm amber light from the interior lamp spilled out of the opening. A woman sat on one of the black velvet seats. She was dressed in an expensively cut black cloak that concealed all but a glimpse of the black gown underneath. Her face was a pale blur behind a black lace veil. He could see that she was slender. There was a supple, confident grace about her form that told him she was no green, gawky girl fresh out of the schoolroom. He really ought to have paid more attention to the bits and bobs of gossip concerning her that had come his way in the past year, he thought. Ah well, too late now.

"It was good of you to respond so quickly to my note, Mr. Hunt. Time is of the essence."

The voice was low with a throaty undercurrent that ignited a spark of sensual awareness deep inside him. Unfortunately, although her words were laced with crisp urgency, he could detect no promise of passion. Apparently the Wicked Widow had not lured him into her carriage with the intent of seducing him into a night of wild, reckless lovemaking. Artemis sat down and closed the door. He wondered if he ought to be disappointed or relieved.

"Your message reached me just as I was about to play a hand of cards that I was quite certain to win," he said. "I trust that whatever it is you have to say to me, madam, it will make up for the several hundred pounds I was obliged to forgo in order to meet with you."

She stiffened. Her fingers, sheathed in black kid gloves, tightened around the large black reticule on her lap. "Allow me to introduce myself, sir. I am Madeline Reed Deveridge."

"I know who you are, Mrs. Deveridge.

And, as you obviously know who I am, I suggest we skip the formalities and go directly to business."

"Yes, of course." Behind the veil, her eyes glittered with something that might have been irritation. "My maid, Nellie, was kidnapped near the west gate of the Dream Pavilions less than an hour ago. As you are the owner of those pleasure gardens, I expect you to take full responsibility for criminal actions that occur on or near your property. I want you to help me find Nellie."

Artemis felt as if he had plunged into an icy sea. *She knew about his connection to the Dream Pavilions.* How was that possible? When he had received her note, he had considered and discarded half a dozen reasons for tonight's unlikely rendezvous, but none of them came anywhere near this. How could she have learned that he owned the gardens?

He had known the risks of exposure from the outset. But he had thought himself sunk so deep into the Strategies of Concealment and Distraction that no one, with the possible exception of another master of Vanza, could have discovered the truth. And there was no reason another master would come looking for him.

"Mr. Hunt?" Madeline's voice sharp-ened. "Did you hear what I said?"

"Every word, Mrs. Deveridge." To conceal his anger, he deliberately infused his voice with the touch of ennui expected from a gentleman threatened with acute boredom. "But I must admit, I do not comprehend. I believe you have come to the wrong address. If your maid has truly been kidnapped, you must instruct your coachman to drive to Bow Street. There you will no doubt be able to hire a runner to look for her. Here in St. James, we prefer other, less strenuous pursuits."

"Do not play your Vanza games with me, sir. I do not care if you are a full master. As the owner of the Dream Pavilions, it is your responsibility to ensure the safety of those who patronize your establishment. I expect you to take immediate action to find Nellie."

She knew he was Vanza. That was even more alarming than the news that she was aware of his ownership of the Pavilions.

The chill in his gut began to spread. He had a sudden, maddening vision of his carefully wrought scheme brought down in ruins. This extraordinary female had somehow acquired a dangerous amount of information about him.

He smiled to cover his fury and disbelief.

19

"Curiosity impels me to inquire just how you came up with the outlandish notion that I am in any way connected to the Dream Pavilions or the Vanzagarian Society."

"It hardly matters, sir."

"You are wrong, Mrs. Deveridge," he said very softly. "It matters."

Something in his voice obviously affected her. For the first time since he had entered the carriage, she appeared to hesitate. About time, he thought grimly.

But when she finally responded, she was astonishingly cool. "I am aware that you are not only a member of the Vanzagarian Society, but a full master, sir. Once I had ascertained that much about you, I knew to look beneath the surface. Those who are trained in that philosophy are rarely what they seem. They are fond of illusion and inclined toward eccentricity."

This was a thousand times worse than he had feared. "I see. May I ask who told you about me?"

"No one told me, sir. At least, not in the way you mean. I discovered the truth through my own efforts."

Not bloody likely, he thought. "You will explain yourself, madam."

"I really do not have time to go into this now, sir. Nellie is in grave danger. I insist that you help me locate her."

"Why should I bother to help you track down your runaway maid, Mrs. Deveridge? I'm sure you can acquire another readily enough."

"Nellie did not run away. I told you, she was kidnapped by villains. Her friend Alice saw it all."

"Alice?"

"The pair went to see the newest attractions at the Pavilions this evening. When they left the gardens by the west gate, two men snatched Nellie. They bundled her into a carriage and drove off before anyone realized what had happened."

"I think it far more probable that your Nellie ran off with a young man," Artemis said bluntly. "And her friend concocted the kidnapping story so that if Nellie changes her mind, you'll allow her to return to her post."

"Rubbish. Nellie was seized straight off the street."

Belatedly he reminded himself that the Wicked Widow was reputed to be mad. "Why would anyone kidnap your maid?" he asked, reasonably enough, he thought, under the circumstances.

"I fear she was taken away by some of those vile men who supply innocent young women to the brothels." Madeline picked up a black parasol. "Enough of these explanations. We have not a moment to lose."

Artemis wondered if she intended to use the point of the parasol to prod him into action. He was relieved when she grasped the handle and rapped the tip smartly on the roof of the carriage. The coachman had obviously been listening intently for the signal. The vehicle rumbled immediately into motion.

"What the devil do you think you're doing?" Artemis said. "Has it occurred to you that I might object to being kidnapped myself?"

"I do not particularly care about your objections, sir." Madeline settled back into her seat. Her eyes glittered through the lace veil. "Finding Nellie is the only thing that matters at the moment. I shall apologize to you later, if necessary."

"I'll look forward to that. Where are we going?"

"Back to the scene of the kidnapping. The west gate of your pleasure garden, sir."

Artemis narrowed his eyes. She did not sound mad. She sounded extremely determined. "What, precisely, do you expect me to do, Mrs. Deveridge?"

"You own the Dream Pavilions. And you

are Vanza. Between the two, I suspect that you have connections in places I do not."

He considered her for a long while. "Are you implying that I am acquainted with members of the criminal class, madam?"

"I would not presume to guess the extent, let alone the nature, of your web of associates."

The scorn in her voice was particularly interesting, coming as it did on top of her unsettling knowledge concerning his very private business affairs. One thing was certain: He could not get out of the carriage and walk away at this juncture. Her knowledge of his ownership of the Pavilions was, on its own, more than enough to wreak havoc with his carefully laid plans.

He was no longer amused by his own curiosity and anticipation. It was imperative that he discover not only how much Madeline Deveridge knew, but how she had come to learn such carefully concealed facts.

He lounged in the corner of the black velvet seat and studied her veiled features.

"Very well, Mrs. Deveridge," he said. "I will do what I can to help you recover your missing maid. But do not blame me if it transpires that young Nellie does not wish to be found."

She reached out to lift a corner of the window curtain and peered into the fog-bound street. "I assure you, she will want to be rescued."

His attention was caught and briefly held by the graceful, gloved hand that grasped the edge of the curtain. He was unwillingly fascinated by the delicate curve of wrist and palm. He caught the faint, tantalizing scent of some flowery herbs she must have used in her bathwater. With an effort he brought his attention back to the more pressing issue.

"Regardless of how this matter is concluded, madam, I had better warn you that when it is finished, I will want some answers of my own."

She turned her head quite sharply to stare at him. "Answers? What sort of answers?"

"Do not mistake me, Mrs. Deveridge. I am extremely impressed with the quantity and quality of the information you possess. Your sources must be excellent. But I fear you know a bit too much about me and my affairs."

It had been a desperate gamble, but she had won. She was face-to-face with the mysterious Dream Merchant, the secret owner of London's most exotic pleasure garden. Madeline was well aware that she had taken a great risk by letting him know that she knew his identity. He had good reason to be concerned, she thought. He moved in high circles in the Polite World. He was on the guest list of every important hostess of the ton, and he was a member of all the best clubs. But even his fortune would not protect him from the social disaster that would ensue if Society discovered that it had admitted to its most exclusive ranks a gentleman who had *gone into trade.*

She had to acknowledge that he had carried off an audacious performance. Indeed, Hunt had crafted a role for himself that was worthy of the great Edmund Kean. He had successfully managed to keep his identity as the Dream Merchant a secret. No one thought to question the source of his wealth. He was a gentleman, after all. Gentlemen did not discuss such matters unless it became obvious that a man had run out of money altogether, in which case he became the subject of considerable scorn and a great deal of vicious gossip. More than one man had put a pistol to his head rather than face the scandal of financial ruin.

There was no getting around it. She had virtually blackmailed Hunt into helping her tonight, but she'd had no other choice. There would certainly be a price to pay. Artemis Hunt was a Vanza master, one of the most skilled gentlemen who had ever studied the arcane arts. Such men tended to be extremely secretive by nature.

Hunt had gone to great lengths to hide his Vanza past — a very ominous move indeed. Unlike his ownership of the Dream Pavilions, a membership in the Vanzagarian Society would do him no harm in social circles. Only gentlemen studied Vanza, after all. Yet he was intent on cloaking himself in mystery. That did not bode well.

In her experience the majority of the members of the Vanzagarian Society were harmless crackpots. Others were no worse than enthusiastic eccentrics. A few were quite mad, however. And some were truly dangerous. Artemis Hunt, she began to believe, might well be in that last category. When this night's business was finished, she could find herself facing an entirely new host of problems.

As if she did not already have enough to keep her occupied. On the other hand, given her inability to sleep through the night lately, she might as well keep busy, she thought glumly.

A shiver went through her. She realized that she was very conscious of the manner in which Hunt seemed to occupy a great deal of the interior of the small carriage. In overall size he was not as large as her coachman, Latimer, but there was an impressive breadth to his shoulders and a dangerously languid grace about him that disturbed her senses in some peculiar manner she could not explain. The watchful intelligence in his eyes only served to heighten the unsettling sensation.

She realized that in spite of all that she knew about him, she was fascinated by him.

She wrapped her cloak more tightly around herself. *Don't be a fool,* she thought. The last thing she had ever wanted to do was become involved with another member of the Vanzagarian Society.

But it was too late to change her mind. She had made her decision. Now she must follow through on her scheme. Nellie's very life might depend upon this bold stroke.

The carriage clattered to a stop, shaking her out of her uneasy thoughts. Artemis reached out and turned down the carriage lamp. Then he grasped the curtain and pulled it aside. She watched, unwillingly riveted by the controlled power of his movements as he looked out into the night.

"Well, madam, we have arrived at the west gate. As you can see, it is quite busy, even at this hour. I cannot believe any young girl could be spirited off in a carriage in front of so many people. Not unless she wished to be carried away."

Madeline leaned forward to examine the scene. The grounds were lit with a multitude of colorful lamps. The low price of a ticket made it possible for people from all walks of life to purchase an evening's entertainment inside the Dream Pavilions. Ladies and gentlemen, members of the country gentry, shopkeepers, apprentices, maids, footmen, dandies, military officers, rakes, and rogues — all came and went through the brightly illuminated gates.

Hunt had a point, she thought. There were any number of people and vehicles in the vicinity. It would have been difficult for a woman to be dragged forcibly into a carriage without someone taking notice.

"The kidnapping did not take place directly in front of the gate," Madeline said. "Alice told me that she and Nellie were standing at the entrance to a nearby lane waiting for the carriage I sent to fetch them when the ruffians appeared." She studied the dark entrance to a narrow street. "She must have meant that corner over there where those young boys are loitering about."

"Hmm."

His skepticism was palpable. Madeline glanced at him, alarmed. If he did not take the matter seriously, they would achieve nothing tonight. She knew that time was running out. "Sir, we must hurry. If we do not move swiftly, Nellie will disappear into the stews. It will be impossible to find her."

Artemis allowed the curtain to fall back into place over the window. His hand closed on the door handle. "Remain here. I shall return in a few minutes."

She sat forward quickly. "Where are you going?"

"Calm yourself, Mrs. Deveridge. I have no intention of abandoning the quest. I shall return after I have made a few inquiries."

He vaulted lightly down from the carriage and shut the door before she could demand further details. Irritated and dismayed by the manner in which he had suddenly taken charge, she watched him walk toward the entrance to the dark lane.

She saw him make a few deft adjustments to his greatcoat and hat and was astonished at the result. Within a few steps he had completely altered his appearance.

Although he no longer looked like a gentleman who had just come from his club, he still moved with a fluid self-confidence that she recognized immediately. It was so very similar to the way Renwick had carried himself that it sent a shudder through her. She would forever associate that sleek, prowling stride with skilled practitioners of the fighting arts of Vanza. She wondered again if she had made a grave mistake.

Stop it, she scolded herself. *You knew what you were about tonight when you sent the message into his club. You wanted his assistance and now, for better or worse, you have got it.*

On the positive side, in terms of his physical appearance, Hunt bore no resemblance at all to her dead husband. For some reason she found that fact oddly reassuring. With his blue eyes, pale hair, and romantically handsome features, Renwick had mocked the golden-haired angels in the paintings of the great artists.

Hunt, on the other hand, could have posed for the devil himself.

It was not just his near-black hair, green eyes, and stark, ascetic face that gave the impression of dark, unplumbed depths. It was the cold, knowing expression in his gaze that sent icy little frissons along her nerves. This was a man who had explored the outer reaches of hell. Unlike Renwick, who charmed everyone who came near him with a sorcerer's ease, Hunt looked every bit as dangerous as he no doubt was.

As she watched, he disappeared into the waves of shadow that lapped at the island of bright lights that was the Dream Pavilions.

Latimer climbed down from the box. He appeared at the window, his broad face creased with anxiety.

"I don't like this, ma'am," he said. "Should have gone to Bow Street to find a runner instead."

"You may be right, but it is too late to try that approach now. I have committed us to this path. I can only hope —" She broke off as Hunt materialized behind Latimer. "Oh, there you are, sir. We were beginning to worry."

"This is Short John." Artemis indicated a thin, wiry, unkempt lad of no more than ten or eleven years. "He will accompany us."

Madeline frowned at Short John. "It's quite late. Shouldn't you be in bed, young man?"

Short John's head came up in an unmistakable gesture of deeply offended pride. He spit quite expertly on the pavement. "I'm not in that line o' work, ma'am. I'm in a respectable trade, I am."

Madeline stared at him. "I beg your pardon? What do you sell?"

"Information," Short John said cheerfully. "I'm one of Zachary's Eyes and Ears."

"Who is Zachary?"

"Zachary works for me," Artemis said, cutting short what would obviously have proved to be an involved explanation. "Short John, allow me to present Mrs. Deveridge."

Short John grinned, jerked off his cap, and gave Madeline a surprisingly graceful bow. "At yer service, ma'am."

Madeline inclined her head in response. "It is a pleasure, Short John. I hope you can help us."

"I'll do me best, ma'am."

"Enough, we cannot waste any more time." Artemis glanced at Latimer as he reached for the handle of the carriage door. "Hurry, man. Short John here will guide you. We are going to a tavern in Blister Lane. The Yellow-Eyed Dog. Do you know it?"

"Not the tavern, sir, but I know Blister Lane." Latimer's face darkened. "Is that where the villains took my Nellie?"

"So Short John tells me. He will ride with you on the box." Artemis opened the door and glided into the carriage. "Let us be off."

Latimer bounded back onto his seat. Short John scrambled up behind him. The carriage was in motion before Artemis got the door closed.

"Your man is certainly anxious to find Nellie," he observed as he took his seat.

"Latimer and Nellie are sweethearts," Madeline explained. "They intend to wed soon." She tried to read his face. "How did you learn that Nellie had been taken to this tavern?"

"Short John saw the entire event."

She stared at him, astonished. "Why on earth didn't he report the crime?"

"As he told you, he's a man of business. He can't afford to give away his stock-in-trade. He was waiting for Zachary to make his usual rounds to collect information, which would, in turn, have been turned over to me in the morning. But I showed up to-night instead, so the boy sold his wares to me. He knows that I can be trusted to give Zachary his usual fee."

"Good heavens, sir, are you telling me that you employ an entire network of informants such as Short John?"

He shrugged. "I pay them much higher wages than the receivers to whom most of them used to sell the odd stolen watch or candlestick. And when Zachary and his Eyes and Ears deal with me, they do not risk being clapped into prison as they did when they were employed in their former careers."

"I don't understand. Why would you pay

for the sort of rumors and gossip a gang of young ruffians might collect on the streets?"

"You'd be amazed at what one can learn from such sources."

She sniffed delicately. "I do not doubt that the information would indeed be quite astounding. But why would a gentleman in your position want to know any of it?"

He said nothing. He just looked at her. His eyes gleamed with humorless amusement as he withdrew into some dark place within himself.

What had she expected? she wondered. She should have guessed that he would be a thorough-going eccentric.

She cleared her throat. "No offense, sir. It is just that it all sounds somewhat, uh, unusual."

"So very arcane, complex, and secretive, do you mean?" Artemis's voice was far too polite. "So very Vanza?"

Best to change the subject, Madeline thought. "Where is this Zachary person tonight?"

"He is a young man of a certain age," Artemis said dryly. "He is out courting his young lady this evening. She works in a milliner's shop. This is her night off. He will be sorry to learn that he missed the adventure."

34

"Well, at least we know what happened. I told you Nellie did not run off with a man."

"So you did. Are you always so quick to remind people when you have the right of the matter?"

"I cannot be bothered to beat about the bush, sir. Not when it comes to something as important as an innocent young woman's safety." She frowned as a thought struck her. "How did Short John learn the location where Nellie was taken?"

"He followed the carriage on foot. He told me it was not difficult because the traffic was moving so slowly on account of the fog." Artemis smiled grimly. "Short John is a bright lad. He knew that a young woman being carried off near one of the entrances to the Pavilions was just the sort of tidbit for which I would pay very well."

"I should think that you would indeed want to be aware of such criminal activity taking place in the vicinity of your place of business. After all, as the proprietor of the Pavilions you do have a certain responsibility."

"Quite right." Artemis seemed to withdraw even deeper into the shadows. "Can't have that sort of thing going on in the neighborhood. Bad for business."

Chapter Two

The thick glass panes in the windows of the Yellow-Eyed Dog glowed with an evil light. The fire on the hearth created menacing shadows that lurched and swayed like so many drunken ghosts.

The inhabitants were no doubt drunk, Artemis thought, but they were certainly not harmless phantoms. Most were likely armed. The Yellow-Eyed Dog was a gathering place for some of the roughest elements of the stews.

Madeline studied the scene intently through the carriage window. "Luckily, I thought to bring along my pistol."

He managed not to groan aloud. He had been in her company for no more than an hour, but he already knew the lady well enough not to be startled by that piece of news.

"You will be good enough to keep it in your reticule," he said very firmly. "I prefer not to resort to pistols if they can be avoided. They tend to precipitate untidy messes."

"I am well aware of that," she said.

He recalled the rumors he had heard concerning the demise of her husband. "Yes, I imagine you are."

"Nevertheless," Madeline continued, "snatching a young woman off the street is hardly a tidy crime, sir. I suspect it will not have a tidy solution."

He set his jaw. "If your Nellie is inside the Dog, I should be able to retrieve her without the use of a pistol."

Madeline still looked doubtful. "I don't think that will be possible, Mr. Hunt. The patrons appear to be a rough lot."

"All the more reason to avoid loud noises that would draw their attention." He fixed her with a meaningful look. "My plan will work unless you fail to follow instructions, madam."

"I have agreed to abide by your scheme, and I will do so." She paused delicately. "Unless, of course, something goes awry."

He would have to be content with that weak promise, he thought. The Wicked Widow was obviously accustomed to giving orders, not taking them. "Very well, let us be about the business. You understand your role?"

"Do not concern yourself, sir. Short John and I will have the carriage waiting at the mouth of the alley."

"See that you do. I will be more than a little annoyed if I come out the back door with Nellie and see no handy means of leaving the vicinity." Artemis tossed his hat down onto the seat and got out of the cab.

Latimer turned the ribbons over to Short John and climbed down from the box to join Artemis. He looked even larger standing on the street than he had huddled on the driver's box. The coachman's massive shoulders blotted out much of the glow of the single carriage lamp.

Artemis remembered his early impression of Latimer. *More guard than coachman.*

"I've got me pistol, sir," Latimer assured him.

"Do you and your employer always go about armed to the teeth?"

Latimer appeared surprised by the question. "Aye, sir."

Artemis shook his head. "And she thinks me eccentric. Never mind, are you ready?"

"Aye, sir." Latimer glowered at the windows of the Yellow-Eyed Dog. " 'Od's teeth, if they've harmed my Nellie, I'll make every last one of 'em pay."

"I doubt that there has been enough time to harm the lass." Artemis started across the street. "To be blunt, if she was kidnapped with the intention of selling her to a brothel, the bastards will have been careful not to do anything that would lower her, ah, value in that particular market, if you take my meaning."

Latimer stiffened with dread and rage. "I comprehend ye well enough, sir. I've heard they sell the girls in auctions the same way horses are sold off at Tattersall's. The poor things go to the highest bidder."

"Never fear, we will get to her in time," Artemis said quietly.

Latimer turned his head. His face was a bleak mask in the yellow light that flared through the tavern windows. "If we get my Nellie safely out of here tonight, I want ye to know that I'll be in yer debt for the rest of me life, sir."

The poor man was in love, Artemis thought. Unable to think of any further words of reassurance, he squeezed Latimer's shoulder briefly. "Remember," Artemis said, "give me fifteen minutes, no more, and then create a distraction." He moved into the shadows.

"Aye, sir." Latimer stalked to the door of the tavern door, opened it, and disappeared inside.

Artemis went into the alley that led to the back of the tavern. Within three steps he was enveloped in a tide of foul odors. The narrow passage had obviously been used as a privy as well as a place to toss refuse. His boots would be badly in need of cleaning when this affair was finished tonight.

He reached the rear of the alley, turned the corner, and found himself in what had once been a garden. The tavern privy loomed in the corner. The door to the kitchen stood open to admit the night air. One floor above, a light glowed from a window.

Artemis pulled the collar of his greatcoat up to conceal his profile as he strode toward the kitchen door. If anyone noticed him, he would pass himself off as just one more drunken rake who had wandered into the stews in search of debauchery and entertainment.

He found the rear stairs and took them two at a time to the upper floor. On the landing he heard the muffled voices of two men. A fierce quarrel was in full boil behind one of the doors that opened off the darkened hall.

"She's a prime bit o' muslin, I tell ye. We can get twice as much for her from that old bawd who operates the house in Rose Lane."

"I made a bargain, damn yer bloody eyes, and I ain't goin' back on it. Got me reputation to think of."

"This is a business we're in, ye great fool, not a gennelman's sport with proper rules and the like. The point is to make money, and I'm tellin' ye, she'll fetch a lot more blunt if we market her to the brothel keeper in Rose —"

The argument was interrupted by a sudden uproar from the ground floor. Shouts and cries of alarm echoed up the stairwell. Artemis recognized the loudest of the voices. It belonged to Latimer.

"Fire! Fire in the kitchen! Run fer yer lives, the place is goin' up like a torch!"

A thunderous pounding ensued. The sound of heavily booted feet heading toward the door, Artemis surmised. He heard a rumble and crash as a large object, a table perhaps, overturned.

He tried the first knob he came to in the hall. It turned easily. He opened the door partway and paused. His senses told him that the unlit room was empty. He stepped inside, leaving the door slightly ajar.

"Sound the alarm!" Latimer's muffled voice rose in a yell. "The smoke is so thick in the kitchen ye can't see yer bloody hand in front o' yer face now."

The second door in the upstairs hall slammed open. Artemis watched from the shadows as a broad, muscular man appeared. He was followed by a thin, rat-faced companion. The light from the lamp inside the room revealed their rough clothing and uncertain expressions.

"What the bloody hell is goin' on?" the large man asked of no one in particular.

"Ye heard the cry." The thin man tried and failed to edge around the other man. "There's a fire. I can smell the smoke. We've got to get out of here."

"What about the girl? She's worth too much to leave behind."

"She's not worth me life." The thin man finally managed to force his way out into the hall. He dashed toward the front stairs. "Ye can carry her if ye feel like goin' to the trouble."

The big man hesitated. He glanced back into the lamp-lit room. Frustration warred with desperation on his coarse features. "Bloody, friggin' hell."

Unfortunately, greed won out. The man swung around and started back into the small chamber. He reappeared a minute later with an unconscious woman slung over his beefy shoulder.

Artemis moved out into the hall. "Allow me to assist you in rescuing the young lady."

The big man scowled furiously. "Get out

o' me bleedin' way."

"Sorry." Artemis stepped aside.

The big man stormed past, heading for the front stairs. Artemis stuck out a boot and simultaneously struck the villain with a short chop to the vulnerable area between neck and shoulder.

The man howled as his left arm and most of his left side went numb. He stumbled and tripped headlong over Artemis's outstretched boot. He released Nellie to put out his right arm in a vain attempt to break his fall.

Artemis scooped up Nellie before the man hit the floor. He draped the girl across his own shoulder and made for the rear stairs. Down below he could hear the sounds of people attempting to flee through the kitchen door.

A figure loomed halfway up the narrow stairs.

"Have ye got her?" Latimer demanded. Then he caught sight of Artemis's burden. "*Nellie!* She's dead!"

"Just asleep. Probably dosed with laudanum or some such concoction. Come, man, we must make haste."

Latimer did not argue. He turned and led the way back down the stairs. Artemis followed swiftly.

When they reached the ground floor, it was obvious that they were among the last to vacate the premises. Smoke roiled in the kitchen.

"You may have overdone things with the lamp oil in the cooking fire," Artemis observed.

"Ye never said how much to use," Latimer growled.

"Never mind, it worked."

They hurried through the garden and turned down the alley. Several people were milling around in the street, but the overall air of panic was diminishing rapidly. The lack of flames was no doubt hampering the effectiveness of the illusion, Artemis thought. He saw one man, possibly the tavern proprietor, tentatively start back into the building.

"Let us be quick about this," Artemis ordered.

"Aye, sir."

The carriage was there, precisely where Artemis had instructed it to wait. At least the woman had followed orders. Short John was on the box, the reins in his hands. The door of the vehicle flew open as Artemis approached.

"You have her!" Madeline cried. "Thank God."

She reached out to help Artemis angle Nellie through the small opening. Latimer jumped up to take charge of the team.

Artemis got Nellie through the door and made to follow.

"Hold right where ye are, ye bloody, thievin' bastard, or I'll lodge a bullet in yer spine."

Artemis recognized the voice. The thin man.

"Latimer, get us out of here." Artemis launched himself through the door and pulled it closed behind him.

He reached out to drag Madeline off the seat and down onto the floor so that she would not be silhouetted in the window. But she resisted for some unfathomable reason. Artemis felt her struggle against him as the coach lurched into motion. She raised her arm. He glimpsed the small pistol in her hand, inches from his ear.

"No!" he yelled. But he knew that it was too late. He released her and clapped his hands over his ears.

There was a flash of light. Inside the small cab the pistol's roar was as loud as a cannon.

Artemis was vaguely aware of the carriage jolting forward, but the accompanying noise of wheels and hooves was a distant buzz. He opened his eyes and saw Madeline gazing anxiously down at him. Her lips were moving but he could not hear a word she was saying.

She grasped him by the shoulders and shook him. Her mouth opened and closed again. He realized she was asking him if he was all right.

"No," he said. His ears were ringing now. He could not be certain of the volume of his own voice. He hoped he was shouting. He certainly felt like shouting. "No, I am not all right. Bloody hell, madam, I can only pray that you have not permanently deafened me."

Chapter Three

The fumes that wafted from the open door of the stillroom smelled of vinegar, chamomile, and elder flowers. Madeline paused and glanced around the corner into the small chamber.

With its collection of flasks, mortars and pestles, and various sized jars, together with the abundant assortment of dried herbs and flowers, the stillroom always put Madeline in mind of a laboratory. Her aunt, enveloped in a large apron and bent industriously over a bubbling flask, could have been mistaken for some mad alchemist.

"Aunt Bernice?"

"One moment, dear." Bernice did not look up from her work. "I am right in the midst of an infusion."

Madeline hovered impatiently in the opening. "I am sorry to interrupt you, but I want to ask your opinion on a very important matter."

"Of course. Just another few minutes. The potency of this particular tonic is entirely dependent upon the length of time the flowers are allowed to steep in the vinegar."

Madeline folded her arms and propped one shoulder against the doorjamb. There was no point in rushing her aunt when she was engaged in concocting one of her potions. Thanks to Bernice, Madeline was quite certain the household possessed the largest assortment of soothing brews, strengthening infusions, medicinal jellies, and other such remedies in all of London.

Bernice was passionate about her tonics and elixirs. She claimed to suffer from weak nerves, and she was forever experimenting with therapeutic treatments for her condition. In addition, she was dedicated to the diagnosis of similar problems in others and was given to preparing special remedies for them based on their temperaments.

Bernice spent hours researching ancient recipes for various concoctions and decoctions designed to treat afflictions of the nerves. She was acquainted with every apothecary in town, especially the select few who sold rare Vanzagarian herbs.

Madeline would have been less patient with her aunt's hobby if it were not for two things. The first was that Bernice's remedies frequently proved remarkably efficacious. The herbal tea she had given to Nellie that morning had had a wonderfully soothing effect on the maid's overwrought nerves.

The second reason was that no one understood better than Madeline did how very necessary such distractions were on occasion. The events of that dark night nearly a year ago had been sufficient to put a severe strain on even the sturdiest nerves. The troubling occurrences of the past few days had only made matters worse.

Bernice was in her early forties, a dainty, spirited, attractive woman with a quick mind. Years ago she had been a high flyer in social circles, but she had given up the glitter of Society to take charge of her brother's infant daughter after Elizabeth Reed died.

"Finished." Bernice whisked the flask off the flame and poured the contents through a strainer into a pan. "Now it must cool for an hour."

She wiped her hands on her apron as she turned toward Madeline. Her silver-blue eyes gleamed with satisfaction. "What was it you wanted to discuss with me, dear?"

"I fear that Mr. Hunt will make good on his promise to pay a call on us this afternoon," Madeline said slowly.

Bernice arched her brows. "He is not intending to call upon us, dear. It is you he wishes to visit."

"Yes, well, the thing is, last night after

seeing us safely home, he told me quite bluntly that he will have some questions to ask."

"Questions?"

Madeline exhaled slowly. "Concerning how I came to know so much about him and his business affairs."

"Well, of course, dear. One can hardly blame the man. After all, he has gone to a great deal of trouble to hide several aspects of his private life. Then, one night, from out of nowhere, a woman he has never met summons him from his club and demands his assistance in rescuing her maid. In the process, she informs him that she knows full well that he is not only the secret proprietor of the Dream Pavilions, but a master of Vanza. Any man in his position would be quite naturally alarmed."

"He was not at all cheerful about the matter, that is for certain. I don't expect it will be a pleasant discussion. But after what he did for us last night, I feel it would be churlish to refuse to see him today."

"Churlish indeed," Bernice said. "From the sound of things, he rose to the status of hero last night. Latimer has been exclaiming over Mr. Hunt's exploits all morning."

"It's all very well for Latimer to paint

Hunt as a heroic figure. I'm the one who must confront him today and explain to him how I came to know the intimate details of his business affairs."

"I can see how that will be a trifle awkward." Bernice eyed her shrewdly for a few seconds. "You are anxious because although you were content to make use of Mr. Hunt's skills last night, you do not know what to do with him this morning."

"He is Vanza."

"That does not automatically make him a devil. Not all gentlemen who are members of the Vanzagarian Society are like Renwick Deveridge." Bernice took a step forward and put her hand on Madeline's arm. "You need look no farther than your own dear father to know the truth of that."

"Yes, but —"

"There is nothing in your records to indicate that Hunt is inclined toward evil, is there?"

"Well, no, but —"

"Indeed, he was evidently quite reasonable about matters last night."

"I gave him very little choice."

Bernice cocked a brow. "Do not be too sure of that. I have a hunch that Hunt could have made himself far more difficult to manage had he wished to do so."

51

A flicker of hope went through Madeline. "Do you know, Aunt Bernice, you may have a point. Hunt was amazingly cooperative last night."

"I'm sure you will be able to explain everything to him this morning in a manner that will satisfy him."

Madeline thought about the relentless intent she had glimpsed in his eyes when he had left her at the door last night. The brief flare of relief faded. "I'm not so certain of that."

"Your problem is nothing more than overwrought nerves." Bernice reached for a small blue bottle that stood on the table. "Here, take a spoonful of this when you have your tea. You will be feeling yourself in no time."

"Thank you, Aunt Bernice." Absently, Madeline took the bottle.

"I wouldn't worry too much about Mr. Hunt," Bernice said briskly. "I expect his chief concern is that you do not reveal his identity as the Dream Merchant. One cannot blame him. He is moving in some very exclusive circles at the moment."

"Yes." Madeline frowned. "I wonder why. He does not seem the sort who would give a fig about the Polite World."

"Looking for a wife, no doubt," Bernice

said with airy assurance. "If it got out that he was in trade, his search would be considerably narrowed."

"A wife?" Madeline was startled by her own response to Bernice's deduction. Why was she taken aback at the notion that Hunt was concealing his business connections because he was shopping for a wife? It was a perfectly logical conclusion. "Yes, of course. I hadn't thought of that possibility."

Bernice gave her a knowing look. "That is because you are far too busy envisioning dire conspiracies and reading ominous portents into the smallest, most ordinary occurrences these days. No wonder your nerves are so inflamed that you cannot sleep well."

"You may be right." Madeline turned to go down the hall. "One thing is certain, I must convince Hunt that his secrets are safe with me."

"I'm sure you'll accomplish that with very little trouble, my dear. You are nothing if not resourceful."

Madeline went into the library. She paused to empty the contents of the blue bottle into the potted palm near the window. Then she sat down behind her desk and thought about Artemis Hunt.

Bernice was right. Hunt had been remarkably cooperative last night. He had also displayed a useful degree of skill. Perhaps he could be induced to be even more helpful in the future.

Artemis lounged in his chair, propped an ankle on one knee, and idly tapped a letter opener against his boot. He regarded the sturdy looking man who sat across from him on the other side of the wide desk.

Henry Leggett had been Artemis's man of affairs since before he'd had anything significant in the way of business affairs to handle. He'd more or less inherited Henry from his father.

Not that Carlton Hunt had had much use for Henry's services. Artemis had been fond of his sire, but there was no denying that Carlton had had little interest in investing for the future. After the death of his wife, the small concern he'd had for managing what was left of the Hunt family fortune had vanished altogether.

Henry and Artemis had both been obliged to watch helplessly while all of Henry's sound advice was ignored by a man who lived for gambling and reckless adventures in the stews. In the end it had been Henry who had come up to Oxford to inform Artemis that Carlton had got himself killed in a duel over a disputed hand of cards. It was

Henry who had sadly reported that there was nothing left in the family coffers.

Alone in the world, Artemis had resorted to the gaming hells himself in order to survive. Unlike his father, he'd had a certain knack for cards. But the life of a gamester was precarious at best.

One night Artemis had encountered an elderly gentleman who had won with methodical efficiency. The others had all played with bottles of claret at their sides, but the old man had had nothing to drink. Unlike his companions, who picked up their cards and tossed them down with fashionable indifference, the winner had paid strict attention to what he held in his hand.

Artemis had quietly excused himself from the table midway through the game because he could see that, in the end, they would all lose to the unknown gentleman. Eventually the stranger had picked up his winning vouchers and left the club. Artemis had followed him out into the street.

"What would it cost me to learn to play cards the way you do, sir?" he asked just as the man was about to climb into a waiting carriage.

The stranger examined Artemis with cool, considering eyes for a full moment.

"The price would be quite high," he said.

"Not many young men would wish to pay it. But if you are serious in your intentions, you may call on me tomorrow. We will discuss the matter of your future."

"I don't have much money." Artemis smiled wryly. "In point of fact, I have considerably less now than I did earlier in the evening, thanks to you, sir."

"You were the only one who had the sense to quit when you saw the way things were going," the stranger said. "You might have the makings of an excellent student. I shall look forward to meeting with you in the morning."

Artemis had been on the stranger's doorstep at eleven o'clock the next day. The moment he had been admitted, he had realized that he was in the home of a scholar, not a professional gamester. He soon discovered that George Charters was a mathematician by inclination and training.

"I was merely experimenting with a notion I came up with a few months ago concerning the probability of certain numbers appearing in a series of card hands," he'd explained. "I have no great interest in making my living at the tables, however. Much too unpredictable for my taste. What about you, sir? Do you intend to spend your life in the hells?"

"Not if I can help it," Artemis had replied readily. "I would prefer a career that was rather more predictable myself."

George Charters had been Vanza. It had suited him to instruct Artemis in some of the basic notions of the philosophy. When he had realized that he had a willing and adept pupil, he had offered to pay Artemis's passage to the Isle of Vanzagara. Henry Leggett had agreed that he should seize the opportunity.

Artemis had spent a total of four intense years in the Garden Temples, returning to England every summer to visit with George and Henry, and with his lover, Catherine Jensen.

On his last visit, Artemis had arrived to discover that George was dying of a heart ailment and Catherine had been killed in a mysterious fall.

Henry had stood at his side during both funerals. When they were over, Artemis had announced that he would not return to Vanzagara. He intended to stay in England and make his fortune and seek his revenge. Henry had not been keen on the notion of vengeance, but he had approved of the fortune-making scheme. He had accepted his offer of a post.

Henry had proved quite brilliant, not only

at managing investments with great discretion, but also at learning intimate details concerning the financial affairs of others. Henry provided Artemis with the sort of information that Zachary's Eyes and Ears could not be expected to learn on the streets, the sort that only a respectable man of affairs could hope to discover.

But this morning, Artemis decided, it was not enough.

"Is that all you could learn about Mrs. Deveridge, Henry? Rumors, gossip, and secondhand scandal-broth? I already know most of what you have just told me. It's common knowledge in the clubs."

Henry looked up from his notebook. He peered at Artemis over the round gold rims of his spectacles.

"It is not as though you allowed me a great deal of time for the task, Artemis." He glanced meaningfully at the tall clock. "I received your message at approximately eight o'clock this morning. It is now two-thirty. Six and a half hours is simply not sufficient for the sort of inquiries you wish to be made. I shall have more to offer in a few days."

"Bloody hell. My fate is in the hands of the Wicked Widow and all you can tell me is that she has a habit of murdering her husbands."

"One husband, not several," Leggett said in his maddeningly precise way. "And the tale is based on gossip, not fact. I would remind you that Mrs. Deveridge was never considered a suspect in her husband's death. She was not even questioned, let alone taken up on charges."

"Because there was no proof. Only speculation."

"Indeed." Henry glanced down at his notes. "According to the facts that I was able to learn, Renwick Deveridge was alone in his house late at night when a housebreaker entered. The villain shot Deveridge dead, set a fire to conceal the murder, and made off with the valuables."

"But no one in Society really believes that is what happened."

"It was no secret that Deveridge was estranged from his spouse. Mrs. Deveridge had moved out of the house within weeks of the marriage. She refused to return to live with her husband as man and wife." Henry paused to clear his throat. "She is said to be somewhat, ah, headstrong."

"Yes. I can vouch for that." Artemis tapped the letter opener against his boot. "What can you tell me about the unfortunate husband?"

Henry's bushy gray brows bunched together as he consulted his notes. "Very little, I'm afraid. As you know, his name was Renwick Deveridge. No family that I could discover. He appears to have spent some time abroad on the Continent during the war."

"What of it?" Artemis gave him a knowing look. "So did you."

Henry cleared his throat. "Yes, well, I think it safe to say he was not gadding about spying on Napoleon. In any event, Deveridge returned to London approximately two years ago. He made the acquaintance of Winton Reed and soon afterward became engaged to Reed's daughter. Madeline Reed and Deveridge were married a short time later."

"Not a long engagement."

"They were, in fact, married by special license." Henry rattled his papers in a disapproving manner. "As I noted, the lady is said to be somewhat rash and impetuous. As it transpired, within two months of the wedding night Deveridge was dead and the gossip began to circulate that she had murdered him."

"Deveridge must have proved a very disappointing husband indeed."

"In point of fact," Henry said deliberately, "there was talk that, before Deveridge was so conveniently dispatched, Mrs. Deveridge's father, Winton Reed, had instructed his solicitor to make inquiries about the possibility of an annulment or formal separation."

"An *annulment*." Artemis tossed the letter opener onto the desk. He sat forward abruptly. "Are you certain?"

"As certain as I can be with the limited facts at hand. Given the great difficulty and expense of obtaining a divorce, an annulment, although time-consuming, no doubt seemed the simpler approach."

"But hardly a flattering one for Renwick Deveridge. There are very few grounds for an annulment, after all. In this instance I would assume that the only ones that would apply would have involved an accusation of impotence against Deveridge."

"Indeed." Henry cleared his throat again.

Artemis reminded himself that Henry was something of a prude when it came to matters of physical intimacy. "But even with the aid of skilled solicitors, it would have taken years for Mrs. Deveridge to establish a case for impotence."

"Undoubtedly. The assumption of nearly everyone in the Polite World is that she lacked the patience to go through the legal proceedings." Henry paused. "Or perhaps she discovered that her father could not afford the cost."

"So she took steps to end the marriage in her own fashion, is that it?"

"That is certainly how the gossips would have it."

Artemis had seen enough of her last night to know that she was a lady of formidable determination. If she had been truly desperate to end her marriage, would she have gone so far as to murder Deveridge?

"You said Renwick Deveridge was shot before the fire was set?"

"According to the doctor who examined the body, yes."

Artemis rose and went to stand at the window. "I must tell you that last night Mrs. Deveridge displayed a certain expertise with pistols."

"Humph. Hardly the sort of skill that is suited to a lady."

Artemis smiled to himself as he gazed out into his high-walled garden. Henry held traditional views concerning female deportment. "No. Do you have anything else for me?"

"Mrs. Deveridge's father was one of the very first members of the Vanzagarian Society. He held a master's status."

"Yes, I know."

"He was considerably advanced in years before he married and fathered a daughter. It is said that after his wife's death he doted on Madeline. Went so far as to instruct her in matters that most would not deem appropriate for a young lady."

"Such as the use of a pistol, it seems."

"Apparently. Reed had become something of a recluse in recent years. Devoted himself to his study of dead languages."

"I believe that he was a noted expert in the old tongue of Vanzagara," Artemis said. "Go on."

"Reed died early on the morning after the fire. The scandalmongers claim that the knowledge that his daughter had gone mad and murdered her husband gave him such a shock that his heart failed him."

"I see."

Henry coughed discreetly. "As a man of business, I feel compelled to point out that, due to the series of unfortunate deaths in the family, Mrs. Deveridge is now in sole control of the inheritances of both her father and her husband."

"Good God, man." Artemis turned to stare at him. "Surely you're not about to suggest that she murdered both men in order to get her hands on their fortunes?"

"No, of course not." Henry's mouth

tightened with distaste. "It is difficult to believe that any daughter could be so unnatural. I was merely pointing out the, uh, results of the untimely events."

"Thank you, Henry. You know that I rely on you for that sort of insightful analysis." Artemis walked back to his desk and propped himself on the edge. "While we are on the subject of glaring facts, I cannot help but note another one."

"What is that, sir?"

"Renwick Deveridge had studied Vanza. He would not have been an easy man to kill."

Henry blinked several times behind the lenses of his spectacles while he absorbed the implications. "I take your point. Difficult to believe that a female could manage the business, eh?"

"Or a common, garden-variety housebreaker, either, for that matter."

Henry gave him a troubled look. "Indeed."

"I think," Artemis said slowly, "that, of the two possible suspects in Deveridge's death, his wife or an unknown footpad, I'd stake my wager on the lady."

Henry looked pained. "I vow, the notion of a female resorting to such violence sends a cold chill down a man's spine, does it not?"

"I'm not sure about the cold chill, but it certainly raises a few interesting questions."

Henry groaned heavily. "I was afraid of this."

Artemis looked at him. "What do you mean?"

"I knew from the moment I got your message this morning that there was something amiss about this entire affair. You are far too curious about Madeline Deveridge."

"She presents me with a problem. I am attempting to gather information relating to that problem. You know me, Henry. I like to be in possession of all the facts before I take any action."

"Do not try to fob me off with such watery explanations. This is more than merely another matter of business for you, Artemis. I can tell that you are fascinated with Mrs. Deveridge. Indeed, I have not known you to take such a keen personal interest in a female in an exceedingly long time."

"I should think you would be happy for me, Henry. You have been telling me for some time now that I have become much too obsessed with my plans for revenge. At the very least, my association with Mrs. Deveridge will serve to broaden my range of interests and activities for a while."

Henry gave him a dour look. "Unfortunately, I do not think they will be broadened in any positive way."

"Be that as it may, I have some time to kill while I await the completion of my other plans." Artemis paused. "I believe that I shall occupy myself with a more detailed investigation of Mrs. Deveridge."

Chapter Four

He examined the small house at the end of the lane as he went up the steps. It was not large but it had well-proportioned windows to admit the light and provide a fine view of the park. The neighborhood appeared to be quiet and sedate, but it was not what anyone would call fashionable.

Mrs. Deveridge might control the not inconsiderable inheritances left to her by her father and husband, but she had not spent her money on a lavish mansion in a stylish neighborhood. From what Henry had been able to determine, she lived an almost reclusive life with her aunt.

The mysteries surrounding the lady grew more intriguing with each passing moment, Artemis thought. So did his anticipation at the thought of seeing her for the first time in the full light of day. Memories of eyes provocatively veiled by black lace had kept him awake for several hours last night.

The door opened. Latimer loomed in the small hall. He looked even larger in the daylight than he had last night in the fog.

"Mr. Hunt." Latimer's eyes brightened.

"Good day, Latimer. How is your Nellie?"

"Hale and hearty, thanks to you, sir. She don't remember much about what 'appened, but I expect that's for the best." Latimer hesitated. "I want to tell ye again, sir, how grateful I am for what ye did."

"We made a good team, did we not?" Artemis stepped over the threshold. "Please tell Mrs. Deveridge that I am here to see her. I believe I am expected."

"Aye, sir. She's in the library. I'll announce ye, sir." He turned to lead the way.

Artemis glanced back at the shutters on the windows. They were heavily barred and fixed with stout locks and tiny bells that would tinkle a warning if anyone attempted to force them open. When they were closed at night, they would prove a sturdy defense against intruders. Did the lady fear ordinary housebreakers or some greater threat?

He followed Latimer down a long corridor to the rear of the house. The big man halted at the entrance to a room that was crammed from floor to ceiling with leatherbound books, journals, notebooks, and papers of every description. The handsome windows that looked out onto a well-tended but severely pruned garden were also fitted with barred shutters, locks, and bells.

"Mr. Hunt to see you, ma'am."

Madeline rose from behind a heavy oak desk. "Thank you, Latimer. Do come in, Mr. Hunt."

She wore a black gown cut in a fashionable, high-waisted style, but there was no lace veil to conceal her features that morning. Artemis looked at her and knew that Henry had been right about the depth of his interest in this woman. It went far beyond curiosity and into the dangerous realm of fascination. His awareness of her seemed to shimmer in the air around him. He wondered if Madeline sensed it.

There was a startling mix of intelligence, determination, and wariness in her clear blue eyes. Her dark hair was parted in the middle and bound at the back of her head in a neat, no-nonsense style. She had a soft, full mouth, a firm chin, and a self-possession that presented a subtle challenge to everything that was male in him.

Latimer hovered in the doorway. "Will you be needin' anything, ma'am?"

"No, thank you," Madeline said. "You may leave us."

"Yes, ma'am." Latimer let himself out of the library and closed the door.

Madeline looked at Artemis. "Please be seated, Mr. Hunt."

"Thank you." He took the japanned and gilded beech wood armchair she indicated. A glance at the rich carpet, heavy drapes, and elegantly carved desk confirmed Leggett's assessment of Mrs. Deveridge's finances. The house was small, but the furnishings were of excellent quality.

She sat down behind her desk. "I trust you have recovered your hearing, sir?"

"My ears rang for a time, but I am happy to tell you that my senses all appear to be completely restored."

"Thank heavens." She looked genuinely relieved. "I would not have wanted to be responsible for an injury to your person."

"As it happens, there was no permanent damage done, either to me or" — he raised his brows slightly — "to the villain you attempted to shoot."

Her mouth tightened. "I am actually a rather decent shot, sir. But the carriage was moving and it was dark and you *had* seized my arm, if you will recall. I fear the combination of so many impediments took its toll on my aim."

"I pray you will forgive me, madam. Violent solutions have their place from time to time, but as a general rule, I prefer to avoid that sort of thing."

She narrowed her eyes. "I find that somewhat surprising, given your training."

"If you know anything at all about the ancient arts of Vanza, you must know that subtlety is always stressed over the obvious in the philosophy. Violence is hardly subtle. When the occasion does call for it, the strategy should be crafted with precision and carried out in such a way that the results do not leave a trail that leads directly back to the one who initiated the action."

She grimaced. "You are indeed a true student of Vanza, Mr. Hunt. Your thinking on such subjects is clever, crafty, and labyrinthine."

"I realize the fact that I am Vanza does not elevate me in your opinion, madam. But allow me to remind you that shooting a man dead in the street last night could have produced a variety of complications that both of us might have found most inconvenient this morning."

"What do you mean?" Her eyes widened in surprise. "You assisted me in rescuing a young woman. How could anyone object to that?"

"I prefer not to attract attention, Mrs. Deveridge."

She flushed. "Yes, of course. You no doubt fear that word might get out about your connection to the Dream Pavilions.

Rest assured I will say nothing to anyone."

"I appreciate the reassurance. As it happens, I have a great deal at stake at the moment."

"I have no wish to meddle in your, ah, financial affairs."

He went cold. Just how much did the woman know? Was it possible that she had also learned of his carefully wrought plans for vengeance?

"You do not intend to meddle, you say?" he repeated neutrally.

She waved a hand in casual dismissal. "Heavens, no, sir. Your plans to select a wife from the higher circles of the ton are of absolutely no interest to me. Marry where you wish, Mr. Hunt. And the best of luck to you."

He relaxed slightly. "You relieve my mind, Mrs. Deveridge."

"I quite understand that your search for a well-connected bride would be severely hampered if it were to get out that you are in trade, sir." She paused, her brows drawing together in a vaguely troubled frown. "But are you sure that it is a wise notion to contract a marriage under what might be construed as false pretenses?"

"As a matter of fact, I hadn't thought about the matter from that perspective," he said blandly.

"What will you do when the truth comes out?" There was more than a hint of frosty disapproval in the question. "Do you expect your wife to simply ignore the fact that you are in trade?"

"Mmm."

She leaned forward and glared. "Allow me to give you a word of advice, sir. If you have any intention of establishing a marriage based on mutual respect and affection, you will be honest with your future spouse right from the start."

"As I have absolutely no intention of establishing that sort of marriage in the near future, I don't think I need be overly concerned with the finer points of your lecture on the subject."

She flinched in surprise. Then she unclasped her fingers and sat back quickly. "Good Lord, I *was* lecturing you, was I not?"

"That is certainly what it sounded like to me."

"Forgive me, Mr. Hunt." She propped her elbows on the desk and dropped her head into her hands. "I vow, I do not know what came over me. I had no right to involve myself in your personal affairs. My thinking has been rather muddied of late. My only excuse is that I have had some difficulty sleeping and I —" She broke off, raised her head, and winced. "Now I am rambling."

"Do not concern yourself about the rambling." He paused a beat. "But I wish to make it clear that I would be very displeased if my business affairs became snarled at this particular juncture. I'm sure you can appreciate that I am involved in some extremely delicate matters."

"Yes, of course. You have made your point, sir. There is no need to threaten me."

"I was not aware that I had uttered any threats."

"Sir, you are Vanza." She gave him a steely look. "It is unnecessary to spell out your warnings. I assure you, they are quite clear."

For some reason her disgust of all things Vanza was beginning to irritate him. "For a lady who stooped to blackmail in order to coerce me into assisting her last night, you have considerable nerve to insult me today."

"Blackmail?" Her eyes widened in outrage. "I did nothing of the kind."

"You made it plain that you knew of my ownership of the Dream Pavilions and you are aware that I do not want any gossip in that direction. Forgive me if I misunderstood your intent, but I got the distinct impression that you used your information to force me to assist you."

She went very pink. "I merely pointed out your obligations in the matter."

"Call it what you wish. I call it blackmail."

"Oh. Well, you are entitled to your opinion, of course."

"Yes. And I should add that blackmail is not my favorite parlor game."

"I regret the necessity —"

The twinge of panic in her eyes satisfied him. He interrupted her explanations with a wave of his hand. "How is your maid bearing up today?"

Madeline looked briefly disconcerted by the abrupt change of topic. She made a visible effort to collect herself. "Nellie is very well, although the kidnappers apparently poured a great deal of laudanum down her throat. She is still a bit groggy and her recollection of events is extremely vague."

"Latimer told me that she does not recall much about the affair."

"No. The only thing she remembers with any clarity is that the two men argued over how to get the best price for her. She gained the impression that they had been commissioned to abduct her but one of them thought they could get more by selling her to another client." Madeline shuddered. "It is revolting to think that the brothel keepers are actively engaged in the buying and selling of young women."

"Not only young women. They deal in young boys, as well."

"It is a terrible trade. One would think the authorities —"

"The authorities can do very little about it."

"Thank heavens we were able to find Nellie in time." Madeline met his eyes. "If it had not been for your assistance, we would have lost her. Last night I did not have an opportunity to thank you properly. Please allow me to do so now."

"You may thank me by answering my questions," he said very softly.

A wary expression lit her eyes. She gripped the edge of her desk as though bracing herself. "I expected no less. Very well, you are entitled to some explanation. I suppose your chief concern is to discover precisely how I came to know of your connection to the Dream Pavilions."

"Forgive me, Mrs. Deveridge, but my curiosity on that point was strong enough to keep me awake for quite some time last night."

"Really?" She brightened with what could

only be a sympathetic interest. "Do you suffer much difficulty in sleeping?"

He smiled thinly. "I am sure I will sleep like the dead once I have the answers to my questions."

She started a bit at the word *dead*, but she caught herself immediately. "Yes, well, I suppose I ought to begin by telling you that my father was a member of the Vanzagarian Society."

"I am already aware of that fact. I also know that he had achieved the rank of a master."

"Yes. But he was interested primarily in the scholarly aspects of Vanza, not the metaphysical notions or the physical exercises. He studied the ancient language of the Isle of Vanzagara for many years. Indeed, he was a noted expert within the Society."

"I know."

"I see." She cleared her throat. "In the course of his work he communicated with many other Vanza scholars scattered throughout England, the Continent, and America. Here in London he frequently consulted with Ignatius Lorring himself." Madeline paused. "That was, of course, before Lorring became so ill that he stopped seeing his old friends and colleagues."

"As the Grand Master of the Society, Lorring knew more about its members than anyone else. Are you telling me that your father discussed such matters with him?"

"I regret to say that they did more than merely discuss the personal affairs of the members of the Society. Toward the end of his life, Lorring became obsessed with information concerning gentlemen in the Society." She rolled her eyes. "One might say that he became the Grand Master Eccentric of the Society of Eccentrics and Oddities."

"Perhaps we could skip your personal reflections on the members of the Vanzagarian Society?"

"Sorry."

She did not look at all sorry, he decided, merely frustrated because he had stopped her in mid-lecture.

"I comprehend that you hold strong views on the subject," he said politely, "but I fear that if you take the time to describe them all to me, we shall not finish this conversation by nightfall."

"You may be right," she shot back. "There are, after all, so many things to criticize about the Society, are there not? But for the sake of brevity, I shall move on to the essentials. Suffice it to say that, driven by a desire for the most minute details, Lorring appointed my father to keep a record of the members."

"What sort of record?"

She hesitated, as if torn by some internal debate. Then, quite suddenly, she got to her feet. "I will show you."

She removed a gold chain from around her throat. He saw that a small key, which had been hidden from sight beneath her fichu, dangled from the delicate, gold links. She crossed the room to a small cupboard secured with a brass lock.

She opened the cupboard with the key and removed a large journal bound in dark leather. She carried the volume back to her desk and set it down with great care.

"This is the record Lorring requested my father to compile and maintain." She opened the book and glanced down at the first page. "It has not been kept current since my father's death, so the information on the members is now a full year out of date."

A whisper of unease went through him. He got to his feet and went to look at the first page of the old journal. He saw at once that it was a record of names that went back to the earliest days of the Vanzagarian Society. Slowly he turned the pages, examining the contents. There were lengthy notes beneath each entry. The details covered far more than such minor facts as the date a gentleman had been admitted to the Society and the level of expertise he had achieved. They included business and personal affairs as well as comments on the temperaments and extremely private inclinations of the various members.

Artemis knew that a good deal of what he was looking at would have made excellent scandal-broth, at the very least. Some of it was blackmail material. He paused to read the notes concerning himself. There was no mention of his affair with Catherine Jensen or the three men he intended to destroy. His plans for vengeance appeared to be safe for the moment. Nevertheless, there was far too much information concerning his personal affairs in the damned book. He frowned at the sentences that had been added at the bottom of the page.

Hunt is a true master of Vanza. He thinks in dark and devious ways.

"Who else knows about this book?" he asked.

She took a step back. He realized it was his tone of voice, not the simple question, that had alarmed her.

"Only my father and Ignatius Lorring knew about this record," she said hastily. "They are both dead."

He looked up from the page that was headed with his name. "You are forgetting yourself, Mrs. Deveridge," he said softly. "You appear to be very much alive."

She swallowed visibly, blinked, and then produced a dazzling smile and a small, wholly artificial chuckle. "Yes, of course. But you have no need to concern yourself with the trifling fact that I possess this old book, sir."

Artemis closed the journal deliberately. "I wish I could be certain of that."

"Oh, you can, sir. Indeed, you can be absolutely certain."

"That remains to be seen." He picked up the book and carried it back to the cupboard. "Old volumes connected to Vanza can be dangerous. It was not so very long ago that rumors concerning an ancient text resulted in some mysterious deaths."

He heard a thud as something heavy landed on the carpet. The sound was accompanied by a sharp gasp. He ignored both as he put the book into the cupboard. He closed and locked the door and turned slowly to look at Madeline.

She was crouched on the carpet, busily retrieving a heavy silver figure that had fallen from the desk. He noticed that her fingers trembled slightly as she rose and placed the little statue precisely next to the inkwell.

"I assume you refer to the rumors about the so-called *Book of Secrets*, sir," she said smoothly. She made a show of brushing off her hands. "Utter rubbish."

"Not in the opinion of some members of the Society."

"I must point out, sir, that many members of the Society hold a variety of extremely odd notions." She made a sound of exasperation. "*The Book of Secrets*, if, indeed, it ever existed, was destroyed in a fire that consumed a certain villa in Italy."

"One can only hope that is the case." Artemis went to stand at her heavily protected window. He looked out into the little garden and noted that there were no large trees, hedges, or other masses of foliage that could give cover to an intruder. "As I said, books can be dangerous things. Tell me, Mrs. Deveridge, do you intend to use the information your father set down in that journal to blackmail anyone else? Because if that is the case, I must advise you that there is some risk involved."

"Will you kindly cease employing the word *blackmail* at every turn in the conversation?" she snapped. "It is most an-noying."

He glanced at her over his shoulder. Her expression of severe disgruntlement would have been amusing under other circum-stances. "Forgive me, madam, but given that my future is in your hands, I feel in need of constant reassurance."

Her lips tightened with irritation. "I have already told you that I have no sinister in-tentions, sir. Last night I was forced to use desperate measures, but such a situation is highly unlikely to occur again."

He looked at the little bells that dangled from the heavily barred shutters. "I do not think that you are as confident of that as you would have me believe, madam."

Silence gripped the library. Artemis turned completely around to confront Madeline. Her expression was one of unwa-vering determination, but he could see the haunted look beneath the surface.

"Tell me, Mrs. Deveridge," he said qui-etly. "Who or what do you fear?"

"I cannot imagine what you are talking about, sir."

"I realize that because I am Vanza, you assume that I am something of an eccentric, if not a complete crackpot, but kindly credit me with some elementary reasoning ability."

She began to have the appearance of a creature that has been cornered. "What do you mean?"

"You employ an armed coachman who clearly performs the services of a bodyguard. You barricade your windows with shutters that are designed to keep out intruders. Your garden has been stripped of foliage so that no one can approach the house unseen. You yourself have learned to use a pistol."

"London is a dangerous place, sir."

"It is indeed. But I think you feel more at risk than many other people." He held her eyes. "What do you fear, madam?"

She gazed at him for a long time. Then she went back behind her desk and sank down into her chair. Her shoulders were rigid with tension.

"My personal affairs are none of your concern, Mr. Hunt."

He studied her averted face, taking in the evidence of her pride and courage. "Everyone has dreams, Mrs. Deveridge. I comprehend that yours is to be free of the fear you feel."

Her gaze turned curiously speculative. "What do you think you can do on my behalf, sir?"

"Who knows?" He smiled slightly. "But I

am the Dream Merchant. Perhaps I can make your dream come true."

"I am in no mood for jests."

"I assure you, I am not particularly amused myself at this moment."

Her hand clenched around a small brass paperweight. She studied it intently. "Even if what you say is true, if you *could* just possibly be of some assistance to me, sir, I suspect there would be a price for such services."

He shrugged. "There is a price for everything. Sometimes it is worth paying. Sometimes it is not."

She closed her eyes for a moment. When she opened them, her gaze was steady, penetrating.

"I will admit," she said carefully, "that last night after I returned home, a certain notion did cross my mind."

He had her, he thought. She had taken the bait. "What notion was that?"

She put the brass paperweight down. "I spent a great deal of time pondering a pair of old sayings. One was the adage that it is best to fight fire with fire. The other was that it takes a thief to catch a thief."

Understanding flashed through him. "Bloody hell, madam, this is a Vanza matter, is it not?"

She blinked twice at his leap of comprehension. Then she scowled. "In a way. Possibly." She sighed. "I cannot be certain."

"What are you thinking? That you will employ a master of Vanza to deal with an affair of Vanza? Is that your logic?"

"Something along those lines, yes." She drummed her fingers on the desk. "I am still pondering the matter, sir, but it has occurred to me that you might be uniquely qualified to assist me in resolving an issue that is causing me a great deal of concern."

"You mean that you have thought of a way to use my skills as a master to solve your problem."

"If we were to come to an agreement," she said deliberately, "I would see our association as being in the nature of employer and employee. I would, of course, pay you for your expertise."

"This becomes more intriguing by the moment. Just how the devil do you plan to reimburse me, Mrs. Deveridge?" He held up a palm. "Before you answer that question, let us be clear on one point. As you have noted, I am in trade and I do very well in my business affairs. I do not need or want your money, madam."

"Perhaps not." Her eyes narrowed. "But I think I have something you do want, sir."

He let his gaze slide coolly over her. "Do you indeed? I will admit that the offer is an interesting one." He thought about the standing wager in the betting books. "And not without its rewards."

She stared at him. "I beg your pardon?"

Her expression of blank incomprehension told him that she did not know about the wager. "It is not often that a man is afforded the opportunity of an affair with the Wicked Widow. Tell me, madam, can I expect to survive the experience? Or do your lovers run the same risks as your husbands?"

Her jaw dropped. An instant later icy fury leaped in her eyes. "If I decide to employ you, Mr. Hunt, there will certainly be some risk involved, but that risk will not emanate from me."

He raised his brows. "I hate to sound crass, but about the nature of my reimbursement . . . ?"

She glanced meaningfully at the cupboard that contained the journal of Vanza members. "I saw from your expression that you do not relish the notion that so much personal information concerning your private affairs has been set down in that book."

"You are correct. I do not like it at all." And one way or another, he would find a way to get his hands on the bloody volume.

He glanced at the foolish little bells on the shutters. They would prove no great obstacle to his skills.

She watched him with shrewd intensity. "If we come to terms, sir, I will pay you for your time and trouble with that journal."

"Are you saying that you will give me that damned book if I help you?"

"Yes." She hesitated. "But first I must decide whether or not to employ you. I must think on it some more before I come to a decision. There is a great deal at stake."

"For your own sake, Mrs. Deveridge, I suggest that you do not hesitate too long."

She raised her chin with chilly disdain. "Another threat, sir?"

"Not at all. I was merely referring to your attempts to fortify your home." He motioned toward the shutters. "If what you fear is Vanza related, I can assure you that the ringing of those bells may well come too late to do you any good."

She went pale and gripped the arm of her chair so tightly that her knuckles whitened. "I think you had better go now, sir."

He hesitated and then inclined his head formally. "As you wish, madam. You know where to reach me when you make up your mind."

"I will let you know when I —" She broke

off as the door of the library opened without warning. She glanced quickly at the newcomer. "Aunt Bernice."

"Sorry, dear." Bernice beamed at Artemis. "I didn't realize you were still with your guest. Aren't you going to introduce us?"

"Yes, of course," Madeline muttered.

She made the introductions swiftly and grudgingly. Artemis refused to be hurried. He liked Bernice Reed on sight. She was an elegant, dainty woman of a certain age who had an obvious instinct for fashion and style. The glint of laughter in her bright blue eyes appealed to him. He bowed over her hand and was rewarded with a gracious response that told him the lady was not without some experience of the ballroom.

"My niece has informed me that we have every reason to be grateful to you for your assistance last night," Bernice said. "You are a hero in this household today."

"Thank you, Miss Reed. I appreciate your kind words." He flicked a glance at Madeline. "But I have been assured by Mrs. Deveridge that I was not exactly a hero in the affair. I was merely fulfilling my obligations as the proprietor of the establishment where the kidnapping took place, you see."

Madeline winced. Artemis took some

small satisfaction from the expression.

Bernice stared at Madeline, clearly aghast. "Good heavens, dear, surely you never said such a thing to poor Mr. Hunt. He went far beyond the call of responsibility last night. I do not see how you can possibly claim that he had any obligation at all in the situation. Nellie was kidnapped outside the pleasure garden, not inside the grounds."

"I made it quite clear to Mr. Hunt that his services were appreciated," Madeline said through obviously gritted teeth.

"She did indeed," Artemis said. "In fact, I proved so useful that she is contemplating hiring me for another task. Something to do with the notion of employing a thief to catch a thief, I believe."

Bernice gasped. "She called you a *thief*, sir?"

"Well," Artemis began.

Madeline threw up her hands. "I never called you any such thing, sir."

"True enough," Artemis allowed. He turned back to Bernice. "She never actually called me a thief."

"I should hope not," Bernice said.

Madeline groaned.

"Being in trade," Artemis said, "I am naturally quite excited by the prospect of continued employment." He winked at Bernice as he went toward the door. "Between you and me, Miss Reed, I have every expectation of obtaining the post. There are very few other qualified candidates, you see."

He walked into the hall and let himself out the front door before either woman could get her mouth closed.

Chapter Five

"He is Vanza," Madeline said. "That means that he is playing some deep game. Hiring him to assist us will be quite risky."

"I do not think that it is wise to use words such as *hire* or *employ* when one discusses the prospect of asking Mr. Hunt to aid us." Bernice pursed her lips. "It is difficult to envision him as a paid employee, if you see what I mean."

"On the contrary, thinking of Mr. Hunt as a paid employee is the only sensible way to view any connection to him." Madeline sat forward on the chair behind her desk and studied the brass paperweight in front of her as though it were an ancient oracle. "If we pursue this plan of mine, we must take great care to ensure that Hunt knows his place."

Bernice sipped her tea, which Nellie had brought in. "Hmm."

"My greatest fear is that we no longer have any choice in the matter."

Bernice blinked. "I beg your pardon?"

"He knows about Papa's book, you see."

"Oh dear."

"Yes, I know, it was a mistake to show it

to him." Madeline got restlessly to her feet. "I told him about it in the course of explaining how I came to learn of his connection to the Dream Pavilions. I thought it would reassure him to know that I hadn't actively spied on him."

Bernice's eyes no longer gleamed with amusement. "Now that he is aware that some of his secrets are recorded, he will want to get his hands on that journal at all costs."

"I fear you are correct." Madeline gazed out into the severely trimmed garden. "I saw the look in his eyes when he came to the page with his name on it. I knew at once that I had made a grave error."

"So you offered him a bargain." Bernice nodded. "Not a bad notion. He seemed willing enough to entertain the prospect of such an arrangement."

"A bit too willing, if you ask me, but I don't know what else to do except continue on this course." Madeline glanced at Bernice. "There is no doubt but that he could be of use to us. I saw him in action last night. The scheme he devised for rescuing Nellie from that tavern was quite clever. And he carried her over his shoulder for the entire length of the alley. He appeared to be quite physically fit for a man of his age."

"He is hardly in his dotage."

"No, of course he isn't," Madeline said hastily. "I was merely pointing out that he is not an extremely *young* man."

"No."

"Nor an old one, as you just pointed out," she continued doggedly. "Indeed, one could say that he appears to be exactly the right age. Mature yet still quite agile."

"Mature yet still agile," Bernice repeated neutrally. "Yes, that does describe Hunt, I think."

"I am entertaining a few doubts about your conclusions concerning Mr. Hunt's reasons for keeping his ownership of the Dream Pavilions a dark secret."

"Are you?"

"Yes. I am no longer entirely certain that he is doing so because he wishes to find himself a wealthy, highborn wife."

Bernice looked mildly surprised. "Why? Forming an alliance with a powerful family seems a perfectly logical thing for an ambitious gentleman to do."

"It is easy to believe that Mr. Hunt has a few ambitions." Madeline tapped a finger against the window ledge. "But I'm not so sure they involve marriage. Something tells me that if that had been his goal, he would have achieved it by now."

"A good point."

"There should have been an announcement of an engagement. At the very least, we ought to have heard some gossip connecting his name to that of some eligible young ladies of the ton."

"There is that." Bernice paused. "Interesting that we have heard no names dropped, as it were. What do you think is going on?"

"Who can tell with a Vanza master?" Madeline swung around and began to pace the library. "But there is something about him."

"Something?"

"Yes." Madeline waved a hand as she struggled to find words to explain what her intuition told her was true. "He is certainly not your typical gentleman of the ton. It is as if he were made of something more substantial than the usual denizens of the social world. He is a hawk among moths."

"Presumably a mature yet still agile hawk among moths, eh?" A distinctly amused gleam lit Bernice's vivid eyes. "What an interesting description. So poetical. Almost metaphysical in tone."

Madeline glared. "You find my description of Hunt humorous?"

Bernice chuckled. "My dear, I consider it

95

to be vastly reassuring."

That brought Madeline to a halt. "Whatever do you mean by that?"

"After your experience with Renwick Deveridge, I had begun to fear that you would never again take a healthy interest in the male of the species. But now it seems I had no reason to be concerned, after all."

Shock left Madeline speechless. When she finally pulled herself together, she still could not think of anything coherent to say.

"*Aunt Bernice.* Really."

"You have kept yourself closeted away from the world for a year now. Perfectly understandable, given all that you went through. Nevertheless, the entire affair would have amounted to an even greater tragedy if it transpired that you never recovered your natural womanly feeling. I take your evident interest in Mr. Hunt as an excellent sign."

"I am not *interested* in him, for heaven's sake." Madeline stalked back toward the bookcase. "At least not in the way you mean. But I am convinced that now that he knows about Papa's journal, it will be extremely difficult to get rid of him. So we may as well make good use of him, if you see what I mean."

"You could simply give Hunt the

96

journal," Bernice said dryly.

Madeline stopped in front of the book-case. "Believe me, I thought of that."

"But?"

"But we are in need of his expertise. Why not strike a bargain for his skills? Two birds with one stone and all that." She was falling back on a great many proverbs this morning, she reflected.

"Why not, indeed?" Bernice looked thoughtful. "It is not as if we have a lot of choice in this affair."

"No, we do not." Madeline glanced at the bells on the shutters. "In fact, I suspect that if we do not offer to give Mr. Hunt the journal in exchange for his services, he will pay us a visit some dark night and help himself to the bloody book."

The following morning Madeline put down the pen she had been using to make notes and closed the slim, leather-clad book she had been attempting to decipher.

Decipher was, indeed, the appropriate word, she decided. The little book was very old and well worn. It was a handwritten jumble of apparently meaningless phrases. As far as she could determine, the words were a mix of ancient Greek, Egyptian hieroglyphs, and the old, long-dead language of Vanzagara. It had been delivered three weeks earlier after a long and complicated journey from Spain and had intrigued her immediately. She had set to work on it at once.

Thus far she had made no headway, however. The Greek was simple enough, but the words she had translated made no sense. The hieroglyphs were a great mystery, of course, although she had heard that Mr. Thomas Young was developing an interesting theory concerning Egyptian writing based on his work with the Rosetta stone. Unfortunately, he had not yet published his analysis.

When it came to the ancient language of Vanzagara, she knew herself to be one of a very small handful of scholars who stood any chance of translating even a portion of the text. Very few people outside the family were aware of her skill. The study of Vanza and its dead tongue was considered to be the province of gentlemen. Ladies were not admitted to the Society, nor was it considered suitable to instruct them in subjects connected to it.

Even if they had been informed that Winton Reed had taught his daughter everything he knew, few members of the Vanzagarian Society would have believed a female capable of comprehending the complexities of the strange language of the old books.

Madeline had been working on the small volume in her spare moments for several days now. The project, difficult and demanding as it was, had been a welcome distraction from her other concerns. But this morning it was not proving effective.

She found herself looking up frequently from her work to check the clock. It annoyed her to realize that she was counting the minutes and hours since her message had been sent off to Artemis Hunt, but she could not help herself.

"It's here!" Bernice's voice rang out in the hall. "It has arrived!"

"What on earth?" Madeline stared at the closed door of the library and listened to her aunt's footsteps hurrying along the corridor.

A few seconds later the door was flung wide. Bernice sailed triumphantly into the room, waving what appeared to be a white card. "This is so exciting."

Madeline peered at the card. "What is it?"

"Mr. Hunt's response to your note, of course."

Relief poured through Madeline. She leaped to her feet. "Let me see that."

Bernice handed the card to her with the air of a magician producing a dove out of thin air.

Madeline tore open the note and read it through once, quickly. At first she thought she had misread the contents. Stunned, she went back to the beginning and went through it again. It made no more sense the second time around. She lowered the card and stared, bemused, at Bernice.

"What is the problem, dear?"

"I sent Mr. Hunt a message informing him that I wished to pursue a discussion of our business arrangement. He sent back this . . . this . . ."

"This what?" Bernice took the note from Madeline. She whipped out a pair of spectacles, plunked them on her nose, and read the note aloud.

"I request the honor of escorting you to the masquerade ball that is to be held on the grounds of the Dream Pavilions on Thursday evening."

Bernice looked up, eyes widening with glee. "Why, dear, it's an *invitation*."

"I can see that." Madeline ripped the note out of Bernice's fingers and glared at the bold, masculine script. "What the bloody hell is he up to?"

"Really, Madeline, you are entirely too suspicious for a woman of your age. What is so odd about being invited to a ball by a respectable gentleman?"

"This is not a respectable gentleman we are discussing, this is Artemis Hunt. I've got every right to be suspicious."

"You are becoming somewhat overwrought, my dear." Bernice frowned. "Have you had trouble sleeping again? You are using my special elixir, are you not?"

"Yes, yes. Very effective stuff." She saw no reason to tell Bernice the truth. She had poured the elixir into the chamber pot last night, just as she did every night, because she dared not use it. The last thing she wanted to do at night was fall asleep. The dreams were getting worse.

"Well then, if it isn't lack of sleep that is affecting your nerves, perhaps it is something else," Bernice said.

"My reaction to this note of Hunt's is not a case of delicate nerves. It is common sense." Madeline snapped the card against her palm. "Think of it: I inform the man that I wish to engage his services for a specified fee and he sends back an invitation to a fancy dress ball. What sort of answer is that?"

"A most interesting one, if you ask me. Especially as it comes from a mature yet still agile gentleman."

"No." Madeline eyed her grimly. "I fear that it is a very Vanza answer. Hunt is deliberately trying to confound me. We must ask ourselves why."

"I can think of only one way to discover the answer to that question, my dear."

"What is that?"

"You must accept his invitation, of course."

Madeline stared at her. "Have you gone mad? Go to a masked ball with Hunt? What a perfectly bizarre notion."

Bernice gave her a knowing look. "You are dealing with a master of Vanza. You will have to handle him with great cleverness and skill. Never fear, I have boundless faith in your abilities to get at the truth."

"Hmm."

"In any event, I do not see how it will do you the least bit of harm to go to a ball," Bernice added. "I vow, you need some entertainment. You are starting to become as eccentric and reclusive and secretive as any of the gentlemen of the Vanzagarian Society."

Chapter Six

"I see Glenthorpe is in his altitudes a bit earlier than usual tonight." Lord Belstead cast a disapproving eye toward the man slumped in a wing-back chair in front of the hearth. "Not yet ten o'clock and the man's already foxed."

"Mayhap we should invite him to play a hand or two with us." Sledmere did not look up from his cards. "Glenthorpe is a fool, especially when he's drunk. We could no doubt win a fair amount off him tonight."

"Too easy." Artemis examined his own hand. "Where's the sport in playing cards with a drunken fool?"

"I was not thinking of the sport involved," Sledmere said. "I was contemplating the profit."

Artemis put down his cards. "Speaking of which, allow me to tell you that I have just made a bit of one."

Belstead glanced at the cards and snorted. "At my expense, it appears. You do have the devil's own luck, sir."

Across the room, Glenthorpe put down his empty glass and lurched to his feet. Watching him, Artemis said, "I have pushed that luck as far as it will go this evening. If you will excuse me, I believe that I am late to an appointment."

Belstead chuckled. "Who's the fair lady, Hunt?"

"Her name escapes me at the moment." Artemis rose from his chair. "No doubt it will come to mind at the appropriate moment. Good evening, gentlemen."

Sledmere laughed. "Make certain you recall the correct name at the right instant, sir. For some odd reason, females take offense if one gets the names mixed up."

"Thank you for the advice," Artemis said.

He left the card room and went into the hall to collect his greatcoat, hat, and gloves from the porter.

Glenthorpe was at the door. He staggered slightly and turned. "I say, Hunt, are you leaving?"

"Yes."

"Care to share a carriage?" Glenthorpe peered blearily through windows. "Difficult to find one on a night like this, y'know. I vow, the bloody fog is so thick you could slice it with a knife."

"Why not?" Artemis put on his greatcoat and went through the door.

"Excellent." Glenthorpe's expression of relief was almost comical. He hurried to follow Artemis out into the mist-shrouded street. "Safer to leave together, y'know. Night like this, there's bound to be footpads and villains abroad."

"So they say." Artemis hailed a hackney.

The carriage clattered to a halt in front of the club steps. Glenthorpe vaulted awkwardly into it and sank down on one of the seats. Artemis followed and closed the door.

"Never known so much fog in early summer," Glenthorpe muttered.

The hackney rattled off down the street.

Artemis contemplated Glenthorpe. The man did not notice the perusal. He was too busy watching the dark street. He appeared anxious. There was a strained, nervous look about his eyes.

"It's none of my affair, of course." Artemis lounged deeper into the shadows of the corner. "But I can't help noticing that you seem a trifle uneasy tonight, Glenthorpe. Is there something worrying you?"

Glenthorpe's eyes jerked from the view through the window to Artemis's face and then back again. "Ever had the sense that someone was watching you, sir?"

"Watching me?"

"*Me*. Not you." Glenthorpe closed the curtains on the window and sank back against the worn, threadbare squabs. "Lately I have had the oddest notion that I am being followed at times. But when I turn to look, there is never anyone behind me. It is very unsettling."

"Why would anyone follow you?"

"How the devil should I know?" Glenthorpe spoke much too loudly and far too vehemently. He blinked in alarm at the sound of his own voice. Hastily he lowered his tone. "But he's there. I can feel it in my bones."

"Who is this man you believe to be following you?" Artemis asked with very little interest.

"You will not credit this, but I think he is —" Glenthorpe broke off.

"Who?" Artemis prompted politely.

"It is difficult to explain." Glenthorpe's fingers twitched on the seat. "Goes back to something that happened a few years ago. Something that involved a young woman."

"Indeed."

"She was just an actress, y'know. No one important." Glenthorpe swallowed convulsively. "Terrible event occurred. Never meant anything of the sort, of course. The others said it would be amusing. Said the girl was only teasing. Playing hard to get. But she wasn't, y'see."

"What happened?" Artemis asked evenly.

"We took her someplace private." Glenthorpe rubbed his nose with the back of his gloved hand. "Thought we'd all have a bit of sport. But she . . . she fought us. Ran off. It wasn't our fault she . . . Never mind. Point is, I didn't have any hand in what happened. The others had their way with her but when it came my turn, I couldn't, if y'see what I mean. Too much to drink. Or maybe it was the way she looked at me."

"How did she look at you?"

"As if she were some sort of witch casting a spell of doom. She said we'd all pay. Well, that was nonsense, of course. But I realized the others were wrong. She wasn't teasing. She didn't want any of us. I . . . I just . . . I couldn't go through with it."

"But you were there that night."

"Yes. But only because the others dragged me along. It's not the sort of thing I enjoy, you know. I'm not . . . that is to say, my nature is not as . . . as physical as that of other men." Glenthorpe twitched again. "In any event, I made some sort of excuse. The others laughed at me but I didn't care. I just wanted to leave. But the girl, she got free. Ran off into the night. There was an accident. She fell."

"What did you do?"

"Me?" Glenthorpe looked horrified.

"Why, nothing. Nothing at all. That's what I'm trying to explain. There's no reason for him to come after me. I didn't touch her."

"Who is after you?"

"She said —" Glenthorpe licked his lips and rubbed his nose again. "She said her lover would destroy us all for what we had done to her. But that was five years ago. *Five long years.* Thought sure it was finished and forgotten."

"But now you're no longer so certain?"

Glenthorpe hesitated and then shoved one hand into a pocket. He withdrew a watch fob seal. "Got this a few months ago. Just showed up on my doorstep."

Artemis glanced at the gold seal engraved with the image of a rearing stallion. "What of it?"

"I think *he* sent it to me. The one she said would avenge her."

"Why would he do that?"

Glenthorpe rubbed his nose. "I have a nasty feeling that he's toying with me. The way a cat does with a mouse, y'see? But it's not fair."

"Why not?"

"Because of the three of us, I'm the only one who didn't hurt her." Glenthorpe slumped into his seat. "I'm the only one who didn't touch her."

"But you were there that night, were you not?"

"Yes, but —"

"Save your explanations, Glenthorpe. I am not interested in them. Perhaps you can try them out on whoever you think is following you." Artemis rapped on the roof to get the attention of the coachman. "If you will excuse me, I shall leave you here. I believe that I would prefer to walk the rest of the way home alone."

"But the footpads —"

"A man must make choices when it comes to the company he keeps."

The hackney lumbered to a halt. Artemis got out and closed the door. He did not look back as he walked off into the dark, swirling fog.

Chapter Seven

He was breaking all of his own rules tonight. The laws he had lived by for so many years were few in number but they were rigid and unyielding: He sold dreams but he never committed the foolish error of allowing himself to believe in them. He had made a career of crafting illusions, but he himself never confused fantasy with reality.

He had told himself that a few waltzes with the Wicked Widow would amount to nothing more than elements in his strategy, clever ploys designed to lure her into his snare. The lady knew too much about him, and he knew that he had to gain the upper hand. The ancient Vanza adage summed it up well: *That which is dangerous must be understood before it can be controlled.*

Madeline gave him an impatient look through the eye openings of her feathered mask. "It is high time that we got down to business, sir."

So much for seducing her with a waltz.

"I had hoped that you would allow yourself to enjoy the evening before we discussed our business affairs in detail."

Artemis drew her closer into his arms and swept her into another turn on the crowded floor. "I certainly intend to do so."

"I do not know what game you are playing, Mr. Hunt, but so far as I am concerned, my reasons for being here do not include dancing and entertainment."

"I must tell you, Madeline, you are not living up to your reputation as a seductive female capable of luring a man to his doom. I confess that I am somewhat disappointed."

"Naturally I am devastated to learn that I am not proving sufficiently exciting, but I cannot say I am surprised that you noticed my failure in that regard. Why, only the day before yesterday, my aunt pointed out the fact that I have become as reclusive and eccentric as any member of the Vanzagarian Society."

"Do not concern yourself, madam. It seems that I am rapidly acquiring a taste for reclusive, eccentric females."

He saw her mouth open in outraged surprise. Before she could administer the setdown that he no doubt deserved, he whirled her into another wide turn. The folds of her black domino billowed around her ankles.

He was grimly determined to enjoy at least a portion of this evening. She felt as good in his arms as he had known she would: vibrantly warm and sensual. The scent of her was more intoxicating than the most exotic incense. A strange recklessness had been brewing in him since the interview in her library. Tonight he would indulge it in spite of the risks.

It took her a quarter of the distance around the dance floor to collect herself. "Why in heaven's name did you insist on this ridiculous charade of a waltz?" she asked tightly.

"It is not a charade. We are indeed performing the waltz, in case you had not noticed. Unlike so much of what is available on the grounds of the Dream Pavilions, there is no illusion involved in our dance. I expect we shall both be quite winded when we finish."

"You know very well what I mean, sir."

He smiled slightly. "I am in the business of selling dreams and illusions, madam. You are in the market for some of my goods. Like any expert tradesman, I insist you sample my wares before we settle to the tawdry details of striking a bargain."

He swept her off in another direction before she could argue. Perhaps if he waltzed her vigorously enough, she would be too breathless to talk business for a while.

They would eventually have to deal with the subject, of course. But he intended the bargaining to take place here on the terrain that he controlled, not at a place of her choosing. Such details mattered greatly in any negotiation. When one did business with a lady reputed to murder gentlemen, one took care to occupy the high ground.

As he whirled Madeline around the floor, the practical side of his nature noted with detached satisfaction that the Golden Pavilion assembly rooms were crowded tonight. The masquerade balls, held every Thursday evening in the summer months, were among the most popular attractions in the pleasure gardens. They were open to anyone who could afford the price of a ticket. The only requirement for admission was that the dancers be masked.

The democratic nature of the events offended many. But the masquerade balls had been declared amusing by some of the more jaded elements of the fashionable world. That was all it took to draw the crowds. The faint hint of scandal and intrigue that hung over the gardens proved infinitely seductive. On any given Thursday night dandies, officers, young rakes, and country gentry mingled with actresses, ladies, merchants, and rogues on the dance floor. They danced amid a fanciful re-creation of the splendors of ancient Egypt and Rome.

The shadowy lighting gleamed on gilded pillars, obelisks, and statuary. One end of the spacious rooms was dominated by a decorator's version of an Egyptian temple, complete with imitation stone sphinxes. At the other end a Roman fountain surrounded by artistically broken columns splashed into a wide, low pool. Fake mummies, lavish thrones, and a great many painted urns were strategically displayed in between. There were also a number of dark alcoves and recesses equipped with small stone benches just large enough for two people.

When he had purchased the run-down pleasure garden three years ago, Artemis had had a vision of what he wished to create. Henry Leggett had faithfully carried out his instructions. It was Henry who dealt with the manager, the architects, and the decorators. They had all been instructed to fill the extensive grounds with the exotic, the sumptuous, and the mysterious.

No one understood the allure of dreams better than a man who did not allow himself to dream.

The music drew to a close too soon for his liking. Reluctantly he brought Madeline to a halt. The black folds of her domino swirled around her trim ankles one last time and fluttered to a rest. Her eyes challenged him through the mask.

"Now that you have amused yourself by teasing me, may we proceed to business, sir?"

Ah well. He had known he could not make the dance last all night. "Very well, Mrs. Deveridge, we shall discuss our bargain. But not here. We require privacy for such a sordid affair."

"Hardly sordid, sir."

"In the eyes of Society, madam, there is nothing quite so vulgar as a matter of business."

He took her arm and guided her through the wide double doors out into the lantern-lit grounds of the Dream Pavilions. The mild night had drawn a large crowd to savor the slightly scandalous thrills of the pleasure gardens.

The careful lighting heightened the eerie effects of the tableaux of triumphal arches, mythical scenes, and classical ruins that were arranged along the winding, wooded paths. High overhead, an acrobat walked a tightrope. Down below, a troupe of dandies placed bets on the results of illusions crafted by a magician dressed in Oriental robes. People strolled about munching hot meat pies and pastries purchased from nearby booths. Men and women flirted in the shadowy garden alcoves and disappeared into the dark walks. Music, laughter, and occasional bursts of applause rose and fell across the grounds.

Madeline glanced at a group of noisy young people who had gathered in front of the anchoress's cave. "I vow, that cavern looks quite real."

"That is the point, Mrs. Deveridge."

He tightened his grip on her arm and drew her toward the far end of the pleasure gardens where the woods lay shrouded in darkness. They passed the entrance to the Crystal Pavilion, where an audience had gathered to watch troupes of clockwork toy soldiers engage in a mock battle.

Applause spilled from the neighboring pavilion. Madeline turned to look at its illuminated entrance. "What entertainment is provided in that hall?"

"That is the Silver Pavilion. I have hired a mesmerist to give demonstrations."

"Oh yes, of course. It was the mesmerist whom Nellie and Alice were so eager to see the other evening." She eyed him curiously. "Do you believe in the powers of mesmerism, sir?"

He listened to the enthusiastic shouts of

approval that echoed from the Silver Pavilion. "I believe in selling tickets, madam. The mesmerist does that quite well."

Instead of smiling at his small bit of irony, her mouth tightened in a vaguely troubled line. "There are elements of Vanza that rely on what might be termed mesmerism."

"I will not argue with that. The mind is an unknown realm. Its mysteries lie at the heart of the philosophy of Vanza."

The crowd began to thin as the graveled path grew darker.

"Where are we going?" Madeline asked uneasily.

"To a section of the gardens that has not yet been opened to the public. We can be private there. I will show you the newest attraction."

"What is that?"

"The Haunted Mansion."

Her head came around swiftly. *Haunted?*

The sharpness of tone surprised him. "Do not tell me that you are afraid of ghosts, Mrs. Deveridge. I would not believe it for a moment."

She said nothing but he could feel the tension in her.

Ghosts?

When they reached the dark hedges that walled off the far end of the grounds, Artemis removed his mask.

"There is no need to be concerned that anyone will see you here, Mrs. Deveridge. This section of the grounds is closed to visitors."

She hesitated and then reluctantly reached up to take off her own mask. The moonlight gleamed on her dark hair.

"The Haunted Mansion is still under construction." Artemis opened a gate and picked up an unlit lantern that had been left nearby. "It is due to open next month. I expect it will be very popular with young people and courting couples."

Madeline said nothing as he lit the lantern and guided her along a graveled path walled in with high hedges. They rounded a corner and confronted a stone gate.

"The new maze," Artemis explained as they went past the gate. "It will open together with the Mansion. I designed it myself, using a Vanza pattern that I trust will confound most of my customers."

"I do not doubt it. My father always claimed that Vanza mazes were the most intricate he had ever encountered."

The disapproval in her voice made him smile. "You do not care for mazes?"

"As a girl I enjoyed them. But later I came to associate them with Vanza."

"So of course you ceased to find them amusing."

She slanted him an enigmatic glance but she did not respond.

He drew her around another corner. The Gothic facade of the Haunted Mansion loomed in the moonlight, its narrow windows appropriately dark and foreboding.

Madeline studied the ominous looking structure. "It looks exactly like a castle in one of Mrs. York's horrid novels. I vow, I would think twice about entering the place myself."

"I shall take that as a compliment."

She gave him a startled look. Then she gave him a reluctant smile. "I collect that you had a hand in the design of this attraction as well as the maze?"

"Yes. I believe this one will send a few chills down the spines of my more adventurous guests."

She gave him a searching look. "The Dream Pavilions are something more than a business investment for you, are they not?"

He contemplated the castle while he considered his answer. "I will tell you a secret that I would admit to no one else, Mrs. Deveridge. I bought these pleasure gardens because I believed them to be an excellent investment. I intended to build houses and shops on the land. Perhaps I will do that, eventually. But in the meantime I have discovered that I rather enjoy the planning and design of the various attractions. Selling dreams is a lucrative trade."

"I see." She gazed at the Haunted Mansion. "Do you intend to continue operating these gardens after you have found yourself a suitable wife?"

"I have not made that decision yet." He propped one booted foot on the low rock wall that marked the path leading to the castle. "This is the second time you have asked about my intentions toward my future wife. You seem quite concerned that I be honest with her."

"I recommend it highly."

"Ah, but what if she objects to my source of income?"

Madeline clasped her gloved hands behind her back. She seemed fascinated by the Gothic pavilion. "My advice is to be honest with her right from the start, sir."

"Even if it means that I shall risk losing her?"

"In my experience, deceit is not a good foundation for a marriage."

"Are you telling me that your marriage was built on that particular cornerstone?"

"My husband lied to me from the

moment we met, sir."

The combination of ice and fear in her voice made him go still. "What did he lie about?"

"Everything. He lied to my father and he lied to me. I discovered too late that I could believe nothing he told me. To this day I am still trying to sort out fact from fiction."

"An unpleasant state of affairs."

"Worse than you can imagine," she whispered starkly.

He reached out and caught her chin on the edge of his hand. "Before our business together proceeds any further, Mrs. Deveridge, I suggest that you and I make a pact."

"What pact would that be?"

"Let us promise that we will not lie to each other during the course of our association together. There may be things that we choose not to discuss. We may each keep our own secrets. Everyone is entitled to privacy, after all. But we will not tell lies to each other. Agreed?"

"Such a pact is easy enough to make, sir." Her eyes were bleak in the moonlight. "But how can either of us be certain that the other will live up to it?"

"An excellent question, Mrs. Deveridge. I have no good answer for it. In the end, it comes down to trust."

Her mouth twisted slightly. "They say that I am quite probably mad and a murderess into the bargain. Are you certain you wish to take the risk of trusting me?"

"We all have our little quirks and foibles, do we not?" He shrugged. "If we make this bargain, you will have much to overlook in me. There is my Vanza past and the unfortunate fact that I am in trade, after all."

She stared at him. Then she gave a short, muffled exclamation that could have been a laugh. "Very well, sir, you shall have my word, for what it's worth. I will tell you no lies."

"And you shall have none from me."

"An interesting bargain, is it not?" she said wryly. "A pact of honesty between a woman said to have murdered her husband in cold blood and a gentleman who conceals the truth about himself from the world."

"I am satisfied with it." He looked at her. "Now that we have made that bargain, perhaps you had better tell me what it is you require of me, Mrs. Deveridge."

"No need to be alarmed, sir. I want nothing more of you than what any reasonable person might expect from a madwoman." She continued to stare fixedly at the castle. "I wish you to help me find a ghost, sir."

He absorbed the implications of that statement for a long while. Then he exhaled slowly. "I cannot imagine that a lady of your intellect and education actually believes in phantoms."

Her jaw tightened. "I can almost believe in this particular specter."

"Does this ghost have a name?"

"Oh yes," she said softly. "He has a name. Renwick Deveridge."

Perhaps the rumors were right after all. Perhaps she truly was crazed, a candidate for Bedlam. Artemis was suddenly aware of the chill in the air. The fog was rising from the Thames to shroud the gardens.

"Do you actually believe that your dead husband has returned from the grave to haunt you?" he asked carefully.

"Shortly before he . . . died in that fire, my husband vowed to kill everyone in my family."

"Good God."

"He succeeded in murdering my father."

Artemis watched her intently. "Winton Reed is said to have died of a heart attack."

"It was poison, Mr. Hunt." She glanced at him and then looked away. "My aunt tried to save him but my father was quite elderly and his heart was weak. He died a few hours after the fire."

"I see." He kept his voice neutral. "I don't suppose you have any proof?"

"None whatsoever."

"Mmm."

"You don't believe me, do you, sir?" She swept out a hand. "I can't say that I blame you. Those who think I murdered my husband would no doubt claim that the guilt I must feel has driven me to seeing his ghost."

"Have you seen his ghost?"

"No." She hesitated. "But I know someone who has."

Mad as a March hare? he wondered. Or a clever murderess trying to use him in some dark scheme? Whatever it was, this conversation was certainly not turning out to be dull.

"What do you think is occurring, Mrs. Deveridge?"

"I know this sounds crazed but lately I have begun to wonder if it is possible that my husband did not die in the fire that night."

"I understood that Deveridge's body was found in the ashes."

"Yes. The doctor identified him. But what if . . . ?"

"What if the doctor was wrong? Is that

what you are trying to say?"

"Yes. I was told that the body was burned but not beyond recognition. Nevertheless, a mistake could have been made." She turned suddenly to face him, her eyes stark in the glare of the lantern. "One way or another, I must discover the truth and I must do so quickly. If my husband is still alive, I can only assume that he has returned to carry out his vengeance against my family. I must take action to protect my aunt and myself."

He eyed her for a long moment. "And if it transpires that you are indeed a victim of a fevered imagination, Mrs. Deveridge? What then?"

"Prove to me that I am wrong to believe that Renwick has come back from the grave. Show me that I am mad. I promise you, sir, I would welcome the knowledge that I have succumbed to a nervous affliction." Her mouth curved grimly. "At the very least, I can begin the cure. My aunt is very skilled at preparing tonics for that sort of thing."

He flexed his hand slowly. "Perhaps you should consult Bow Street, Mrs. Deveridge. Someone there may be able to help you."

"Even if I could convince a Bow Street runner that I was not mad, he would not stand a chance against an expert in the arts of Vanza."

"Deveridge was an expert?"

"Yes. He was not a master, though he longed to become one, but he was quite skilled. I must tell you, sir, that after going through my father's notes on the members of the Society, I have concluded that there is only one person other than yourself whom I might consult. Unfortunately, he is not available."

For some reason it irritated him to realize that she had actually considered employing someone else. "Who was the other man you deemed suitable for this task?"

"Mr. Edison Stokes."

"He's not even in England at the moment," Artemis muttered. "Got married a short while back. Took his bride on a tour of Roman ruins, I believe."

"Yes. Which leaves me with very little choice."

"Always gratifying to know that one is at the top of the list, even if one got there by default."

She met his eyes. "Well, sir? Will you assist me in my inquiries in exchange for my father's journal?"

He looked into her eyes and saw no madness there, only a fierce determination and a hint of true desperation. If he did not aid her, she would take on the task alone or perhaps seek the help of one of the many crackpot members of the Vanzagarian Society. Either way, she would put herself at great risk if her fears proved true.

If they proved true.

There were a thousand reasons not to get involved with this woman, he thought. But he could not seem to think of any of them at the moment.

"I will make some inquiries," he heard himself say cautiously. He saw her lips part. He raised his hand to silence her. "If they confirm your concerns, we will discuss the matter further. But I make no promises beyond that."

She gave him an unexpected smile, one that made the lantern light seem pale in comparison. "Thank you, sir. I assure you that when this is finished, you shall have my father's journal to do with as you like."

"Yes," he said. "I will." *One way or another.*

"Now then," she said crisply, "I expect you have some questions."

"I have a great many questions."

"I realize that what I have to tell you will sound somewhat bizarre, to say the least."

"No doubt."

"But I assure you, I have good reasons for my concerns."

"Speaking of the truth, madam . . ."

She gave him an inquiring look. "Yes?"

"Since we have agreed that we will be honest with each other, you had best know here and now that I find you very attractive, Madeline."

There was a heavy silence.

"Oh dear," she said eventually. "That is most unfortunate."

"No doubt, but there you have it."

"I had rather hoped we could avoid that particular complication."

"That makes two of us, madam."

"Nevertheless," she said briskly, "I expect you have an advantage over the other gentlemen who are similarly afflicted."

"Afflicted." He thought about that. "Yes, the word does appear to apply to the problem."

She frowned. "You are certainly not the first man to suffer this peculiar interest in me."

"I should no doubt be relieved to learn that I am not alone."

She sighed. "There is no comprehending it, but in truth, I have received any number of notes and bouquets from gentlemen during the past year. All of them seeking a romantical connection, if you can believe it."

"I see."

"It is really quite odd, but Aunt Bernice has explained to me that a certain sort of gentlemen is attracted to widows. That sort is apparently under the impression that a lady in my position has had some experience of the world and therefore a man need not concern himself with her, uh, lack of experience, shall we say."

Artemis nodded wisely. "In other words, he need not be held back by a gentlemanly regard for her innocence."

"Precisely. As Aunt Bernice says, there is, apparently, something about a widow."

"Mmm."

"Mind you, I can understand the appeal of experience to a man who is bent on conducting an affair with a lady."

"Mmm."

She shook her head slightly. "But one would think that the rumors surrounding the manner in which I achieved my widowhood would be somewhat off-putting to gentlemen."

"Indeed."

"Experience is all very well as far as it goes, but I confess I cannot comprehend the appeal of a lady who is said to have murdered her husband in cold blood."

"There is no accounting for taste." He decided not to mention the standing wager in the club betting books. The guarantee of a thousand pounds to any man who succeeded in spending a night with her was quite sufficient to explain the bouquets and invitations she had received. But she might not appreciate that fact.

She gave him an admonishing look. "My advice, sir, is to call upon your Vanza training to fortify yourself against any interest you may have in forming a romantical connection with me."

He framed her face with his hands. "I am sorry to tell you that even my status as a master does not seem to be proof against a desire to form a connection with you, Madeline."

Her eyes widened. "Truly?"

"Truly."

She swallowed visibly. "How very odd."

"Yes, isn't it. But as you are forever reminding me, the gentlemen of Vanza are nothing if not odd."

He bent his head and covered her mouth with his own before she could say another word.

He sensed her surprise and confusion but she did not attempt to push herself away. He pulled her into his arms, folding her tightly against his chest. She was closer now, much closer than she had been when they had danced the waltz. He could feel the warmth of her body. He knew that he was growing very hard against the soft curve of her hip. Her subtle scent filled his head.

She gave a small gasp. Then, abruptly, her mouth softened under his. The folds of her domino brushed against his boots.

He slipped his hands inside her domino and fitted his palms around her, just below the bodice of her gown. The gentle weight of her breasts rested tantalizingly on the edge of his hands. Urgency coursed through him. He felt his blood heat swiftly.

Perhaps there *was* something about a widow, he thought.

He drank hungrily from her mouth. Her response was enthusiastic enough, but strangely awkward. He reminded himself that she had not been a wife for a year now and that her marriage had apparently been unsatisfying.

The fierce demands of his body took him by surprise. His training had taught him control in all things, including his relations with women. In addition, he was no longer in the first flush of lustful youth.

But at the moment he felt very lustful indeed.

He slid his mouth to the sweet, vulnerable skin of her throat and tightened his hands around her slender body. Her fingers clenched in his hair. She shivered in his arms.

There was definitely something about a widow, he decided. At least there was something about this widow.

"Artemis." It was as though a dam had been breached somewhere inside her.

Her response sent passion rolling through him in a great wave. It had been years since he had been at the mercy of such a driving thirst. The fact that it threatened to outstrip the control he had spent so much time and effort acquiring should have shaken him to the core. Instead he ached to surrender to its snare.

"I was wrong," he said against her mouth. "You are even more dangerous than the rumors would have one believe."

"No."

"Yes."

"Perhaps it is no more than this peculiar affliction I mentioned a moment ago," she said breathlessly.

"Perhaps. But I must tell you that I do not give a bloody damn."

He tried to think while he deepened the kiss. It was not easy. But one fact hammered at him. He could not take her here on the damp grass.

He picked her up and started toward the steps of the Haunted Mansion. The folds of her cloak cascaded over his arms.

"Dear God." Madeline tore her mouth from his and simultaneously went rigid against him. In the shadows her eyes were huge, but not with passion. "The *window*."

"What?" Jolted back to reality by the shock and fear in her voice, he set her quickly on her feet and looked up at the row of narrow, vaulted windows. "What is it?"

"There is someone in there." She stared up at the panes of dark glass on the second level. "I saw him move, I swear it."

Artemis groaned. "I believe you."

"What?" She whirled to face him. "But who — ?"

"My young friend Zachary or one of his Eyes and Ears, no doubt. I have warned them repeatedly to stay out of this attraction until it is finished. But the bloodthirsty little devils are very excited about it. Gave Henry all sorts of ideas for creating a proper ghostly effect."

He started toward the steps.

"Artemis, wait —"

"Stay here." He picked up the lantern and opened the front door. "This won't take but a moment. I'll soon have the lads on their way."

"I do not like this, Artemis." She hugged herself and gazed uneasily at the door. "Please come away. Send one of your employees to deal with the matter."

Her anxiety was beyond reason, he thought. On the other hand, this was a lady who feared the ghost of a murdered husband. He thought about the stout shutters and warning bells she had installed in her home. What diabolical fate had put him in the hands of this female? But he could not turn away from her, and it was not just her father's journal that chained him now.

"Calm yourself," he said in what he hoped were soothing tones. "I shall return in a moment."

He entered the Haunted Mansion. The light from his lamp flared on the imitation stone hall, creating pockets of deep shadows beneath the twisting staircase.

"Damnation, how can you be so bloody stubborn?" Madeline picked up her skirts and rushed up the steps to follow him into the attraction. "I really did see someone in the window."

"I told you that I do not doubt you."

"Do not pretend to humor me, sir. You are now in my employ. If you insist on confronting the intruder, then it is my responsibility to accompany you."

He briefly considered and rejected the notion of forcing her to go back outside. She was obviously overwrought by whatever it was she had glimpsed in the darkened window. She would only grow more anxious if he made her wait alone out on the path. It was unlikely that the intruder, if he actually existed, would present a serious threat.

"As you wish." He started up the narrow staircase that led to the next floor of the castle. The light of the lantern danced eerily on the walls.

"No offense," Madeline muttered behind him, "but I, for one, have no intention of ever paying good money to view this ghastly attraction."

"It is rather effective, isn't it?" He glanced at the bleached bones dangling in a stone recess. "What do you think of the skeleton?"

"Perfectly dreadful."

"It was Short John's contribution to the decor. When the attraction is completed, there will be several ghosts hanging from the ceiling and a rather nice display of a head-less corpse. One of the other lads suggested some cowled figures for the top of the stairs."

"Artemis, for God's sake, this is no time to conduct a guided tour. There is an in-truder up there somewhere. He may be waiting to pounce on us."

"Highly unlikely. Zachary and his friends are well aware that I would take a dim view of that sort of thing." A very dim view. When he got his hands on the urchin who had interrupted his passionate interlude with Madeline, he would let him know just how much he objected to such interference. "By and large, the Eyes and Ears are a good lot, but once in a while —"

He broke off abruptly, distracted by the shadowy movement at the top of the stairs. The lamplight caught the edge of a cloak, but the figure was already moving away. The intruder vanished down a long hall on near-silent feet.

"Artemis," Madeline breathed.

He ignored her, vaulted the last of the steps, and raced after the fleeing figure. He heard Madeline behind him. For the first time he questioned his decision to allow her to accompany him. He had caught only a glimpse of the intruder, but that was enough to tell him that the person he was chasing was a man, not an urchin.

At the end of the hall, a door slammed shut. Artemis came to a halt in front of it, set down the lantern, and twisted the handle. It turned but the door did not open.

"Bastard has wedged something heavy up

against it," he told Madeline.

He leaned his shoulder against the panels and shoved hard.

"Let me help." Madeline moved into place behind him and planted both hands on the wood.

Artemis felt the door shift as the heavy object that had been placed in front of it scraped across the bare floor. He heard movement inside the room.

"What the bloody hell is he doing in there?" he muttered.

He gave one last shove against the door. It opened far enough to allow him to slip into the darkened chamber.

"Stay here," he said to Madeline. This time he made it a clear command.

"For God's sake, be careful," she said in a voice that carried an edge of authority as sharp as his own.

Artemis lunged into the room, keeping his body low and angled to the side so as to present less of a target. Instinctively he fell back on his old training and sought the deepest shadows.

But he knew already that he was too late.

Cool night air wafted through the window that opened onto the miniature balcony. A net of artificial cobwebs danced on the currents of the light draft. The gossamer curtain billowed in an eerie fashion in the moonlight, silently taunting him.

Bloody idiot, Artemis thought. How did he expect to escape that way? Unless he chose to risk the long drop to the ground, the intruder was well and truly trapped.

Trapped creatures were often extremely dangerous, however.

He circled a recently painted canvas backdrop that featured a pair of specters hovering over a crypt. Easing aside the veil of cobwebs, he edged toward the window. He could see the length of the small balcony. It was empty.

"There is no one out there," Madeline whispered from the middle of the chamber. "He has disappeared."

"He'll be lucky if he did not break his neck when he jumped."

"I heard no sound."

She was right.

Artemis stepped out onto the balcony and looked down. He saw no crumpled figure lying on the grass. Nor could he detect anyone limping away into the woods toward the seldom used south gate.

"Gone," she whispered.

"There is no way he could have jumped that far without injuring an ankle." He stepped back and looked up. "I wonder if he used another route."

"The roof?"

"It's possible, although he would still face the problem of getting down from his perch —" Artemis broke off as the toe of his boot brushed against a soft, pliable object. He looked down. A cold feeling twisted through him. "Bloody hell."

Madeline watched as he reached to retrieve the thing he had trod upon. "What is it?"

"The reason our intruder did not crack his skull when he went over this balcony a few minutes ago." Artemis held up a length of rope with an intricate knot tied in one end. "He no doubt used this to enter the mansion as well as to leave it."

Madeline sighed. "Well, at least you know that I did not see a ghost."

"On the contrary, I do not think that we can be entirely certain of that fact."

She tensed. "What do you mean?"

Artemis drew the heavy cord slowly across the palm of his hand. "The knots he used in his rope ladder are Vanza knots."

Chapter Eight

"Tell me the tale from the beginning," Artemis said.

Madeline looked out at the small, bare garden through the library window. She clasped her hands behind her back and concentrated on composing her thoughts. She was keenly aware of Artemis lounging against the edge of her desk, waiting for her to begin her explanations.

Last night after the incident in the Haunted Mansion, he had brought her straight home, checked the locks on her shutters, and promised to send someone to keep watch on her house for the remainder of the night.

"Try to get some rest," he'd said. "I wish to do some thinking. I will return in the morning and we shall make plans."

She had spent the night trying to decide how much to tell him. Now she must pick and choose her words carefully. "I told you that my husband murdered my father with poison. I found Papa before he died. Bernice tried to save him but even her strongest remedies proved ineffective. She said that Renwick had used some fatal Vanza brew."

"Go on."

His voice was very even in tone. It gave nothing away. She could not tell if he believed her.

"We had all realized by then that Renwick was quite insane. Oh, he hid it well for several months. Long enough to fool my father and me and everyone else. But in the end it became obvious."

"What made it plain to you that your husband was a madman?"

She hesitated. "After our marriage it soon became clear that there was something very strange about Renwick. He spent hours in a special chamber at the top of the house. He called it his laboratory. He always kept it locked. He would not allow anyone inside. But one afternoon while he performed his meditation exercises, I was able to steal the key."

"You searched the locked room?"

"Yes." She looked down at her hands. "I suppose you are thinking that it was not the act of an obedient wife."

Artemis ignored that. "What did you find?"

She turned around slowly to meet his eyes. "Proof that Renwick was deeply involved in the shadowy side of Vanza."

"What sort of proof?"

"Journals. Books. Notes. Alchemical rubbish that my father always disdained. He said that sort of thing was not true Vanza. But I know from my own researches that there has always been a dark undercurrent of magic and alchemy running through the philosophy."

"Bloody occult nonsense. The monks of the Garden Temples do not teach those things. The knowledge is forbidden."

She raised her brows. "You know what they say about forbidden knowledge, sir. For some it holds great allure."

"Your husband was one of those men who are attracted to it, I take it?"

"Yes. That was the real reason he sought out my father and wormed his way into our household. He even went so far as to marry me in an attempt to convince Papa to teach him what he wished to know. He believed that if he made himself a part of our family, Papa would share all his secrets with him."

"What secrets did Deveridge wish to learn?"

"Two things. The first was knowledge of the ancient language of Vanza, the one in which the old books of alchemy and magic are written."

"And the second thing?"

Her jaw tightened. "Renwick wanted to become a full master. Indeed, he was obsessed with attaining that status."

"Your father refused to instruct him in the knowledge of the highest circles?"

She drew a deep breath. "Yes. Papa finally realized, too late, that Renwick was evil. My husband actually believed that if he could decipher the secrets of the occult texts of Vanza, he could transform himself into a sorcerer."

"Deveridge was indeed mad if he believed that."

"More than mad, sir. Murderous. Shortly before he died, my father warned Bernice and me that Renwick had vowed to kill us all. My husband intended to destroy the entire family because of Papa's refusal to teach him what he needed to know in order to decipher the old occult books."

"But Deveridge conveniently died at the hands of a housebreaker before he could complete his vengeance," Artemis said quietly.

"Yes." Madeline met his intent, steady gaze. "Bernice believes that it was nothing less than the hand of fate in action."

"Mmm." Artemis nodded thoughtfully. "Fate is always a handy explanation for that sort of thing, is it not?"

She cleared her throat. "Indeed, I do not know what might have happened if Renwick had lived. With Papa dead, there was no one to protect Bernice and me from him."

"If what you have told me is true, I can certainly comprehend your dilemma."

She closed her eyes for a few seconds, steeling herself. "You do not believe me."

"Let us say that I am withholding final judgment at this point."

"I know it all sounds very bizarre, sir, but it is the truth." She clenched her hands. "I swear to you that I am not mad. The things I have told you are not the product of an overwrought imagination. You must believe me."

He contemplated her for a moment longer. Then, without a word, he rose to his feet and crossed the room to the brandy table. He picked up the heavy crystal decanter, removed the stopper, and poured the liquor into a glass.

He carried the glass to her and folded one of her hands around it. "Drink."

The glass felt cool in her fingers. She gazed down at the contents, aware that her mind had gone numb. She said the only thing that she could think of to say. "But it is only eleven o'clock in the morning, sir. One does not drink brandy at this hour."

"You would be surprised by what some people do at eleven o'clock in the morning. Drink it."

"I vow, you are as annoying as Aunt Bernice with her tonics." Raising the glass, she took a swallow of brandy. It burned all the way down, but the heat felt surprisingly good. So good, in fact, that she decided to take a second sip.

"Now then," Artemis said, "let us get to the meat of the situation. It has been a year since your husband's death. What else besides the incident in the Haunted Mansion last night has happened to make you think that Renwick Deveridge has returned to avenge himself on you and yours?"

"Do not mistake me, sir." She set the glass down forcefully. "I know that gossip has it that I am given to wild fancies and fevered visions. But I have good cause to fear that something very strange is happening."

He smiled slightly. "I see the brandy has had a restorative effect on your spirits, madam. Tell me about the ghost of Renwick Deveridge."

She folded her arms beneath her breasts and began to prowl the library. "I certainly do not believe that Renwick Deveridge has somehow done the impossible and returned from the grave to haunt us. If he is out there somewhere, it is because he managed to survive the fire. I have asked you to hunt for a ghost, but I do not actually believe in specters."

"I will take your word for it." He propped one shoulder against the end of a bookcase. He did not take his eyes off her face. "Allow me to rephrase my question. What has happened recently to arouse your fear of Deveridge?"

Explaining this next bit was going to be somewhat tricky, she thought. "A week ago I received a note from a gentleman who was a colleague of my father's. He, too, is something of an expert in ancient languages, and he has studied the old tongue of Vanzagara."

"What did this note say?"

She braced herself. "In his message he told me that he had seen Renwick Deveridge's ghost in his library. He felt he ought to let me know about the incident."

"Bloody hell."

She sighed. "I know it is an outlandish tale, sir. But you must take portions of it seriously or you will do me no good at all."

"Who is this scholar who claimed to see the ghost?"

Another nasty bit, she thought. "Lord Linslade."

"Linslade?" Artemis gave her an incredulous look. "Everyone knows the man's a crackbrain. He's been seeing ghosts for years. Talks to the shade of his dead wife regularly, I'm told."

"I know." She stopped pacing and sank into the nearest chair. "Believe me, although his note gave me something of a jolt, I did not place any credence in it until . . ."

"Until what?"

"Until four days ago, when I got a message from Mr. Pitney."

Artemis watched her closely. "Eaton Pitney?"

"Do you know him?"

"I met him once or twice years ago. He is also a distinguished expert in ancient languages."

"Indeed."

"I understand Pitney has become every bit as eccentric as Linslade in recent years."

"Yes." She leaned back in her chair and looked at him. "He is definitely odd, even by the standards of the membership of the Vanzagarian Society. For years he has believed that he is being watched by phantoms he calls Strangers. I understand that he fired his entire household staff last year in an attempt to get rid of any Strangers posing as servants."

"Did Pitney claim to have seen Deveridge's ghost, too?" Artemis asked dryly.

"No, Mr. Hunt." She drummed her fingers on the arm of the chair and struggled to hold on to a few shreds of her patience. "He did not mention ghosts in his note."

His expression softened slightly although his eyes remained cool and watchful. "What, exactly, did he say in his message?"

"I will show it to you."

She rose, removed the key she kept around her neck, and went to the cupboard where she kept the journal of the members of the Vanzagarian Society. She opened the door and took out one of the notes she had put inside.

She glanced at the tiny, cramped writing and then handed the message to Artemis without comment.

He took it from her and read it aloud.

"My Dear Mrs. D.,

As a former colleague of your esteemed father, I feel that it is my responsibility to inform you that after years of watching me from the shadows, one of the Strangers recently grew so bold as to attempt to invade my library. Fortunately, he was thwarted by my stout locks and shutters.

148

It is the fact that the Stranger appeared to be intent on gaining entrance to my books and notes that led me to wonder if he might pose a threat to other experts in the old tongue. Your father once told me that he had taught you his skills in the ancient language of Vanzagara. I am also aware that you still possess Winton Reed's books and papers. I thought it best to warn you that someone may be searching for that sort of thing.

As you no doubt know, there were recent rumors about an ancient text of Vanza called the Book of Secrets. Utter rubbish, of course, but the tales may have drawn the Strangers out of the shadows to search for it. . . ."

Artemis refolded the note. He looked thoughtful. Madeline took that as a good sign.

"I realize that it is not much to go on," she said carefully. "A message about a ghost from a gentleman who is known to see them on a regular basis and a warning about a phantom who may or may not have tried to enter the library of a gentleman who has been plagued by strange notions for years. Nevertheless, I cannot bring myself to ignore those notes from Linslade and Pitney."

"You need not explain further, Madeline," Artemis said quietly. "I comprehend now what it is that has alarmed you."

A great sense of relief soared through her. "You do see the links between those two notes then, sir?"

"Of course. Either of these messages, taken separately, could have been dismissed out of hand as the scribblings of a crackpot. But together they comprise a pattern."

"Precisely."

He did understand, she thought. But then, he was Vanza. The willingness to see through the layers of reality to the possibilities beneath the surface was one of the most basic principles of the philosophy.

"The most interesting fact here," Artemis continued, "is Linslade's conviction that it was not just any ghost he encountered, but the specter of your dead husband."

"You see why I felt it necessary to take precautions and to make some inquiries into the matter."

"Indeed." He looked at her. "I presume you wish to start with Linslade?"

"Yes. I thought we might call upon him this very afternoon, if that is agreeable to you."

Artemis shrugged. "I will admit to some

curiosity in the matter. I have never had an extended discussion with a man who claims to converse regularly with ghosts."

"How kind of you to call, Mrs. Deveridge." Lord Linslade dimpled with pleasure as he directed Madeline to a chair. She could have sworn that his bird-bright eyes actually twinkled as he turned to Artemis.

"And you, sir. Delighted to see you again, Hunt." He gave Artemis an elfin smile. "It has been some time since we last met, has it not?"

"Several years, I believe," Artemis said as he took a chair.

"Indeed." Linslade bobbed his head and perched behind his desk. "Much too long, sir. I understand you studied in the Garden Temples and are now a master of the old arts."

Madeline looked at the full-length portrait of Lady Linslade that dominated the wall behind the baron's desk. The picture showed a sturdy, full-bosomed woman who, while she was alive, had towered over her dapper little husband. She was dressed in a low-cut, square-necked evening gown decorated with Greek and Etruscan designs. It was a style that had been in the first stare of fashion at the time of her death twelve years earlier.

Madeline recalled that Lord and Lady Linslade had always been quite keen on keeping abreast of the latest fashions. While Lady Linslade was now forever stuck in a twelve-year-old gown, her husband had continued to stay current. Today Linslade wore an elegantly tailored ensemble that included a rose-pink satin waistcoat and a cravat tied in the latest, most intricate manner.

Linslade folded his small, neatly manicured hands on his desk and beamed at Madeline. "I must tell you, my dear, I have had some extremely stimulating conversations with your father."

Madeline froze. "You have spoken with Papa?"

"Yes, indeed." Linslade chuckled. "I vow, I see more of Reed now than I did when he was alive."

Madeline noticed the amused glint in Artemis's eye and tried to ignore it.

"What topics do you discuss with my father?" she asked cautiously.

"We generally consult each other about our researches into the old Vanzagarian tongue, of course," Linslade said. "Winton Reed always did hold the most interesting notions. I have long been of the opinion that he and Ignatius Lorring were among the most expert authorities on the language in all of Europe."

"I see." Madeline gave Artemis another quick, uneasy glance. She was not sure what to say next.

"Tell me, sir," Artemis said quite casually, "do you hold conversations with Lorring, too, these days?"

"Lorring has not seen fit to call upon me since his death a few months ago. Not surprising, really." Linslade sniffed. "The man always was extremely arrogant and opinionated. Very high in the instep, you know. Considered himself the final authority on every aspect of Vanza. I doubt that he has changed much in that respect since his death."

"He *was* the explorer and scholar who discovered the Isle of Vanzagara," Artemis reminded him. "It was Lorring who made the art and philosophy known to us. He was the founder and the first Grand Master of the Vanzagarian Society. One could say that he had some right to his high opinion of himself."

"Yes, yes, I know." Linslade fluttered one hand in a delicate, dismissive gesture. "No one disputes his position as the discoverer of Vanzagara. To be honest, I had rather hoped that he *would* call upon me after his death. He was very ill toward the end of his life, you know. He did not see many visitors. I never got the opportunity to ask him about a certain rumor I heard shortly before he died."

"What rumor was that?" Artemis asked.

"Surely you heard it, too, sir?" Linslade looked at him. "Several months back, the membership of the Vanzagarian Society was all abuzz with tales of the theft of a certain very old book."

"The *Book of Secrets*," Artemis said. "Yes, I heard the gossip. I did not put any stock in it, however."

"No, of course not," Linslade said quickly. "Utter rubbish. But quite curious, don't you think? It would have been interesting to obtain Lorring's views on the matter."

"According to what little I heard," Artemis said deliberately, "the *Book of Secrets*, if indeed it existed, was destroyed in a fire that consumed Farrell Blue's villa in Italy."

"Yes, yes, I know." Linslade sighed. "Unfortunately, Blue has not called upon me since his death, either, so I have been unable to question him about the matter."

This was going nowhere, Madeline

thought. It was time to take charge of the conversation. "My lord, you mentioned in your note that you had seen my late husband recently."

"Right here in my library." Linslade's cheerful expression dissolved into a troubled frown. "Something of a surprise, you know. We had met on one or two occasions during the time he was a student of your father's, but we were not what you would call close friends."

Artemis stretched out his legs and studied the toes of his gleaming boots. "Would you consider him a colleague?"

"We certainly shared similar scholarly interests, but Deveridge had no use for my theories and opinions. In fact, he made it quite clear that he considered me a doddering old fool. He struck me as rather rude." Linslade paused abruptly and gave Madeline an apologetic look. "Forgive me, my dear, I did not mean to criticize your late husband."

She managed a cool little smile. "I'm sure you're well aware that my marriage was not a happy union, sir."

"I confess I had heard rumors to that effect." Sympathy warmed Linslade's bright eyes. "How very tragic. I am so sorry you did not know the degree of bliss, both

155

physical and metaphysical, that Lady Linslade and I were fortunate enough to experience."

"I understand that sort of happiness in marriage is uncommon, sir," Madeline said crisply. "Now then, about the conversation you had with my late husband. Could you relate it to us?"

"Certainly." Linslade pursed his lips. "It did not last long. In fact, we very nearly did not meet at all. Merest chance, as it were."

Artemis looked up from his boots. "What do you mean?"

"It was quite late when Deveridge appeared here in the library. The household had been abed for hours. If I had not had some trouble sleeping that night and decided to come down here to fetch a book, I would have missed him altogether."

Madeline leaned forward slightly. "What, precisely, did he say to you, sir?"

"Let me think." Linslade's brows bunched together in a meditative frown. "I believe I spoke first. The customary civilities were exchanged. I told him I was surprised to see him. Mentioned that I'd heard about his death in a house fire a year ago."

"What did he say to that?" Artemis asked with what sounded like genuine curiosity.

"I believe he remarked that it had been

most inconvenient."

"Inconvenient?" Madeline felt trickles of icy perspiration beneath her gown. "That was the word he used?"

"Yes, I'm quite sure it was." Linslade wriggled uncomfortably and gave her an apologetic look. "As I said, we chatted. Naturally, I did not go into detail concerning the gossip I'd heard about the exact manner of his, er, demise, my dear."

"Naturally." Madeline coughed slightly to clear her throat. "Very kind of you not to discuss the unfortunate rumors that have been circulating."

"I am always very polite with the dead," Linslade assured her. "They seem to appreciate it. Always felt that what went on between a man and his wife was entirely their affair, in any event."

Artemis looked at Linslade. "How did Deveridge respond when you addressed him?"

"Seemed a bit startled when I first spoke to him." Linslade's brows rose. "It was as if he hadn't been expecting to see me. Can't imagine why. He was the one who had called upon me, and he was in my library, after all."

"Indeed. What else did you talk about?"

"I asked him if he was still pursuing his

157

studies of the old tongue. He said he was." Linslade jiggled his brows. "Mentioned the gossip about the *Book of Secrets*, as a matter of fact. Asked me if I'd heard the latest rumor on the subject."

"What was that?" Artemis asked without any inflection.

"Something about the *Book of Secrets* having survived the fire in Italy, after all. Said he'd heard that the recipes in it had not only been written in the old tongue, but had been set down in a sort of code. Very complicated stuff, even for a great authority on the language. Seemed to feel that some means of explaining or deciphering it would be required in order to translate the thing."

Madeline tightened one gloved hand. "Did you comment on that?"

Linslade snorted delicately. "Told him that any talk of the *Book of Secrets* must be considered as naught but idle gossip."

"Did he say anything else?" Madeline heard the tremor in her own voice and clamped her teeth together.

"Nothing of significance. We chatted for a few moments longer and then he left." Artemis looked at Madeline. "He asked me to mention him to you, my dear. Said something about not wanting you to forget him.

That's why I sent you a note about our meeting."

Madeline stopped breathing for a few seconds. She could not move so much as a finger. She was aware that Artemis was watching her with an enigmatic, sidelong look, but she could not turn her head to meet his eyes.

She stared at Linslade. The man conversed regularly with ghosts. He was not entirely sane. But he did not appear to be utterly mad, either. How much of what he said was truth and how much was fancy? How did one sort out the two?

She glanced at the portrait of Lady Linslade in her twelve-year-old gown. A thought struck her.

"My lord," she said carefully, "I'm curious about one point. When you encounter your lady wife's ghost, how is she dressed?"

"Dressed? Why, in a rather fine gown, of course." Linslade smiled benignly. "Lady Linslade always had excellent taste."

Madeline caught Artemis's eye. He must have realized her intent, because he inclined his head ever so slightly in approval.

"Does Lady Linslade continue to keep up with the latest styles?" Madeline held her breath.

159

Linslade looked surprised and then vaguely regretful. "I'm afraid not. She always appears in that lovely gown she wore for her portrait. She was rather fond of the Greek and Etruscan style, you know."

"I see." Madeline breathed cautiously. "And my father? When you saw his ghost, how was he garbed?"

Linslade beamed. "Exactly as he was the last time I called upon him. He wears that dark blue coat he always wore to the meetings of the Society and a rather unfortunate yellow waistcoat. You recall it, I'm sure."

"Yes." She swallowed. "I recall his yellow waistcoat. What about my husband? Do you remember what his ghost wore when he came to see you the other evening?"

"As a matter of fact, I do. I recall thinking that he presented a very stylish appearance. He wore a dark coat cut away in the latest fashion and his cravat was tied in the Serenade. That particular knot is all the crack at the moment, you know."

"I see," Madeline whispered.

"Oh, and there was one other thing. He carried a walking stick. It had a fine gold handle carved in the shape of a falcon's head. Very handsome."

The hair on the nape of Madeline's neck stirred.

★ ★ ★

Ten minutes later Artemis handed her up into the carriage, got in behind her, and closed the door. He did not like the strain he saw in her eyes. She was composed but much too pale.

"Are you all right?" he asked as the vehicle rumbled forward.

"Yes, of course." She laced her fingers together deliberately. "Artemis, it sounds very much as if Linslade encountered a genuine intruder in his library the other night, not a ghost."

"An intruder who looked enough like your dead husband to make Linslade think it was Renwick Deveridge's ghost." He settled back into the seat. "Interesting. By the way, I must tell you, Madeline, that was an extremely clever line of inquiry you pursued there at the end. Should have thought of asking about the attire the various ghosts favored myself."

She looked surprised by the compliment. "Thank you, sir."

He shrugged. "It would seem that, as a rule, the ghosts who call upon Linslade choose to appear in the clothes they were accustomed to wear when they were alive. But Renwick's shade was dressed in the current fashion, not last year's styles."

161

"Linslade is quite eccentric," Madeline reminded him uneasily.

"I will not quarrel with you on that point. It's possible that we're placing too much emphasis on his responses to our questions. The man is obviously given to wild fancies. Perhaps he conjured up current attire for Deveridge's ghost because his disordered brain could not recall what your husband had worn the last time they had met."

She contemplated that for a few seconds. "I see what you mean. I'm sure that his lordship is too much the gentleman to imagine a nude ghost."

"A nude ghost. What an interesting notion."

She gave him a quelling glance. "I cannot believe that we are sitting here discussing the fashion tastes of specters. Anyone who overheard us would no doubt conclude that we had both escaped from a madhouse."

"Yes."

"Artemis, I must tell you something."

"What is that?"

"Lord Linslade mentioned that the ghost carried a . . . a walking stick."

"What of it? Walking sticks are very much in fashion at the moment. I do not carry one myself, but that is because I find them to be a damned nuisance."

She looked out at the street. "The thing about the stick Linslade described is that it sounded quite unique."

"Ah yes. The gold handle carved in the shape of the head of a bird of prey. What of it?"

She exhaled slowly. "It not only sounded unique, it sounded horribly familiar. Renwick always carried a walking stick that fit Linslade's description exactly."

A stillness welled up inside him. "Are you quite certain of that?"

"Yes." An expression that was disturbingly close to panic flared in her eyes. She got control of herself immediately. "Yes, I am quite certain of it. He once told me that it had been a gift from his father."

Artemis studied her for a long time.

"I think it would be best if you and your aunt moved into my house until this thing is ended," he said eventually.

She stared at him. "Move into your house? But that is ridiculous. Why on earth should we do such a thing?"

"Because I am convinced that your very large coachman and those little bells on your shutters will prove useless against Renwick Deveridge's ghost."

"But, Artemis . . ."

He held her eyes. "You have dragged me

into this affair, madam. So be it. We have a bargain. I will find your phantom for you. But you, in turn, must agree to follow my instructions regarding your safety."

She gave him a suspicious look. "Your orders, you mean."

"You may apply whatever term pleases you. But in affairs such as this, there cannot be two in command. You will put everyone in your household at risk if you challenge me at every turn."

"I am not challenging you, sir. I am questioning the wisdom of your suggestion."

"Oddly enough," he said, "I interpret that as a challenge."

She stirred restlessly. "You are somewhat sensitive on the subject of your authority, are you not, sir?"

"I am extremely sensitive on that particular subject. So sensitive, in fact, that I rarely allow anyone to question it."

She glared at him. "You cannot expect me to turn all of the decisions over to you."

"May I remind you again that you are the one who sought me out, madam? You offered a bargain and I accepted. We made a pact."

She hesitated and then apparently decided to try another tack. "Sir, you must not lose sight of your other goal."

For an unpleasant moment he thought again that she had somehow learned of his plans to avenge Catherine. "My other goal?"

"You know very well that you are in the market for a well-connected wife." She gave him a cross look. "You have made it plain that you are concerned that if it were to get out that you are in trade, you would not be able to form the sort of marital alliance you desire to contract."

"What of it?"

"I must tell you that it is not just your being in trade that might put some people off," she said darkly. "Many families in the best circles might well take exception to the notion of your entertaining the Wicked Widow as a houseguest."

"I hadn't considered that possibility." He cocked a brow. "Do you really believe that some of the high sticklers might actually object to my choice of guests?"

"Yes, I do."

"How very narrow-minded of them."

"The thing is," she said earnestly, "it would not reflect at all well on your sensibilities. You must see that. I can assure you that the sort of ladies who might be on your list of potential wives would not care to learn that you have had me under your roof for an extended stay."

"Madeline, when was the last time you slept through the night?"

Her eyes widened, but once again she collected herself with remarkable speed. "How did you guess?"

"I spoke with the man I posted on the street outside your house last night. He said that the light remained on in your window until dawn. I suspect that is a frequent occurrence."

She turned her head to stare out at the sunlit street. "For some reason, I have assumed that if he came back, it would be at night. He was a creature of the darkness, you see."

"Deveridge?"

"Yes. He looked like an angel but he was, in truth, a demon. It seems to me that whoever or *whatever* has returned to avenge him will also prefer the night."

Artemis leaned forward and gently caged her hands within his. He waited until she met his eyes.

"Your reasoning is sound," he said. "Those who favor the occult gibberish that belongs to the dark strain of Vanza have a taste for the melodramatic. They are known to favor the night for their activities. But I fear you cannot depend upon a practitioner of the dark arts always working in darkness. The very fact that you are more likely to expect him at night might lead him to choose to act in daylight."

"It is all so bloody complicated," she whispered with anguished vehemence. "I wish my father had never gotten involved with Vanza. I wish I had never heard of the philosophy or met anyone who studied it."

"Madeline —"

She clenched her hands into small fists between his palms. "I vow, when this is over, I will never again have anything to do with anything or anyone connected to that horrid philosophy."

A cold sensation gripped his insides. "You have made your sentiments toward Vanza clear. What you choose to do when this affair is ended is your own concern. But in the meantime, you have employed me for my expertise. I expect you to listen to reason. If you will not think of your own safety, you must consider your aunt. Do you wish to put her at risk?"

She studied his face for a long time. His logic was inescapable and he could see that she understood that. *Vanza logic.* He knew her answer before she did.

"No, of course not," she said quietly. "You are quite right. I must consider Aunt

Bernice's safety. I shall make the arrangements immediately. We can move into your home this very day."

"A wise decision, madam."

She gave him a disgruntled glare. "I was not aware that I made the decision, sir. I believe you are the one who made it."

"Mmm."

"Perhaps," she said thoughtfully, "if we are very careful, very discreet, and quite lucky, no one in your social circles will notice that you have houseguests. Or if they do notice, they will not recognize me."

"Mmm."

He decided not to mention the thousand-pound bet in all the club books.

Chapter Nine

Shortly after two in the morning, Artemis put down his cards and looked at his opponent. "I believe you owe me five hundred pounds, Flood."

"Don't worry, you'll get your damned money by the end of the month, Hunt." Corwin Flood scrawled his name on his voucher and tossed it onto the table.

Artemis raised one brow as he picked up the slip of paper. "You'll pay your debts at the end of the month? Can I take that to mean that you are under the hatches at the moment, Flood?"

"Not at all." Flood reached for the bottle that sat on the table. He filled the glass and downed the claret in a long, eager swallow. When he finished he set aside his glass and eyed Artemis with a brooding gaze. "Sank a bloody fortune into an investment opportunity, the sort that comes along only once in a man's lifetime. Scraped together everything I had in order to buy my shares. It'll pay off in a fortnight. That's when you'll get your money."

"I shall look forward to the day your ship comes in."

Flood snorted. "Ain't a friggin' ship. Wouldn't have put so much into a bloody ship. Too damned risky. Ships sink. Ships disappear at sea. Ships get attacked by pirates." He leaned partway across the table and lowered his voice to a confiding tone. "There's no risk in my investment, sir. What's more, it will pay off far more handsomely than shares in a ship." He grinned slyly. "Unless, of course, the ship happened to be carrying a cargo of pure gold."

"I confess, you have got my interest now. Nothing like gold to captivate a man's attention."

Flood's grin faded abruptly. He seemed to realize that he had said too much. "I was merely jesting, sir." He glanced furtively around and then poured himself more claret. "Just a little humor, that's all."

Artemis got leisurely to his feet. "I trust you were not joking about your financial prospects at the end of the month." He smiled slightly. "I would be disappointed if it transpired that you could not pay off your gaming debts, Flood. Very disappointed."

Flood flinched. Then he scowled angrily. "You'll get your money." His voice was slightly slurred.

"I'm glad to hear that. Are you certain you can't tell me about this investment that is due to pay off in a fortnight? Perhaps it is something that would be of interest to me."

"Sorry," Flood said shortly. "All the shares have been sold. Shouldn't have mentioned it at all. The shareholders have been sworn to secrecy." He looked worried now. "I say, you won't tell anyone about this, will you?"

Artemis smiled slowly. "I will say nothing to anyone, Flood. You have my word on it. The very last thing I wish to do is interfere with your investment."

Flood stared fixedly, as though something in Artemis's smile had put him into a trance. Then he blinked once and seemed to give himself a shake. "Right you are. In your own best interests to keep your mouth shut, eh? Won't get your money if you interfere with my investment prospects."

"Very true."

Artemis turned to walk toward the front hall. Three young, fashionably dressed men, all of whom appeared to be thoroughly foxed, lurched into his path.

One of them stepped forth, eyes widening with theatrical astonishment. He thrust out a hand with a dramatic flourish.

"What ho! My friends, who do we see before us? I do believe it is the bravest, boldest, most fearless man in all of England. I give you Hunt."

The other two chanted a chorus.

"Hunt, Hunt, Hunt."

"Look closely upon that noble visage, study him well, for we may not see his like again in this fair club room."

"Hunt, Hunt, Hunt."

"Upon the morrow our brave Hunt will either be a thousand pounds richer, or —"

"Hunt, Hunt, Hunt."

"Or he will have left this mortal plane forever, dispatched to the great beyond by none other than the Wicked Widow."

"Hunt, Hunt, Hunt."

"We wish him well tonight. At the very least, we wish him a stout, unflagging cock so that he may enjoy his last night on this earth."

"Hunt, Hunt, Hunt."

Artemis walked deliberately toward the three young blades. They laughed uproariously and gave him sweeping bows as they scrambled out of his path.

"Hunt, Hunt, Hunt."

Artemis paused at the doorway and turned halfway around. He gave the three a long, thoughtful stare. A hush of expectation fell on the club room. He removed his watch from his pocket. All eyes were riveted on him as he opened the lid and examined the time.

When he was finished, he closed the lid and casually dropped the watch back into his pocket. "I fear I must take my leave somewhat early tonight. I have affairs that require my attention. I'm sure you all understand."

The three rakes snickered. Muffled laughter sounded from a card table.

"But tomorrow —" Artemis paused for effect. "Always assuming I survive the night, of course —"

One of the young dandies guffawed. "Assuming that degree of optimism, sir, what will you do tomorrow?"

"Tomorrow I shall look forward to making dawn appointments with every man in this club who is so impolite as to insult my new houseguest in my hearing."

The three men stared at Artemis, eyes stark with shock, mouths agape. The interested hush that had settled on the club room became an appalled silence.

Satisfied with the effect he had made, Artemis walked out into the hall. He collected his greatcoat and gloves and went down the steps to the street.

He was less than three strides from the front door when he heard hurried footsteps behind him.

"Hold on there, Hunt," Flood called. "I'll share a carriage with you."

"There aren't any available in the vicinity." Artemis indicated the empty, fogbound street with a slight inclination of his head. "I'm going to walk as far as the square. I expect there will be some hackneys for hire there."

"No carriages?" Flood glanced around with an uncertain expression. "But there are always a few waiting out front."

"Not tonight. The fog, no doubt. Perhaps you would rather stay inside until one appears." Artemis turned his back on Flood and started walking again.

"Wait, I'll accompany you," Flood said quickly. There was a thread of underlying anxiety in his voice. "You're right, bound to be some hackneys in the square, and it will be safer if we walk there together."

"Suit yourself."

Flood fell into step beside him. "The streets are dangerous at this hour, especially on a night like this."

"I'm surprised to hear that you are afraid to walk these streets, Flood. I thought you were in the habit of spending a great deal of time in the stews. This is certainly a far less dangerous part of town."

"I'm not afraid," Flood growled. "Just

using a bit of good sense, that's all."

Artemis listened to the unease in Flood's voice. He smiled slightly. Flood was afraid.

Flood angled him a quick, uncertain glance. "I say, what the devil was that all about back there in the club? Do you actually intend to challenge any man who makes a comment concerning Mrs. Deveridge?"

"No."

Flood snorted. "Didn't think so."

"I will challenge only those who make comments that I deem insulting to the lady."

"Bloody hell. You'd risk a meeting at dawn over the likes of the Wicked Widow? Are you mad, sir? Why she's naught but —"

Artemis stopped walking and turned to face him. "Yes, Flood? You were about to say?"

"Damnation, sir, everyone knows she's a murderess."

"There was no proof." Artemis smiled. "And we all know that one cannot convict a person of murder without proof."

"But everyone knows —"

"Is that so?"

Flood's mouth worked but he uttered no intelligible words. He stared at Artemis, who did not move, and took a jerky step backward. In the diffused glow of the nearby gas lamp, his face, coarsened by years of debauchery, looked sullen and fearful.

"You were about to say something else on the subject, Flood?"

"Nothing." He made a show of straightening his coat. "Wasn't going to say anything else. Just asked a question."

"Consider it answered." Artemis started walking again.

Flood hesitated and then, apparently deciding that he did not want to risk walking back to his club alone, he hurried to catch up with Artemis.

They walked without speaking for a time. Flood's footsteps echoed eerily in the night. Artemis, out of long habit and training, moved without making any noise.

"Should have brought a lantern along." Flood glanced back over his shoulder. "These bloody gas lamps are useless in the fog."

"I prefer not to carry a lantern if I can avoid it," Artemis said. "The glare of the lamp makes one an ideal target for footpads."

"Bloody hell." Flood looked back over his shoulder again. "Never thought of that."

There was a faint, skittering sound from a nearby alley.

Flood grabbed Artemis's sleeve. "Did you hear something?"

"A rat, no doubt." Artemis glanced pointedly at Flood's gloved fingers on his sleeve. "You are wrinkling my coat, sir."

"Sorry." Flood released him immediately.

"You seem to be somewhat anxious, Flood. Perhaps you ought to consider a tonic for your nerves."

"Damnation, sir, I'll have you know that my nerves are as stout as iron."

Artemis shrugged and said nothing. A part of him automatically registered the small sounds of the night, sorting out the familiar, cataloging the shadows, listening for the soft scrape of shoe leather on pavement.

Hooves echoed distantly at the other end of the street.

"Maybe that's a hackney," Flood said eagerly.

But the carriage moved off in the opposite direction.

"Should have stayed at the club," Flood muttered.

"Why are you so anxious tonight?"

There was a short hesitation before Flood spoke. "If you must know, I was threatened a few months ago."

"You don't say." Artemis studied the

candle in the window up ahead. "Who threatened you, sir?"

"I don't know his name."

"Surely you can describe him?"

"No." Flood paused again. "The thing is, I've never seen him."

"If you've never even met the man, why in God's name would he wish to threaten you?"

"I don't know," Flood whined. "That's what makes it all so damned odd."

"You have no notion at all why this stranger has singled you out to threaten?"

"He sent —" Flood broke off on a loud gasp as a cat shot across the pavement and disappeared into an alley. "Friggin' hellfire. What was that?"

"It was only a cat." Artemis paused. "You really are in need of something for those nerves, Flood. What did this man send to you?"

"A seal. The sort one attaches to a watch fob."

"How could you possibly consider that a threat?"

"It's . . . it's difficult to explain." Now that he had started to talk, Flood did not seem to be able to stop. "All goes back to something that happened a few years ago. Some friends and I had a bit of sport with a little actress. The stupid woman got away and ran off. It was dark. We were in the country, you see, and there was an accident and she . . . well, never mind. The point is she vowed that her lover would one day avenge her."

"And now you think he's come for you, is that it?"

"It's impossible." Flood looked over his shoulder again. "Can't be the one she told us would avenge her. Even if the silly little lightskirt had had a lover, why would he bother to come after us now? I mean, she was just an actress. And it's been five years."

"You know the old saying, Flood. Revenge is a dish that is best served cold."

"But we didn't kill her." Flood's voice rose. "She fell to her death when she ran off into the night."

"It sounds as though she fell in an attempt to escape you and your friends, Flood."

"I've got to find a way to talk to him, whoever he is." Flood looked around anxiously again. "I can explain to him that we meant no harm. Just a bit of sport. Not our fault that the little fool —"

"Save your breath, Flood. There is no need to explain yourself to me. I do not want to hear your excuses."

A prostitute in a candlelit window smiled at Artemis and let the shawl fall from her shoulder to display one rouge-tipped breast. He looked at her without any interest and then he returned his attention to the street.

"It's been some months now," Flood said after a while. "Mayhap it was only a malicious joke."

"If that is the case, the avenger certainly has an odd sense of humor."

Out of the corner of his eye, Artemis caught the faint shift in the shadows behind him. For a second he could not put his finger on what had altered. Then he understood.

"Bloody hell," he said softly. "She put out the candle."

"The whore?" Flood glanced back at the darkened window. "What of it? Perhaps she —"

He broke off when he saw that Artemis had flattened himself against the stone wall and was paying him no heed.

The attacker did not spring from an alley or shadowed doorway. Instead he plummeted down toward the street from a high window. The swirling folds of a black cloak flared out around him, blotting up what little light emanated from the gas lamps.

There would be a knife, Artemis thought.

Most Vanza moves did not rely on weapons, but there were exceptions. The spider-in-the-cloud attack always involved a knife.

He seized the trailing edge of the cloak so that the garment could not engulf him as his assailant intended. Jerking it aside, he barely avoided a slashing kick from a booted foot.

The Vanza fighter landed deftly on the pavement, facing Artemis. His features were concealed by a mask fashioned from a black cravat. Icy light glinted off the knife. He lunged forward.

Artemis glided aside. He knew that he had already disrupted the pattern of this particular maneuver. He had to act quickly, before the attacker could switch to another strategy.

The masked assailant saw that he was going to miss his target. He tried to recover. He managed not to fetch up against the wall, but he was off balance for an instant.

Artemis kicked out at the fighter's knife arm. The blow connected. There was a grunt and the blade clattered on the pavement.

Having lost his advantage, the attacker apparently decided that he had no wish to pursue the matter. He spun away. His cloak flew out behind him like a great black wing.

Artemis grasped the hem of the garment and hauled heavily on it. He was not surprised when it came free in his hand. The masked man had released the clasp.

The attacker disappeared into the deep shadows of an unlit lane. His footsteps echoed faintly in the distance. Artemis was left holding the wool cloak.

"Hell's teeth, man." Flood stared at Artemis, stupefied. "He went straight for you. The bastard tried to slit your throat."

Artemis looked down at the cloak that trailed from his hand. "Yes."

"I must say, you handled him brilliantly. Never seen that sort of fighting style before. Most unusual."

"I was fortunate. There was a warning." Artemis glanced at the now darkened window where the prostitute had put out the candle just before the attack. "It was not intended for me, but that is neither here nor there."

"These bloody footpads grow bolder by the day," Flood declared. "If the situation gets any worse, a man won't be able to walk the streets without a runner to watch his back."

Artemis caught hold of the rope that dangled from the window. A brief glance at the intricate knots tied in it was sufficient.

London boasted a great variety of footpads and thieves, but few of them were trained in the ancient fighting arts of Vanza.

Chapter Ten

The flames leaped high. They were still confined to the laboratory on the floor above, but they threw a hellish light down the long hall. Smoke unfurled like a dark banner heralding a legion of demons from the Pit.

She crouched in front of the bedchamber door. The heavy iron key was wet with his blood. She tried not to look at the body on the carpet. But just as she was about to fit the key into the lock, the dead man laughed. The key slipped from her fingers. . . .

Madeline came awake with a shivering start. She sat straight up in bed, gasping for breath, hoping that she had not cried out. She was damp with icy perspiration. The thin lawn of her nightgown was stuck to her back and chest.

For a few seconds she could not imagine where she was. A new wave of fear flashed through her. She scrambled out of bed. When her bare feet hit the cold floor, she suddenly remembered that she was in a bedchamber in Artemis Hunt's large, brooding mansion.

His well-guarded, large, brooding mansion, she reminded herself.

Her fingers trembled, just as they did in the dream. She had to concentrate to light the candle. When she succeeded, the small flame cast a reassuring glow that gleamed on the carved bedposts and the washstand. The trunks full of books that she had hurriedly packed herself were stacked in the corner.

A glance at the clock showed that it was nearly three o'clock in the morning. She had actually slept for two full hours before being awakened by the dream. Quite astonishing, really. She rarely slept at all before dawn. Perhaps it was the knowledge that in this household the locks were sturdy and a guard with a very sizable dog prowled the gardens at night that had allowed her to doze off.

She went to the door and opened it cautiously. The corridor outside was dark, but there was a muted glow on the staircase. It came from the downstairs hall. She heard muffled voices. Artemis was home.

It was about time, she thought. He had told her that he intended to make inquiries in the gaming hells and clubs tonight. She was eager to hear what he had learned.

A door closed quietly somewhere down

below. Silence fell. She waited for a few minutes but she did not hear Artemis on the stairs. She realized that he must have gone into his library.

She went back to the bed and took her wrapper down from the post. She put it on, tied the sash, and slipped her feet into a pair of slippers. Her ruffled cap had been dislodged in the course of her dream. She found it on the pillow and plunked it back down on top of her sadly mussed hair.

Satisfied that she was decently attired, she let herself out of the bedchamber and hurried along the shadowy corridor to the wide, curved staircase. Her soft slippers made no sound as she pattered down the carpeted steps.

She crossed the hall and hesitated at the library. There was something forbidding about the firmly closed door. One would think that Artemis did not want company. It occurred to her that he might have come home quite drunk. She frowned. It was hard to imagine Artemis in his cups. There was an aura of self-mastery, an aspect of stern control in his nature that would seem to preclude that sort of weakness.

She knocked lightly. There was no response.

She hesitated a moment longer and then

cautiously opened the door. If Artemis actually was in his altitudes, she would leave him alone and confront him in the morning.

She peeked around the corner of the door. A fire crackled on the hearth but there was no sign of Artemis. Perhaps he was not in the library after all. But why build a fire?

"I trust that is you, Madeline?" The low, dark voice came from the depths of the vast wing-back chair that faced the fire.

"Yes."

He did not sound the least bit intoxicated, she realized. Relieved, she stepped into the library and closed the door. She kept her hands on the knob behind her. "I heard you return, sir."

"And came straight downstairs for a report, I see, even though it is nearly three o'clock in the morning." He sounded coldly amused. "I perceive that you are going to be an extremely demanding employer, Mrs. Deveridge."

He was not drunk, but he was also not in a good mood. She pressed her lips tightly together and released her death grip on the doorknob. She walked across the carpet.

When she reached the rug in front of the fire, she turned to look at Artemis. At the sight of him sprawled with ominous grace in the great chair, she caught her breath. She knew at once that something dreadful had occurred.

There was a dark gleam in his eyes. He had removed his jacket. His cravat hung loose around his neck. The front of his pleated white linen shirt was undone partway down his chest. She could see the crisp, curling hair in the shadows.

In one hand he held a half-finished glass of brandy. The fingers of his other hand were clenched around an object she could not see.

"Mr. Hunt." She stared at him in growing concern. "Artemis. Are you ill, sir?"

"No."

"I perceive that something of an unpleasant nature has happened. What is it?"

"An acquaintance and I were attacked on the street tonight."

"*Attacked?* Dear God. By whom? Were you robbed?" A thought struck her. She searched his face quickly. "Were you or your friend hurt?"

"No. The villain did not succeed in his goal."

She breathed a sigh of relief. "Thank heavens. A footpad, I presume? The streets are known to be quite unsafe in the vicinity of the hells. You really should be more careful, sir."

"This attack did not take place near a hell. It occurred very close to one of my clubs." He paused to take a swallow of brandy. He lowered the glass slowly. "Whoever he was, he was Vanza."

Her skin prickled. "Are you certain?"

"Yes."

"Were you able to — ?" She broke off, swallowed hard, and tried again. "Did you see him?"

"No. He wore a mask. In the end he fled into the shadows. I believe he may have worked his strategy with the aid of a prostitute who gave him the signal when she spotted us on the street. Tomorrow I shall see if I can locate her. She may be able to provide us with a clue to the identity of the villain."

Madeline's stomach clenched. "Another visit from the ghost of Renwick Deveridge, do you think?"

"I admit that I am not well versed in metaphysics, but to the best of my knowledge, ghosts generally do not rely upon knives."

"He had a *knife?*"

"Yes. He gave an excellent demonstration of the spider-in-the-cloud strategy of attack." Artemis swirled the brandy in his glass. "Fortunately, he lost the element of surprise because I had noticed that the prostitute's candle had been put out."

"Your friend was unhurt?"

Artemis tightened his hand around the object he held. "My companion is not a friend."

"I see." She sank slowly down onto a chair and tried to think through the implications of the shocking news. "This man who is playing the role of Renwick's ghost is after you now, isn't he? He must know that my aunt and I are staying with you. Perhaps he is aware that you have agreed to assist me. I did not realize —"

"Madeline, calm yourself."

She straightened her shoulders and looked at him. "He no doubt intended to murder you tonight. We must assume that he will try again."

Artemis appeared unimpressed by that deduction. "Perhaps. But not immediately. He will be far more cautious next time. He knows that after tonight I will be on my guard."

"He knows more than that, sir. You fought with him. That means he is now aware that you are Vanza."

"Yes." Artemis smiled humorlessly. "And given the fact that he was the loser in our encounter, he also knows that I am more skilled than he is in the fighting arts. I think we can assume that he will be considerably less reckless in the future."

She shuddered. "What did you tell your companion? Did you explain any of this to him?"

"I explained nothing. He assumed the villain was a garden-variety footpad. I let that assumption stand." Artemis contemplated his brandy.

"I see," she said again. "I take it from your tone that you do not like this man who was with you tonight."

Artemis did not respond. He swallowed more brandy instead.

She decided to try another approach. "Did you learn anything in your clubs or in the hells tonight, sir?"

"Very little. There were certainly no rumors of ghosts appearing in the libraries of any other gentlemen of the ton."

"Most gentlemen of the ton would be highly reluctant to admit that they had seen a ghost," Madeline pointed out dryly.

"True enough." He raised the brandy to his mouth and drank again.

Madeline cleared her throat. "While you were out, that young man you employ to bring you information came to the kitchen door."

"Zachary? What news did he have for us?"

"He said that Eaton Pitney has not been seen for several days. The neighbors believe that he has gone to his estate in the country. The housekeeper, who apparently goes in only twice a week, has been told that her services will not be required until sometime next month."

Artemis gazed into the flames. "Interesting."

"Yes, I thought so." She hesitated. "I do not know if this is a good time to discuss our next step in this affair, sir, but I did a great deal of thinking after I spoke with Zachary. I find it rather odd that Mr. Pitney left town at this particular time. He does very little traveling these days, yet he chose to go to the country shortly after sending that note to me."

"Odd indeed," Artemis said in melodramatic accents. "One might go so far as to say it is all deeply suspicious."

She frowned. "Are you mocking me, sir?"

His mouth twisted slightly. "I would not dream of doing such a thing. Pray, continue."

"Well, it struck me that Mr. Pitney may have left town because of some new incident. Perhaps the intruder returned and frightened him. In any event, I have concluded that there is only one logical course of action."

"Have you indeed?" A dangerously laconic gleam lit Artemis's eyes. "And what is that, madam?"

She paused, uncertain of his mood. Then she leaned forward slightly and lowered her voice although there was no one else about. "I propose that we search Mr. Pitney's house while he is in the country. Perhaps we shall find something of interest, some clue that may tell us why he left town."

To her surprise, Artemis nodded in agreement. "Excellent notion. The same idea occurred to me earlier this evening."

"You heard that he had left town?"

He shrugged. "Someone mentioned it in passing over a hand of cards."

"I see." Her spirits rebounded. "Well then, obviously we are aligned in our thinking, sir. That is very satisfying, is it not?"

He gave her an enigmatic look. "Not as satisfying as other forms of alignment might prove to be."

She elected to ignore that remark. He really was in a most extraordinary mood, she thought. But then, she did not know him all that well. Perhaps this strange aspect of his temperament was customary for him.

She decided it would be best to keep the conversation on a businesslike footing.

"I suppose we shall have to go to Pitney's at night," she mused aloud.

"And risk having the neighbors notice strange lights in his house? No, I do not think that would be a wise plan."

"Oh." She pondered that for a moment. "You are suggesting that we enter the house during the day? Won't that be somewhat risky?"

"There is a very high wall around Pitney's garden. Once I am inside, no one will be able to see me."

It took a second or two for his meaning to sink in. When it did, anger shot through her. "Hold on, here, sir. You are not going to go about this alone. This is my plan and I intend to carry it out."

His eyes narrowed. "I will take care of the matter. You will remain here while I search Pitney's house."

His arrogant assumption of authority was too much. She leaped to her feet. "I insist upon accompanying you, sir."

"This habit of arguing with me at every turn is becoming irritating, Madeline." He set aside the empty glass with grave precision. "You have engaged me to conduct this investigation, yet you quarrel with every decision I make."

"That is not true."

"It is true. I weary of the process."

She fisted her hands at her sides. "You forget your place, sir."

Artemis did not move so much as an eyebrow, but she knew at once that she had made a dreadful mistake.

"My place?" he repeated in a terrifyingly neutral tone. "I suppose it is difficult for you to consider me your equal in this affair. After all, I am in trade."

Her mouth went dry. "I refer to your place in regard to our bargain, sir," she said hastily. "I did not mean to infer that I consider you anything less than a gentleman simply because . . . uh —"

"Simply because I am the Dream Merchant?" He got to his feet with the languid air of a cat that has spotted a small bird in the garden.

"Your business affairs have nothing to do with this," she said with what she hoped sounded like great conviction.

"I am delighted to hear that, madam." He opened his left hand.

She heard a tiny clink and saw that he had tossed aside the small object he had been toying with earlier. It landed on the table. She could not tell what it was from where she stood, but she thought she saw the glint of gold.

Artemis closed the distance between them. She jerked her gaze back to his face.

"Artemis?"

"It is very kind of you to overlook my unfortunate connections to trade, madam." He smiled coldly. "But then, you really cannot afford to be too choosy, can you?"

She took a step back and found herself up against the wall next to the marble fireplace surround.

"Sir, I perceive that this is not a good time to continue our conversation. Perhaps it would be best if I went upstairs to bed now. We can discuss our plans for searching Mr. Pitney's house at breakfast."

He crowded in very close and flattened his big hands against the wall on either side of her head, caging her. "On the contrary, Madeline. I really think we ought to discuss your views concerning my proper *place*."

"Some other time, sir."

"Now." His smile was cold. His eyes were not. "In my opinion, you do not have the right to object too strenuously to my unfortunate drawbacks. After all, they say you murdered your own husband and burned his house down around his body to conceal the crime."

"Uh, Artemis —"

"I will admit that your particular reputation may put you ever so slightly above the social level of a gentleman who has gone into trade, but surely no more than a step or two at most."

She took a deep breath and immediately decided that was another mistake. The scent of him, a mix of dried sweat, brandy, and the indescribable essence that was unique to him, sent a frisson across her senses.

"Sir, you are obviously not yourself tonight. I suspect that the encounter with that Vanza villain has unsettled your nerves."

"Do you think so?"

"Only to be expected," she assured him earnestly. "Indeed, if it was Renwick who attacked you, you are fortunate to have survived."

"That was no ghost I tangled with tonight, Madeline. And with all due modesty, I would remind you that I did more than merely survive the skirmish. I made the bastard take to his heels. But my nerves are definitely inflamed."

"My aunt has some wonderful tonics for that sort of thing." Her voice sounded much too high. "I could dash upstairs and fetch a bottle or two for you."

"I know of only one cure."

He angled his head and kissed her; it was a heavy, drugging, demanding kiss that flung her senses to the four winds. She was left shaken and breathless. A shiver of excitement swept through her.

She knew immediately that he had felt her response.

He groaned and moved in closer, deepening the kiss. She was gripped by a rising tide of longing and urgency, the same dizzying brew of emotions that she had experienced when he had kissed her the first time outside the Haunted Mansion.

"Madeline." He muttered her name against her mouth. "Bloody hell, woman, you should not have come in here tonight."

A sudden recklessness blossomed within her. It was as though she had just learned that she might be able to fly if she only put her mind to it.

He is the Dream Merchant, she warned herself. *This sort of fantastical illusion is part of his stock-in-trade.*

But some dreams were worth the price.

"I make my own decisions, Artemis." She put her arms around him and sank into his heat. "I wanted to come into this room."

He raised his head just far enough to meet her eyes. "If you stay, I will make love to you. You do comprehend that, do you not? I am in no mood for games tonight."

The fires that burned in him were hotter than those on the hearth. Indeed, she seemed to be growing very warm herself. Something that she had believed forever dead inside her was coming alive. But there was one thing about which she had to be certain, she thought.

"This inclination you have, sir —"

He brushed his mouth across hers. "I assure you, my desire to make love to you is more than an inconvenient inclination."

"Yes, well, the thing is, it is not just because there is something about a widow, is it? Because I really couldn't bear it if I thought that was —"

"There is something about *you*, Madeline." He kissed her hard and deep, underscoring every word. "God help me, there is something about you."

The low, grating urgency in his voice sent a rush of womanly power through her. She suddenly felt light-headed. She put her hands against his shoulders and spread her fingers wide. Beneath the fabric of his fine shirt she could feel muscle and bone. She smiled slowly and looked up at him from beneath her lashes.

There *was* something about being a

widow, she decided. Something that made her feel quite bold tonight.

"Are you certain that you wish to take the risk of making love to the Wicked Widow?" she asked softly.

His eyes darkened at her sultry, provocative tone. "Is it as dangerous to be your lover as it is to be your husband?"

"I cannot say, sir. I have never had a lover. You must take your chances."

"I must remind you, madam, that you are dealing with a man who used to make his living in the gaming hells." He speared his fingers through her hair, dislodging her little cap. His hand closed around the back of her head. "I am willing to take a risk if the stakes are worthwhile."

He swept her up into his arms and carried her to the wide crimson settee. He put her down on the cushions and turned away.

She watched him walk across the room, listened as he turned the key in the lock. Another shiver of anticipation shot through her. She had the sensation that she was standing at the edge of a cliff looking down into the very deep waters of an uncharted sea. The urge to leap was almost unbearable.

Artemis came back toward her. His hands were on the fastenings of his shirt. By the time he reached the settee, the garment was on the floor.

In the glow of the hearth she saw the small tattoo on his chest. She recognized it as the Flower of Vanza. But curiously the sight of it did not bring her crashing back to earth. It did not trigger old fears or bad memories. Instead, all she could concentrate on was the powerful contours of Artemis's chest. The strength in him was both thrilling and alluring and inexplicably satisfying to all of her senses.

He sat down on the cushion near her slippered feet and yanked off his boots. One at a time, they hit the carpet. The soft thuds were like the peals of a warning bell.

But the sight of his broad shoulders warmed to a golden bronze by the firelight muffled the alarms. He was lean and hard and devastatingly male. She was in the grip of a sweet, heady swell of excitement that was infinitely more potent than any drug Bernice had ever concocted.

Unable to resist, she put out a hand and trailed a finger down the curving muscle of his upper arm. Artemis caught her hand, turned it, and kissed the sensitive skin of her wrist.

Then he came down on top of her, crushing her into the cushions. He wore only his trousers, which did nothing to conceal his heavily aroused body. He slid one leg between her thighs. She felt her robe come undone at his touch. Her thin nightgown was no barrier to his hand. His palm closed over her breast. She felt feverish.

He kissed one nipple and then the other, dampening both through the gossamer lawn fabric. His fingers moved on her, gliding down over the curve of her hip. He tightened his palm around her thigh and squeezed slowly, gently.

She gasped when she felt the first stirrings of dampness between her legs. A liquid heat pooled there, making her wildly restless. She clutched at Artemis's bare back, savoring the strong, muscled feel of him. His thick, unyielding manhood pressed against her upper thigh.

He slid one hand up the inside of her leg to the hot, full place where sensation built steadily. He eased a finger slowly, deliberately into her cleft. A shock of energy sang through her.

"Artemis."

"Some risks," he observed on a note of husky satisfaction, "are indeed worth taking."

"I have come to the very same conclusion, sir."

She had already forgotten how to breathe in a normal fashion, but when he caught hold of the hem of her gown and pushed the material up to her waist, she thought she would never require air again.

He paused long enough to unfasten his trousers. Then he pushed his shaft into her palm. She curled her fingers around him, fascinated by the sleek, hard feel of his rigid member.

She heard him suck in his breath at her touch.

Encouraged by his swift response, she tightened her grip. Artemis tensed. "If you continue to do that, we will both be disappointed."

Startled, she hastily released him. "I am sorry. I did not mean to hurt you."

He gave a short, choked laugh and lowered his damp forehead to hers. "I assure you I am far beyond ordinary pain at the moment. But I would not wish to end this too quickly."

She gave him a tremulous smile. "Nor would I. Indeed, I would quite enjoy spending the rest of the night in this fashion."

"If you can even think of spending several hours enduring this degree of torment, you could give lessons in self-control to a Vanza master."

"Good heavens, are you indeed in torment?"

He kissed her throat. "Yes."

"I had not realized," she said anxiously. "I would not wish you to suffer, Artemis."

He gave another wicked laugh. "You are too kind, my sweet. I shall avail myself of the mercy you offer."

He shifted slightly, settling deeper into her. She did not realize how he had altered their positions until she suddenly felt his shaft pushing slowly, relentlessly against the damp, heated place between her legs.

She shivered again. "Artemis?"

"So much for your own self-mastery, eh?" He sounded amused. "It's all right, my sweet," he added hoarsely. "I cannot wait any longer, either."

He moistened himself in her humid heat and then he drove himself into her in a single, solid thrust.

She had known enough about the matter to expect some small pain, but she was not braced for the feeling of being filled and stretched to the very limits of endurance.

"*Artemis.*" She could hardly speak. His name emerged as little more than a squeak.

He had gone utterly still above her. "Bloody hell?"

She realized she had started to pant like a

small dog. "Would you please, uh, remove yourself? There appears to be some sort of problem."

"Madeline." A great shudder went through him. Every muscle in his body was as taut as a drawn bow. "Why didn't you tell me? How is this possible? Damnation, you are a *widow*."

"But never truly a wife."

"The solicitors," he groaned against her breast. "The annulment. I never realized that it might be based on fact."

She set her teeth and pushed at his shoulders. "I am well aware that this is my fault, but in my own defense, I can only say that I did not realize you would be such a poor fit. Kindly dislodge yourself immediately."

"Don't," he said very urgently when she heaved against him. "Please, do not wiggle about like that."

"I would like for you to remove yourself at once."

"This is not quite the same thing as throwing me out of your drawing room. Madeline, I warn you, *do not move.*"

"How many times must I tell you that I do not take orders from you." She twisted beneath him, attempting to escape his crushing weight and the intense fullness between her legs.

It was as if she had branded him. He started to pull back but something went terribly wrong. His big frame convulsed heavily against her.

He gave a low, muffled groan.

Alarmed, she sank her nails into his shoulders. She held herself very still, not daring to move, as he pumped himself into her.

When it was over, he collapsed on top of her.

A great silence fell.

"Bloody, frigging hell," he said with great depth of feeling.

Gingerly, she took stock.

"Artemis?"

"What is it now, madam? I warn you, I do not think my nerves will sustain any more shocks this evening. I may have to send you upstairs for your aunt's tonic after all."

"It is nothing, really." She moistened her lips. "Just that, well, I wanted to tell you that this position is no longer quite so uncomfortable now as it was a few minutes ago."

For two heartbeats he did not move. Then, very slowly, he raised his head and looked down at her with grim eyes.

"I beg your pardon?" he said with ominous politeness.

She managed a small, placating smile. "It

206

is all right now, truly it is. In spite of my initial impression, I do believe you fit quite well."

"Bloody, frigging hell." This time the oath was uttered so softly that it was almost inaudible.

She cleared her throat. "Perhaps you would like to try it again?"

"What I would like," he said through his teeth, "is an explanation."

He eased himself out of her body and got to his feet. A sense of loss and dismay went through her as he turned his back to her and closed his trousers.

Without a word he handed her a large, white linen handkerchief. Mortified, she took it from him. She could only be grateful that her heavy, quilted wrapper had absorbed most of the evidence of their recent activities. At least she would not have to face the knowing look of the housekeeper in the morning.

She put herself to rights as best she could, took a deep breath, and got to her feet too quickly. Her knees promptly gave way beneath her. She reached out to grab hold of the scrolled end of the settee arm. Artemis caught her and steadied her with surprising gentleness, given his obviously foul mood.

"Are you all right?" he asked roughly.

"Yes, of course." Anger and pride came to her rescue. She retied the sash of her wrapper. She realized she was still holding the handkerchief he had given her. She glanced down and saw that it was stained. Embarrassed, she hastily shoved it into her pocket.

Artemis released her and went to stand in front of the fire. He braced one forearm on the mantel and gazed down into the flames.

"There was talk that your father had made inquiries about an annulment," he said flatly. "Now I comprehend that you truly had grounds."

"Yes." She gazed forlornly into the fire. "But in truth I would have accepted any way out of the marriage."

He met her eyes across the room. "Deveridge was impotent?"

"I cannot say." She shoved her cold hands into the sleeves of her wrapper to warm them. "I know only that he had no interest in me. Not in that way. Unfortunately, I did not discover that truth until our wedding night."

"Why did he marry you in the first place if he could not perform the most fundamental duties of a husband?"

"I thought I made it clear that Renwick did not love me. He had no interest in marriage. What he wanted was the deepest, darkest secrets of Vanza. He believed that my father could bestow them on him by teaching him the old tongue."

Artemis's hand tightened around the edge of the mantel. "Yes, of course. I'm not thinking clearly. You must forgive me."

"You've had a difficult night," she ventured.

"One might say that."

"I could fetch some of my aunt's tonic —"

He gave her a look. "If you mention that bloody tonic one more time, I will not be responsible for my actions."

She was starting to grow irritated. "I was only trying to help."

"Believe me, madam, you've done more than enough for one night."

She hesitated and then decided to try to explain what little she knew about Renwick's behavior. "I told you that I searched my husband's laboratory one day."

Artemis gave her a sharp glance. "What of it?"

"I had a chance to read some of his notes. It appeared that he had convinced himself that his impotence was brought on by his dedication to Vanza. He wrote that he had to concentrate all of his life's energy on his studies in order to unlock the ancient alchemical secrets of the philosophy."

"I see." Artemis drummed his fingers on the mantel. "And you had no clue that he was not interested in his husbandly duties until your wedding night?"

"I know that it is hard to understand, sir." She sighed. "Believe me, I have gone back to the weeks before my marriage a thousand times in my mind, asking myself how I could have been so foolish."

He frowned. "Madeline —"

"All I can tell you is that Renwick was a mad demon who had the appearance of a brilliant angel." She hugged herself. "He thought he could charm us all. And he succeeded for a time."

Artemis's jaw jerked. "You fell in love with him?"

She shook her head. "With hindsight, I could almost believe that he used some sort of magic to hide the truth of himself. But that explanation is too easy. I must be honest — Renwick knew precisely how to seduce me."

For the first time since the incident on the sofa Artemis looked coldly amused. "Obviously he did not overwhelm you with passion."

"No, of course not," she shot back. "Passion is all very well in its way, I suppose. But I was never so young or so naive as to mistake that sort of thing for true love."

And she must not make that mistake tonight, she reminded herself grimly.

"Of course not," he muttered. "No woman possessed of your unique temperament and strength of mind would allow such a trifling affliction as passion to sway her good sense and sound logic."

"Precisely, sir. I have many quarrels with the philosophy of Vanza, and as you know, I do not approve of it."

"You've made your feelings on the subject very clear."

"But I was raised in a household that was guided by Vanza principles, and I confess some of the philosophy's disdain for strong passions did rub off on me." She hesitated briefly. "Renwick was clever enough to comprehend that. I fear he wooed me with a tactic that was infinitely more alluring than passion."

"What the bloody hell is more alluring than passion to a woman of your temperament, madam?" He slanted her an odd, glittering look. "I admit to a great curiosity on the point."

"Sir, I do not understand your tone. Are you annoyed with me?"

211

"I don't know," he said with startling honesty. "Just answer the question."

"Well, the thing is, he pretended to be enthralled with my intelligence and learning."

"Aha. Yes, I see it all quite plainly now. In other words, he made you think that he loved you for your mind."

"Yes. And dim-witted idiot that I was, I believed him." She closed her eyes against the memories. "I thought that we were destined for each other. Twin souls united in a metaphysical connection that would transcend the physical and allow us to unite on a higher plane."

"That is a devilishly strong bond."

"Actually, it proved to be merely an illusion."

Artemis looked down into the flames. "If even half of what you say is true, then Renwick Deveridge was indeed quite mad."

"Yes. As I said, he was able to conceal the fact in the beginning. But after our wedding night it became increasingly obvious that something was dreadfully wrong."

"Insane or not, the man is dead and buried." Artemis continued to gaze into the fire. "Yet it would appear that someone is attempting to make us believe that he has returned from the grave."

"If it is not Renwick's ghost, then it must

be someone who knew him well enough to imitate him. Someone who is also Vanza."

"We must enlarge the scope of our inquiries to encompass Deveridge's past. I shall set Henry Leggett to work on the matter in the morning." Artemis turned away from the fire to face her. "In the meantime we must deal with the situation that now exists between us, madam."

"What do you mean?"

"You know very well what I mean." He glanced at the red settee and then looked back at her. "It is obviously too late for me to apologize for what took place in this chamber tonight —"

"There is no need for an apology," she interrupted swiftly. "Or if there is, it should come from me."

He raised one brow. "I will not quarrel with that."

She flushed. "The thing is, sir, in a sense, nothing has changed."

"Nothing?"

"I mean to say, I am still a widow with a certain reputation. I am living under your roof. If word gets out, people will no doubt assume the worst, that we are engaged in an affair."

"That assumption is now correct."

She gripped the lapels of her wrapper

more securely and raised her chin. "True or not, as I said, nothing has altered in our situation. We are in the same position we were in before the, uh, events occurred on the settee."

"Not quite." He started toward her. "But we will not discuss the matter any further tonight. I think we have both had enough excitement for one evening."

"But, Artemis —"

"We shall deal with this at another time." He took her arm. "When we have both had some sleep and a chance to think. Come, Madeline. It is time you went back to bed."

She tried to dig in her heels. "Surely we should make plans. There is the business of searching Mr. Pitney's house —"

"Later, Madeline."

He tightened his grip on her elbow and steered her toward the door. When they went past the small end table that sat next to the wing-back chair, something small and shiny caught her eye. She glanced down and saw the object Artemis had been toying with earlier.

Before she could question him about it, she found herself at the door.

"Good night, Madeline." His gaze softened slightly as he ushered her through the opening. "Try to get some sleep. I fear you have been deprived of a good night's rest for too long. Plays havoc with the nerves, you know. Just ask your aunt."

He kissed her with surprising gentleness and then he shut the door very firmly in her face. She stared at the closed door for a long time before she turned and made her way up the stairs to her room.

As she climbed beneath the covers she thought about the small object on the end table. She was almost positive that it had been a watch fob with a small, gold seal dangling from the end.

Chapter Eleven

A Stranger had entered the house. His worst fears had come true. They had sent someone to stop him.

He had known for years that he was being watched by the Strangers, had understood that he was being stalked and spied upon. He had long since ceased trying to explain to his friends why he could no longer trust anyone. They believed him to be mad, but he knew the truth: The Strangers haunted him because they were aware that he was getting close to the greatest secrets of Vanza. They were waiting for him to discover the scientific knowledge that had been concealed by the ancients. When he uncovered it, they intended to move in on him and steal it.

The fact that one of them had entered the house tonight meant that he must be very, very close to a great revelation.

He clutched the volume he had been studying when he had first detected the intruder. His hands trembled around the old book as he pressed his ear to the wall. Thank God for the secret passageway in which he stood. He had built it years ago shortly after his wife had died. He had been much younger and far more fit in those days. Done all the work himself, of course. Couldn't trust the carpenters and laborers. They could easily have been spies for the Strangers.

Even in the old days he had sensed that he would one day make a great discovery in the ancient texts of Vanza. He had understood that he would need to protect himself. The Strangers had begun to watch him early on. At first the feeling of being spied upon had been sporadic. But gradually it had become a constant sensation. He had made his preparations. Today he would employ them.

He stood perfectly still in the dark passageway, willing his mind into the Strategy of Invisibility. He was alone in the old stone mansion. Until recently he had allowed the housekeeper in only twice a week, but even then he'd kept an eye on her every minute when she was in the house. Above all, he'd made certain that she never tried to sneak down into the basement. He took care of the cooking himself. Not the work of a gentleman, of course, but when one was being watched by the Strangers, one could not afford to stand on ceremony. One did what one must. The great aim of deciphering the secret knowledge at the core of Vanza was infinitely more important than his gentle-manly pride.

The floor creaked in the hallway on the other side of the wall. The Stranger must have concluded that the house was empty, because, although he had entered very stealthily, he was now making a good deal of noise for a Vanza-trained man.

Inside the passageway Eaton Pitney smiled grimly. Obviously the ruse he had concocted to convince his neighbors that he had gone off to rusticate in the country had worked, although not quite as he had in-tended. He had hoped that if the Strangers believed him to be at his estates, they would leave town in an attempt to follow him and he, in turn, would have a bit of peace.

Instead they had sent one of their number to search his home.

He heard a muffled thud. It was followed by other, similar noises. It took him a moment to understand that the Stranger was on the floor above. He permitted him-self a small sense of satisfaction. Did the in-truder think he was so foolish as to leave his notes lying about where they could be easily found and stolen?

The younger generation of Vanza-trained men had a few things to learn from their elders.

He listened to the sound of drawers being opened and closed. The floorboards creaked overhead. There were more muffled slams and thuds. Eaton huddled in the passageway and waited. Maintaining the serenity of mind required for the Strategy of Invisibility was difficult these days. He had been under an enormous strain for years, and his nerves were not as sturdy as they had once been.

He pressed an ear to the wall, listening for the feel as well as the sound of movement. He could only hope that the intruder would not discover the secrets of the basement.

It seemed an eternity before he detected the Stranger coming back down the stairs. Eaton held his breath when he heard the intruder open the door that led to the rooms below the ground floor. The Stranger descended into the storage rooms and roamed around downstairs for a time. But eventually he returned to the ground floor. Eaton shut his eyes briefly and allowed himself a small shudder of relief. The villain had not discovered the hidden chamber.

After a while the faint noises ceased. Eaton waited another half hour to make absolutely certain that the Stranger had departed. When he was convinced that he was once more alone in the house, he straightened slowly. His muscles ached from being in one position for so long.

When he felt steady on his feet, he made his way to the wall panel that functioned as a concealed doorway to the hidden passage. He paused before opening it, listening intently.

He heard nothing.

He slid the panel aside and stepped out into the darkened hall. There he paused and listened once more.

The silence was as thick as the fog outside in the streets.

Eaton hurried along the hall to the hidden staircase that led down into the bowels of the old mansion. He seized a candle, lit it, and descended the stone steps. He had to be certain that all was secure in his hidden study.

He went past the old storage rooms, opened a secret door, and went down yet another staircase, down into the long-forgotten chambers that had once served the original owners as a dungeon and an escape route that could be used in times of siege.

When he had discovered the underground rooms years ago, he had told no one about them. Instead he had set about making some modifications. He had created a secret study and a laboratory where he could carry out his important researches without fear of being seen by the Strangers. He had taken pains to secure his hidden chamber with a true Vanza snare.

At the bottom of the last set of ancient stone stairs, he slid aside another panel and prepared to enter the most secret chamber in his house.

The scrape of boot leather on the landing above nearly stopped his heart. He whirled around so swiftly that his bad leg went out from under him. He dropped the candle as he clutched wildly at the edge of the panel door. Shadows flickered on the stone walls.

"Did you think you could conceal your secrets from me, you old fool? I knew that all I had to do was wait. The first thing anyone does after an intruder has departed is check his valuables to make certain that they are still safely hidden. So distressingly predictable."

Eaton could not see the Stranger's face in the shadows of the landing, but the candle on the floor had not yet gone out. The flaring light flickered on the barrel of the pistol in the intruder's hand. It also glinted on the gold handle of a handsome walking stick.

As Eaton watched in horror, the Stranger

raised the pistol slightly, aiming it with casual precision.

"No," Eaton whispered. He staggered back a step.

Why hadn't he thought to bring a pistol with him? There was one in his desk in his hidden study, but it might as well have been on the moon for all the good it did him at that moment.

"The thing is," the Stranger said, "I no longer need you to lead me to your secrets. You have just opened the door for me. Very kind of you, sir."

Eaton flung himself back at the instant he sensed the Stranger's finger tighten on the trigger. The sudden, twisting motion sent another jolt of pain down his leg, but he knew that the quick, unexpected movement was his only hope.

There was a flash of light. The roar of the pistol was deafening in the stone chamber. He felt the bullet strike him. *Not as fast as you were in the old days, Eaton.* The impact sent him reeling farther into the secret chamber.

On the floor the candle sputtered one last time and died. Intense, impenetrable darkness flooded the space.

"Bloody hell," the Stranger muttered. He sounded thoroughly irritated by the sudden descent of night.

Eaton was amazed to discover that he was not as dead as his taper. Too high, he thought. The bullet had taken him in the shoulder, not the heart. Or perhaps the Stranger's aim had been slightly off, the result of the wildly dancing shadows cast by the dying flame.

Whatever the reason, he had only seconds. He could hear the intruder growling oaths as he attempted to light another candle.

Eaton pressed one hand tightly against his jacket above the wound, hoping to keep the blood from dripping to the floor. He flattened his palm against the nearest wall. The surface was slick and glassy. He kept his fingers in contact with it and made his way to the first intersection. He turned the corner, relying on his sense of touch to guide him.

Light flared dimly behind him. He did not look back. He could see nothing ahead but he could feel the glassy wall beneath his hand. That was all he needed.

He was the one who had designed the maze. He knew its secrets by heart.

"What the devil?" The Stranger's voice was muffled by the thick, stone walls that formed the floor-to-ceiling canyons of the underground labyrinth. "Come out of

223

there, Pitney. I will let you live if you come here at once. Do you hear me? I will let you live. All I want is the damned key."

Eaton ignored the furious command. He pressed his hand more tightly against the wound, praying that the blood would be absorbed by his jacket. If it dripped onto the floor, it would create a trail that the Stranger could follow through the maze.

He had to get to his study and the pistol in his desk, Eaton thought.

"Come back here, you stupid old man. You don't stand a chance."

Eaton ignored him. He clamped his hand fiercely against his wound and plunged into the darkened maze.

Artemis stood with Zachary in the small, gloom-filled room. Together they looked out the window into the narrow street.

"This was where he concealed himself." Artemis ran his gloved hand along the scratches beneath the windowsill. "You can see where the hooks of his climbing rope were anchored."

Zachary shook his head once. "Good thing ye noticed the whore's candle and realized it was a signal."

"Do you have a name for the woman yet?"

"Lucy Denton. She took the room downstairs a year ago and worked there regularly until today."

"Any word of her whereabouts?"

"Not yet. She disappeared into the stews. Short John says one of the lads picked up a couple of rumors outside a coffeehouse this morning, but so far no one's seen her."

Artemis glanced at his companion. Zachary's brows were bunched together in a troubled frown. His narrow face was tight with tension. His customary cocky mien had been replaced by an unfamiliar brooding air.

Zachary was a bastard. He had a last name but, as was the case with many of those who lived on the streets, he rarely used it. He had been in Artemis's employ for a little more than three years. They had become acquainted when one of the members of Zachary's small, loosely knit gang of street urchins had attempted to relieve Artemis of his gold watch outside his club one night.

The bold effort had failed spectacularly when Artemis had captured the young ruffian by the collar. Instead of abandoning the younger boy to his fate, Zachary, who had been watching from the shadows of a nearby alley, had made a desperate bid to save his small associate.

He had dashed out of the alley, waving a knife with which he had threatened Artemis. Artemis had relieved Zachary of the blade with a simple move, but the young man had thrown himself at him in a desperate bid to get him to free the urchin.

Artemis had been impressed with Zachary's fierce efforts to save the smaller boy. When everything had been sorted out, he had taken him aside. "You're a smart, clever lad," he had told him before allowing him to escape with his young companion. "I have room in my service for someone with your sort of loyalty. If you ever decide you'd like a post that guarantees a quarterly wage, come and see me."

He had found Zachary waiting for him outside his club three nights later. The lad had been wary but determined. They had talked for some time and eventually come to an agreement.

The relationship between himself and Zachary had begun with the cool, business-like distance expected between employer and employee. But somewhere along the line it had evolved into a friendship based on mutual loyalty and respect. Artemis trusted Zachary more than he had ever trusted any of the gentlemen of the ton.

"Never fear, we'll find her eventually."

Artemis clapped him lightly on the shoulder. "In the meantime we'll look in other directions."

Zachary did not appear relieved. If anything, he was more concerned than ever. "He's Vanza, Mr. Hunt."

Artemis smiled. "So am I."

Zachary flushed but he held his ground. "Aye, and now he knows it. That'll make him all the more dangerous. He'll be more cunning the next time he tries his tricks."

"I know you think I'm in my dotage, but age has some benefits. I've learned a few tricks, too."

"I know that better than most, sir. But are ye certain ye don't want me to guard ye?"

"I need you out on the streets gathering information, Zachary, not watching my back. I can take care of myself."

Zachary hesitated and then nodded once. "Aye, sir."

Artemis gazed thoughtfully around the chamber. "He no doubt paid Lucy well. Enough to allow her to bury herself in the stews for a good length of time if she chooses."

Zachary shot him another troubled frown. "We'll find her, but it may take a while. You know what it's like in that part of town. A regular maze, it is."

"The money won't last forever. Sooner or later she'll venture out to find herself some clients. We'll have her then."

"Aye, but it could be too late to do us any good," Zachary muttered.

Artemis smiled faintly. "That is why we will not pin all of our hopes on finding her. Remember the old Vanza saying, 'When one searches for answers, one must look where one does not expect them to be concealed.' We have other places to search besides the stews."

Zachary met his eyes. "We've got some old sayings on the street, too, Mr. Hunt. 'Don't go down any dark alleys unless ye've got a pistol in yer hand and a friend at yer back.' "

"Good advice," Artemis said. "I'll keep it in mind."

Madeline awoke to discover that she had slept more deeply and for a longer stretch of time than she had in ages. Best of all, there had been no dreams of fire and blood tinged with the laughter of a dead man.

Her spirits soared as she pushed aside the covers. When she glanced out the window, she noticed that the city was once again choked with a thick, gray fog, but it did not diminish her sense of well-being. She felt full of energy, ready to take on the task of re-solving the mystery of Renwick's ghost.

Then it struck her that she might very well have to confront Artemis at the breakfast table.

Her enthusiasm for the new day instantly plummeted. A specter might prove easier to face than Artemis. She stared at her sleep-rumpled image in the dressing table mirror. It was one thing to blackmail the Dream Merchant into helping you hunt for a missing maid and then bargain for his assistance in tracking down the vengeful phantom of your late husband. It was another matter altogether to make casual conversation with him over eggs and toast the morning after you had allowed him to seduce you.

Her trepidation irritated her. Why was she so anxious about the prospect of seeing Artemis today? As she had been at pains to explain to him last night, when one considered the matter closely, one could see quite clearly that *nothing had changed*. She was still the Wicked Widow this morning, just as she had been yesterday morning. A lady could hardly become any more notorious in the eyes of a gentleman simply because he had discovered that she had been a *virgin* widow.

Her hands clenched around the edge of the basin. Why did it all have to seem so bloody complicated today?

She glowered at her reflection in the mirror. The sight of herself glowing a shocking shade of pink was extremely annoying.

The flash of anger rallied her spirits. Why should she feel awkward? It was not as though Artemis had any room to be arrogant or mocking. After all, he was a gentleman who had *gone into trade.*

She groaned aloud and seized the pitcher of water. With any luck he would sleep late, she thought. Or perhaps he was one of those gentlemen who rose early and ate before the rest of the household. Her father had had that habit.

She poured cold water into the large white basin and splashed her face vigorously. Shivering, she gave herself a quick sponge bath and then donned her most severe gown, a black bombazine trimmed with gray satin flowers at the hem.

Steeling herself, she opened the door and went downstairs to brave the breakfast room.

Luck was not with her. Artemis had not slept late. He had not even had the common decency to eat early and discreetly disappear into his library. Instead he was at the table, larger than life, conversing amiably with Bernice, for all the world as if nothing out of the ordinary had occurred last night.

Which was precisely the case, she reminded herself grimly. *Nothing had changed.*

"Good morning, dear." Bernice's blue eyes twinkled with delight when she caught sight of Madeline. "My, don't you look fresh as a daisy today, dear. I see my new tonic worked very well. I shall have to give you another bottle tonight."

Madeline saw the glint of amusement in Artemis's eyes. She gave him a frosty look and turned back to her aunt.

"Good morning," she said politely.

A strange expression flashed in Bernice's eyes. It was gone in an instant.

Madeline turned at once to the sideboard and pretended to study the contents of the silver dishes that had been set out.

To her horror Bernice continued to prattle on with innocent good cheer. "I vow, I have not seen you looking so refreshed in ages, Madeline. Doesn't she look wonderfully rested, Artemis?"

"Nothing like a good night's sleep," Artemis agreed in stunningly bland accents.

In spite of her resolve to carry on as though *nothing had changed,* Madeline prayed that the floor would open up beneath her and swallow her whole.

"Mr. Hunt has just informed me about the dreadful events of last night," Bernice said.

"He *told* you?" Madeline dropped the serving spoon back into the tray and whirled around. She glowered ferociously at Artemis. "He actually told you what happened last night?"

"Yes, of course, dear." Bernice made a tut-tutting sound. "I must say I was shocked to the core."

Madeline swallowed. "Yes, well, I can explain. . . ." She trailed off helplessly.

Artemis's mouth curved in a sardonic line. "Your aunt is naturally concerned."

"I have every right to be concerned," Bernice said briskly. "Attacked on the street outside your club, sir. Outrageous. This villain grows too bold for my liking. I trust you will catch him quickly."

The sense of relief that washed through Madeline left her feeling dizzy. She sat down very quickly on the nearest chair and beetled her brows at Artemis. "Have you any news, sir?"

"As a matter of fact, I met with Zachary early this morning," Artemis said. He looked more amused than ever now. "We discovered the room where the Vanza fighter hid and had a look around. I regret to report that we didn't find anything helpful, but Zachary's Eyes and Ears are hard at work as we speak. Sooner or later one of them will bring me something I can use."

Madeline was stunned. He had been up for hours. He had left the house, consulted with Zachary, searched the villain's lair, and returned for breakfast — all before she had even left her bed.

He had been busy with just the sort of tasks she had employed him to perform, she told herself. Nevertheless, his businesslike attitude was somehow unnerving.

He was carrying on just as if *nothing had changed.*

An hour later Bernice cornered Madeline in her bedchamber. She did not bother with pleasantries, but came straight to the point.

"You are falling in love with Mr. Hunt, are you not?"

Madeline dropped the pen she had been using to make some notes. "Good heavens, whatever can you mean, Aunt Bernice?"

"Oh dear, this is even more complicated than I had believed." Bernice looked thoughtful as she sank down onto the edge of the bed. "The two of you have begun an affair."

"*Aunt Bernice.*"

"Naturally, I realized right at the start of this business that the two of you were attracted to each other."

Madeline felt her jaw drop. "What on earth gave you that peculiar notion?"

Bernice held up a hand and ticked off her points on her fingers. "First, you asked him to assist you in dealing with our problem. Second, he agreed to assist you."

"And from that you deduced that we were attracted to each other?"

"Yes."

Madeline shook her head. "That is the most ludicrous, ridiculous, nonsensical assumption I have ever heard. How could you have leaped to such a conclusion on such flimsy evidence?"

"Am I wrong?"

"I asked him to assist us because we required the services of a man who comprehends how one who is trained in Vanza thinks. Mr. Hunt agreed to make himself useful because he wants to get his hands on that journal that Papa kept. It was a simple business arrangement, nothing more."

"Just as I thought. You are having an affair with him."

Madeline drummed her fingers on the escritoire. "It is not quite so straightforward as you seem to think, Aunt Bernice."

"My dear, by virtue of your status as a widow, you are a woman of the world, whether you feel like one or not. I would not presume to give you advice."

"Hah. You know perfectly well you will not hesitate to do so."

"Quite right. As I was saying, I would not presume to give you any advice, but I would suggest you keep one fact in mind."

Madeline was instantly wary. "What is that?"

"You say he agreed to the bargain you offered because he wants Winton's journal."

"Yes."

"He is a master of Vanza."

"That is precisely why I employed him."

Bernice gave her a pitying look. "Really, Madeline, you are an intelligent woman. How can you overlook the obvious?"

"What is so bloody obvious?"

"Mr. Hunt had no need to accept your bargain in order to get hold of the book. Don't you recall? You said yourself that with his skills he could have helped himself to that journal without so much as a by-your-leave."

"Hah." Triumph surged through

Madeline. "That is where you are wrong. I have done some more thinking on that point, and it occurs to me Mr. Hunt knows perfectly well that any attempt on his part to steal that journal would involve a serious risk for him."

"What risk?"

"Why, that I might retaliate by exposing his ownership of the Dream Pavilions, of course. He cannot take the risk of having the ton discover that he is in trade. You see? He had no choice but to make the pact with me."

Bernice studied her for a long time. She said nothing.

Madeline began to fidget. "What is it now? What are you thinking?"

"You know as well as I that, had he wished to do so, he could have found a way to ensure that you did not spill his secrets to the world."

Madeline stilled. A tiny shiver set her nerves to tingling. She glanced down at the cryptic little volume she had been working on. She gazed blankly at the red calf binding for a long time, her thoughts in chaos.

Bernice was right.

After a while she pulled herself together and looked up to meet Bernice's concerned eyes. "You may be correct when you say that he is not helping us because it is the only way he can get hold of the journal. But if that is true, then we have an even more uncomfortable problem on our hands, do we not?"

Bernice gave her an inquiring look. "What is that, dear?"

"If he is not assisting us because of that bloody journal, then why is he doing so?"

"I just told you, dear. He is attracted to you. I expect it pleases him to play the hero."

"If he is attracted to me, it is entirely beside the point," Madeline said steadily. "It does not explain why he has come to our aid. After all, a Vanza master is trained not to allow himself to be ruled by his physical passions."

Bernice looked briefly amused. "I would not assume that the training is always entirely successful, if I were you. Physical passions can be extraordinarily powerful."

Madeline shook her head slowly. "Artemis would never allow himself to be controlled by his sentiments. If he is not assisting us because of Papa's journal or because he wishes to keep me silent, then that can only mean that he has some other, very dark reason for agreeing to our bargain."

"But what other reason could there be?"

Madeline grimaced. "Who can say? He is Vanza."

"My dear —"

"I really do not want to discuss this, Aunt Bernice."

"I see." Bernice paused. "Very well, then, are you all right?"

"Of course I'm all right. Why shouldn't I be perfectly fit?"

"I do not wish to be indelicate, but I am well aware that last night was a somewhat novel experience for you."

"It was not quite what I expected, but there was no harm done," Madeline said briskly.

"Not quite what you expected?" Bernice pursed her lips. "That surprises me. I would have thought that Mr. Hunt would be as skilled in his lovemaking as he appears to be at everything else."

"Really, Aunt Bernice, I thought I made it clear that I do not want to discuss the subject."

"Of course, dear."

"If you must know," Madeline muttered, "Mr. Hunt proved to be exactly as I described him at the start of this affair. Mature yet agile."

Chapter Twelve

He was being followed.

Artemis came to a halt in a doorway and listened. The footsteps were light and muffled in the swirling fog, but he caught the pattern.

They stopped.

He moved out of the doorway and continued down the street. After a few seconds he heard the occasional brush of a shoe on the pavement behind him. The footsteps did not move closer or fall too far behind. He knew that if he turned his head he would see nothing except an indistinct shape because of the thick gray mist.

For most of the distance from his house, there had been enough street clatter to conceal the quiet steps. But even then he had sensed that he was being followed.

He turned left at the corner. There was a large park across the street. The trees were only vague skeletons looming in the fog. A carriage went past cautiously, as though feeling its way in the murk. The horse's hooves rang with an eerie, hollow sound. He took advantage of the covering noise of the wheels to move into another doorway.

He waited.

The carriage rattled off into the distance, and then he heard the footsteps again. Slower now. Very hesitant. The follower had no doubt sensed that the quarry had gone to ground.

After a few seconds of uncertain silence, the footsteps abruptly picked up speed. The follower was moving quickly now. All attempt at stealth had been abandoned.

From the doorway Artemis watched a cloaked and hooded figure move through the mists directly in front of him. The hem of the garment whipped out as the follower hurried down the street.

Artemis glided out of the doorway and fell into step beside his pursuer.

"Lovely afternoon for a stroll, is it not?" he said politely.

"*Artemis.*" Madeline's voice rose on a tiny shriek. She whirled around and came to a halt. Beneath the hood of her cloak, her eyes were very large. "Good God, sir, kindly do not startle me like that again. It is very hard on the nerves."

"What are you doing here? I told you that I would handle this business of searching Pitney's house on my own."

"And I made it equally clear to you that I

had no intention of allowing you to do so. Searching Pitney's home was my plan, if you will recall."

He studied her out of the corner of his eyes. She was thoroughly annoyed, but he wondered if some of the anger was merely an attempt to cover up deeper, more disturbing emotions. He reminded himself that although she was a widow and quite possibly a murderess into the bargain, until last night she had also been an innocent. He thought about how she had blushed at breakfast.

"How are you feeling this morning?" he asked gently.

"I am in excellent health, sir, as usual," she said impatiently. "Yourself?"

"Wracked with guilt. But thank you for asking."

"Guilt?" She halted again and swung around to confront him. "What on earth have you to feel guilty about, sir?"

He stopped, too. "Have you forgotten last night so soon? I am devastated to learn that I made such a tepid impression."

She fixed him with a bristling expression. "Of course I have not forgotten last night. But I assure you that there is absolutely no reason for you to be mired in guilt about the events that transpired in your library."

"You were an innocent virgin."

"Rubbish. I was a virgin but I was hardly innocent." She adjusted her gloves. "I assure you, no woman who went through what I did while I was married to Renwick Deveridge could possibly remain innocent."

"I take your point."

"As I told you last night, nothing has changed."

"Mmm."

She cleared her throat. "Furthermore, there was nothing the least bit tepid about the impression you made."

"Thank you. You cannot know what your kind if somewhat lukewarm compliment means to me. At least I can retain a shred or two of my manly pride."

She scowled. "Humility does not sit properly on you, sir. You may as well save yourself the trouble and effort."

"If you insist."

"If you wish to feel guilty about something, I suggest you experience some severe pangs of remorse for sneaking out of the house without me a short while ago."

He contemplated the fog-cloaked street. There were not many people about, and those few who were making their way through the thick mist could see very little.

It was highly unlikely that anyone would take note of Madeline. If he employed a few precautions, she would be reasonably safe. It was not as though he had much choice, he reminded himself. If he refused to accept her company, he could easily envision her attempting to follow him into Pitney's mansion.

"Very well." He took her arm and started forward. "You may come with me. But you will do as you are told once we are inside the house. Understood?"

He could not see her roll her eyes because the hood of her cloak shielded her face, but he was quite certain she was doing precisely that.

"Really, sir, I despair of your attitude. You do not seem to be able to grasp the very simple notion that you are supposed to follow my instructions, not vice versa. You are involved in this endeavor solely because of the business arrangement I suggested to you. Why, if it were not for me, you would not even be aware of this problem concerning Renwick's ghost."

"Believe me, madam, I never allow myself to forget for so much as a moment that this is all your fault."

The high wall that surrounded the gardens at the rear of Eaton Pitney's big house proved no obstacle to Artemis's skills. Madeline held the small, unlit lantern he had brought along and watched impatiently as he ascended the stone barrier. When he reached the top of the wall, he lowered a length of rope that had been knotted with a loop for her foot.

She seized hold of the rope, thrust the toe of her half boot into the knotted circle, and held on tight while Artemis hoisted her lightly up to the top of the wall. A moment later they descended into the fogbound garden.

"Do you know, Artemis, this is really quite exhilarating."

"I was afraid you would think so." He sounded glumly resigned.

The mist was so heavy that the looming mansion was only a great, hulking shape. No light glowed in any of the windows. Artemis found the kitchen door and tried it.

"Locked," he said.

"Just as one would expect, given that the owner of the house is in the country." Madeline studied the shuttered window. "I trust you can pick the lock."

"What makes you think I can pick locks?"

She shrugged. "You are Vanza. In my experience, men who are trained in the ancient arts are very good at getting through locked doors."

"Obviously you do not approve of such skills," he said. He took a set of lock picks out of the pocket of his coat.

Scenes from her nightmares fluttered through her mind. She saw herself crouched in front of the door of the bedchamber, probing the lock with a key that kept slipping from her fingers.

"I will admit that such skills have their uses," she said bleakly. "And I can hardly object to your abilities with the picks. My father was very good with them, too. Indeed, he taught me . . . Never mind. It does not signify now."

Artemis gave her a quick, searching look before he set to work, but he did not comment.

Madeline grew anxious as the seconds ticked past. "Is something wrong?"

"Pitney's concern with the so-called Strangers he believes are stalking him apparently made him invest in specially designed locks." Artemis's face was set in lines of intense concentration. "These are not the ordinary sort one gets from the average locksmith."

She watched him probe delicately with the picks. "You will be able to manage them, won't you?"

245

"Perhaps." He bent closer to the heavy iron lock. "If you cease distracting me."

"Sorry," she mumbled.

"Ah, there we go. A clever device based on a classic Vanza pattern. I must remember to ask Pitney which locksmith crafted it for him."

The professional interest in his voice worried her. "Don't be absurd. You cannot ask Mr. Pitney about his locks without admitting that you broke into his house."

"Thank you for pointing out that small oversight." He dropped the picks back into his pocket and opened the door.

Madeline found herself gazing into a narrow, gloom-filled hall. No housekeeper or footman appeared to demand explanations or sound the alarm.

She stepped gingerly over the threshold. "The house does seem to be unoccupied. I wonder where Mr. Pitney went?"

"With any luck we shall find something to indicate his destination." Artemis followed her inside and closed the door. He stood quietly for a moment, examining the darkened corridor. "If we do discover a clue, I will send Leggett after him to ask him some questions. I would very much like to know precisely why Pitney felt it necessary to leave town."

"Indeed, I —" Madeline halted in the doorway of the kitchen and stared at the wedge of cheese and the half-eaten loaf of bread that sat on the trestle table.

"What is it?" Artemis came to stand behind her. He looked at the food over the top of her head and went still. "I see."

Madeline went to the table and picked up the bread. "Mr. Pitney must have left in a great hurry. And quite recently. This bread is fresh."

Artemis's eyes narrowed. "Come, we must move quickly. I do not want to spend any more time here than necessary."

He turned away and disappeared down the hall. Madeline followed swiftly. She caught up with him when he paused at another door.

"The library?" she asked as she came up behind him.

"Yes." Artemis did not move. He gazed intently into the chamber. "Either Pitney is in need of a housekeeper or someone else got here before us."

"What do you mean?" She stood on tiptoe to look over his shoulder and caught her breath at the sight of the tumbled books and papers that littered the faded carpet. "Good heavens. Surely Pitney did not create this mess. This goes far beyond eccentricity. In any event, Vanza eccentrics tend to err on the side of too much order and precision. Clutter disturbs them."

"An excellent observation." Artemis stepped back and continued swiftly down the hall.

"Wait," she called softly after him. "Aren't you going to search this room?"

"I doubt that there is any reason to bother with the effort now. Whoever went through the place ahead of us will have taken anything of interest that might have been in there."

"Artemis, maybe Mr. Pitney was right all along. Perhaps he was being watched by someone."

"Perhaps." He sounded more than a little noncommittal.

A thrill of dread went through her. "You're thinking that it was no Stranger who did this, aren't you? It was Renwick's ghost."

"I suggest we cease referring to the man as a ghost. It only complicates the matter. Whoever he is, he's flesh and blood."

"And Vanza."

He did not respond to that.

She trailed after him, halting once more when he paused briefly at the entrance to the drawing room. Inside, the furnishings were covered with heavy, protective cloths. The thick drapes were drawn shut across the windows.

"It does not look as if Pitney did much entertaining," Artemis said dryly.

"A very strange man," Madeline agreed. "But then, he is —"

"Don't say it. This is not a good time to remind me of your sentiments on the subject."

She closed her mouth.

Together they made a quick survey of the upstairs floors. Chaos reigned. Clothes had been pulled out of wardrobes. Dressers had been emptied of their contents. Trunks had been pried open and overturned.

"What was he looking for, do you think?" Madeline asked.

"The same thing he was looking for when he searched Linslade's library, no doubt. The Book of Secrets perhaps, although how any sane man could believe it actually exists is beyond me."

She paused. "I think I have already mentioned the fact that Renwick Deveridge was not sane."

"Yes, you did say something along those lines." Artemis glanced at the narrow, cramped staircase at the end of the hall. "We may as well go back down that way."

"What of the basement? There will surely be storage rooms and such," Madeline said as she followed him down the rear stairs. "Perhaps the ghost, I mean the intruder, did not think to examine them."

"I suspect he was very thorough, but we may as well have a look."

In the hallway outside the kitchen, Artemis found the door that opened onto the basement staircase. He paused long enough to light the lantern, and then he started into the depths of what proved to be a series of dusty storage rooms.

Madeline studied the still-sealed chests and locked trunks. "It does appear that the intruder did not bother to search these chambers. Perhaps he did not discover the basement."

At the bottom of the steps, Artemis came to a halt and raised the lantern. "He was here."

She stopped behind him. "Why do you say that?"

"Footsteps in the dust on the floor. Two sets." He angled the light. "One stops there at that wall. The second returns to this staircase. Two men came down here recently, but only one left."

Madeline stared at the place where the first set of footsteps ended. "It would seem that one of them is able to walk through walls."

"Mmm." Artemis crossed to the stone wall and studied it for a long while. Then he ran his fingers along a crack. He pushed cautiously. There was a faint, muffled whine.

Madeline hurried forward. "There is some mechanism inside the wall?"

"Yes."

By the time she reached his side, one stone had shifted to reveal another heavy iron lock. Artemis set down the lantern and took out his picks.

"We are fortunate that Pitney favors classic Vanza patterns and devices," he said after a moment's work. "Something to be said for tradition."

A short time later he breathed a sigh of satisfaction. Inside the wall, well-oiled pulleys and cables whined again. Madeline watched, fascinated, as a door-sized section of the stone slid aside.

"Another flight of stairs," she whispered. "There must be a chamber beneath this one."

"This portion of the house is very old." Artemis contemplated the flight of ancient stone steps that led down into a sea of darkness. "This staircase probably descends into what must have once been the dungeon. There may have been an escape route down there, also. Such retreats were quite common in old castles and fortresses."

Madeline gazed into the deep gloom at the bottom of the steps. "Perhaps Pitney used it to escape from the intruder."

Artemis looked thoughtful. "I will return later to see where this staircase leads."

"After you take me home, do you mean? Rubbish." She spotted a small heap of candles on the floor. "Come, we must not waste any more time."

He eyed her warily. "Madeline, I can see that I shall have to be firm this time —"

"Save your breath, Artemis." She picked up one of the candles and lit it. "If you do not want to accompany me, I shall find my own way."

For a moment she thought he would argue the point. Then, with a grim expression, he hoisted the lantern and started forward.

"Has anyone ever told you that many gentlemen do not find stubbornness to be an attractive quality in a lady?" he asked in a conversational tone.

She winced and tried not to let his words hurt. But she could not deny the little jab of pain. "As I am not in the market for another husband at the moment, I do not consider it a serious problem. In any event, when it comes to stubbornness, I believe that we are well matched, sir."

"I beg to disagree. The honors go entirely to you." He broke off abruptly. "Well, well, what have we here?"

He had stopped so suddenly on the last step that she nearly collided with him. She paused on the step above and peered down over his shoulder. For a moment she could only stare in amazement.

The lantern light played across what at first appeared to be a narrow corridor lined with flat, diamond-shaped jewels set into intricate patterns. It took her a few seconds to comprehend that she was looking through a narrow doorway into a hallway lined on all sides with small tiles.

"Why would Pitney take the time and trouble to design such elaborate tile work down here?" she asked. "He must indeed be a very strange man."

"I think we can accept that verdict once and for all." Artemis went down the last step and walked a short distance into the tile-lined corridor. "But, as you keep re-minding me, he is Vanza."

She gazed about the passage in growing astonishment. The light of the lantern glowed on thousands of gleaming tiles set in strange patterns that disturbed and deceived the eye. Here the glare revealed an endlessly repeating series of tiny squares that appeared to vanish into infinity. Rows upon rows of parallel lines of various dimensions marched up the walls, shot across the ceiling, and plunged down the opposite side in an effect that left Madeline dazzled and slightly dizzy.

She studied a section of the wall that featured a strange array of triangles within triangles. She could not seem to focus on the pattern. She raised her eyes and found herself gazing at an endless set of circles that looked as though they formed a tunnel large enough to enter. The effect was so real that she put out her hand to touch the opening. She felt only cold tile beneath her fingertips.

"These are Vanza patterns," she whispered. "I have seen some in the old books."

"Yes." Artemis examined a design that tricked the eye into seeing a great chamber where there was only flat wall. "Illustrations from the ancient texts on the Strategy of Illusion. I used some in one of the tableaux in the Dream Pavilions."

He walked to the end of the tiled corridor, turned to the right, and promptly disappeared. It was as though he had simply vanished through one of the walls. The reassuring glow of the lantern disappeared together with him. Madeline was left with only the candle.

A disquieting sense of dread gathered around her in an invisible shroud. She felt another cold draft.

"Artemis?"

He reappeared at the end of the corridor, bringing the light with him. "It's a maze."

She wrinkled her nose. "Fashioned entirely of tiles set in these dreadful patterns?"

"Apparently."

"How very odd."

"Actually," Artemis said slowly, "it's a rather clever way to conceal a secret exit. And perhaps other things as well."

She looked at him as the implications struck her. "Do you think Pitney might have hidden something important in here?"

"Something that was extremely important to a man as eccentric as Eaton Pitney might not be deemed of much interest by anyone else," Artemis cautioned.

"True, but given our general lack of clues, perhaps we had better pursue this one."

"I agree. We will need some string."

"String? Oh, yes, of course. To mark our route through the maze. I expect we can find some in the kitchen."

Artemis started back toward her down the slim passage. He was only a step away when she saw his gaze go straight past her to the dark staircase at the entrance to the maze.

"Bloody hell," he muttered.

He turned down the lantern suddenly and blew out her candle. They were instantly plunged into a stygian darkness.

"What's wrong?" Instinctively Madeline spoke in a whisper.

"There's someone standing in the shadows halfway up those stairs," he said very quietly.

"Pitney?"

"I don't know. I could not see his face. Come."

He took her arm and drew her deeper into the maze. She realized that he was feeling his way along the path. Panic shot through her. The thought of being lost in the unlit labyrinth unleashed an elemental fear. It was suddenly difficult to breathe. She reminded herself that they still had the lantern.

She heard a whoosh of air and then a solid, jarring thud.

"What was that?" she asked.

"The bastard closed the door at the top of the staircase," Artemis said quietly.

There was a muffled clang of iron-on-iron.

"Locked it, too," he added, sounding thoroughly disgusted. "No more than I deserve for allowing you to talk me into exploring this place."

"I'll wager it's Eaton Pitney up there." Anger surged through Madeline, devouring some of the fear that had squeezed her chest. "He probably thinks he just surprised a pair of his so-called Strangers in his maze."

"He did surprise a pair of strangers." Artemis turned up the lantern. "Us, to be precise."

"Perhaps we should call out to him. Explain that we mean no harm."

"I doubt that we could make ourselves heard through that heavy door. Even if it proved possible, I do not think that we will be able to convince him that we are harmless. After all, he caught us prowling through his damned basement." Artemis paused thoughtfully. "And there is always the possibility that it was not Pitney who just locked us in here."

She stilled. "Do you think it was the intruder who searched the house before we arrived?"

"Perhaps." Artemis removed a pistol

from his pocket, checked it briefly, and then looked up at the ceiling with an expression of grave interest.

He was either fascinated by his own reflection in the overhead tiles or he was praying for divine guidance, Madeline decided. Neither effort promised much in the way of immediate help as far as she could tell.

"Artemis, I hesitate to point this out, but we cannot stay here indefinitely."

"Mmm? No, of course not. Cook will be concerned if we do not return for dinner, to say nothing of your aunt. I should likely never hear the end of it."

"It is not only your cook and my aunt who will be worried." She looked around uneasily. "I am likely to become somewhat anxious myself if we are forced to stay in here for any great length of time. I would remind you that we do not have any of Bernice's tonics with us."

"Must remember to pack some the next time we go adventuring."

She scowled at him with sudden suspicion. "Bloody hell, sir, I do believe that you are starting to enjoy yourself."

"It seems only fair that I get some amusement out of this affair." He continued to contemplate the ceiling of the passageway.

"After all, you were the one who said that breaking into Pitney's house was quite exhilarating."

"This is no game, sir. How long do you think the intruder will watch the door?"

"I haven't any notion." Artemis stopped looking at the pattern on the ceiling tiles and gave her an amused smile. "Nor do I intend to discover the answer. Come, let us be off or we shall be late for supper."

"What do you mean? Where do you think you're going?"

"This is a Vanza maze."

"Yes, I know that. What of it?"

"There will be another exit." He turned a corner and disappeared.

"Artemis, don't you dare tease me." She picked up her skirts and hurried around the corner in his wake. She found him in the adjoining tiled passage. "What are you about?"

"I intend to find the other exit. What else would I be about?"

She glowered at his back as she followed him around another turn in the labyrinth. "And just how, pray tell, do you intend to find the second maze entrance?"

"By following the trail, of course."

"*What* trail?" She tried not to look at the eerie, unsettling patterns of the tiles surrounding her. "Artemis, if this is some bizarre Vanza game you are playing, I must tell you that I do not find it at all amusing."

He looked at her over his shoulder. There was more than a hint of arrogant satisfaction in his faint smile. "The path through this maze has been clearly marked. It is obvious to anyone who thinks to look for it."

She glanced around quickly but all she saw was a series of lines that appeared to extend to some far distant horizon and another false opening in the wall. "I don't see any markings."

He swept one hand up to indicate the ceiling. She followed the movement. At first she saw only a whirling pattern of tiny tiles that made it difficult to concentrate. Then she looked closer and saw the faint trace of smoky residue on the glossy surface of some of the paler tiles.

She recognized the sooty evidence left by the innumerable candles and oil lamps that Eaton Pitney must have used to light his way through the maze over the years. The relief that flooded through her was so strong, she decided she could almost forgive Artemis his smug cleverness.

"Very shrewd of you to notice the marks," she said gruffly.

"Have a care with your praise and adulation, my sweet. You cannot know the effect it has on me." He turned another corner and started along a glittering passageway covered in more weird patterns. "I vow, your glowing words make my head spin."

She made a face, which he did not see because he had his back to her, and decided to change the subject. "Poor Mr. Pitney. He must be literally terrified of his mythical Strangers to act in such a fearful manner. Imagine, locking us in his silly maze. When we get out of here, I shall try to speak with him."

"What good will that do?"

"I have had a great deal of experience with my father's eccentric Vanza cronies. I am certain that if I can talk to Mr. Pitney directly, I shall be able to reason with him."

"I hope you are right, because I have a few questions for Pitney myself." Artemis came to a halt once more and stood gazing down at something on the floor. "I trust that it will not be necessary to locate him in the metaphysical realm in order to question him, however."

She stared at the dried brown spots on some pale yellow tiles. A chill went down her spine. "Blood?"

Artemis crouched to get a closer look. "Yes. Only recently dried. Whatever happened here took place within the past few hours." He rose and glanced back the way they had come. "There were no stains on the floor until this point. Either this is where the victim was injured or he was hurt at some other place in the maze and managed to stanch the bleeding until he got this far."

Madeline was aghast. "Do you think Mr. Pitney actually shot someone who dared to enter his maze? That is hard to believe. He is a noted eccentric, but on the few occasions when I have met him, he always seemed like such a pleasant, harmless old man."

"He may be pleasant, but he most certainly is not harmless, even if he is advanced in his years."

"You need not elaborate on that point."

"We do not know yet if he was the victim or the attacker," Artemis said. "You will wait here while I investigate further."

"But, Artemis —"

He did not argue, merely fixed her with a look of such blazing intimidation that she was left speechless. It was, she realized, the first time he had ever shown her this particular side of his nature. It was quite daunting. She blinked and reminded herself that she had sought his help precisely because of his training. She must let him do his work.

She nodded once to indicate that she understood.

Apparently satisfied, Artemis raised the pistol to waist level and went forward with a soundless, gliding stride. He rounded a corner and vanished from view.

She relit her candle with unsteady fingers and listened intently to the echoing silence. She breathed in slowly and deliberately, attempting to quiet her mind as she did on those occasions when she meditated.

She did not know when she first became aware of the slight, almost undetectable fragrance in the air. She sniffed cautiously and caught a faint, sharp-sweet odor. *Incense.* She could not name the herbs but she was almost positive that she had smelled that blend on some other occasion.

The acrid scent grew stronger. From out of her store of memories, she recalled the morning long ago when she had stood in the doorway of Bernice's stillroom and watched as her aunt ground Vanzagarian herbs with a mortar and pestle.

"What are you experimenting with this time, Aunt Bernice?"

Fragments of Bernice's answer flitted through her head.

". . . In small amounts the mixture is said to cause hallucinations and strange visions, but in larger doses it induces sleep, even in the most restless. . . ."

Shock held her immobile for a few seconds. Then, with a wrench of willpower, she unstuck herself from the floor and rushed forward.

"Artemis, where are you? Something terrible is happening."

"This way," Artemis called with grim urgency. "Come quickly. Use the bloodstains as a guide. They are quite clear."

She hurried along the twisting corridors, following the dreadful brown spots on the tiles. She turned one last corner and found herself in a small chamber furnished in the manner of a miniature library.

It was an astonishing sight. There was an aging mahogany desk stacked with papers and a notebook. A handsome rug covered the cold stones. Two unlit lamps stood at attention behind the chair. Three glass-fronted bookcases overflowing with leather-bound volumes stood against a wall patterned with innumerable triangles within triangles.

A gentleman's study situated in the heart of a maze. Not so great an oddity, she thought, when one considered that the gentleman in question was Vanza and therefore constitutionally inclined toward oddities.

Then she saw Artemis crouched behind the desk. She circled the massive piece of furniture and caught her breath at the sight of Eaton Pitney.

He was slumped on the floor, half propped up by the desk. A small pistol lay on the carpet near his limp, bloodstained fingers. He had made an awkward but evidently successful attempt to bind the wound in his upper left shoulder with his cravat.

"Mr. Pitney." She went down beside him and touched his wrist. He did not stir or open his eyes but he was breathing fairly steadily. "Thank God, he is still alive."

"Well, this does answer one or two pressing questions," Artemis said. "Obviously it was not Pitney who locked us in here."

Madeline raised her gaze from Pitney's sallow face. "I smelled incense a moment ago. I believe that it is made of some herbs that are used to promote hallucinations and, eventually, sleep. Someone is deliberately tainting the air in this chamber."

He inhaled deeply and shook his head slightly. "I smell nothing unusual."

"I assure you, I have an excellent nose,

sir, and I *do* smell the sleeping herbs. My aunt once did some experiments with them. We must get out of here quickly."

He met her eyes, his gaze steady and intent. "I will not argue with you."

"You must locate the second exit you mentioned."

He glanced up at the ceiling. "It will be here in the heart of the maze."

"How can you tell that?"

"The soot on the tiles is heaviest at this point and there is no path of smoke leading off in any other direction. In any event, it only makes sense that Pitney would locate his escape route in a location convenient to his study."

He slipped a knife from a sheath that he wore beneath his coat and walked to the nearest section of wall. He slid the point of the blade into the thin crevasse between two tiled panels. Only the tip disappeared. He moved to the next line of joinery and tried again. He was unable to insert the point more than a short distance.

Madeline watched impatiently as he tried every line between panels with methodical precision. When he finished the walls he went down on one knee and began to test the tile joints on the floor. The scent of herbs grew stronger.

"I should have brought the knife my father gave me." Madeline glanced uneasily at Pitney's bandage. "Two could have made short work of this business. Next time I will not forget it."

"I am loath to tell you this, Madeline, but the fact that you are acquainted with the use of pistols and knives and the like will be even more off-putting to many prospective husbands than your stubbornness."

"Obviously if I am ever again in the market for a husband, I shall have to look for one who is open-minded on such matters."

"Yes, you will, won't you? But if he is that open-minded, I fear he will fall into the category of eccentric, and you have already made your position on eccentrics abundantly clear." Artemis took a deep breath and frowned. "You are correct about the incense. I can smell it now."

"Tie your cravat around your face," she said urgently. "It will help to keep out some of the vapors." As she spoke, she wrapped her light woolen scarf so that it covered her nose and mouth. She could still smell the pungent herbs, but the scent was not so strong now.

Artemis made a makeshift mask for himself and then went back to work. He lifted the corner of the carpet and continued to insert the point of his blade between the narrow cracks. Madeline was starting to wonder if his theory of a second exit was badly flawed, but she said nothing because she could not think of a better notion.

She stared at one of the patterns on the wall and thought it shifted slightly. She blinked and tried to clear her vision. The pattern wavered again.

"Artemis, the hallucinating effects of the herbs are beginning to take effect. We have very little time."

Two squares in from the edge of the carpet, Artemis probed another space between two tiles.

The knife sank to the hilt.

"I think we have found our exit." Artemis sheathed the blade.

He probed swiftly, found a niche for his fingers, and hauled upward on the edge of the stone. Madeline heard the squeak of hinges. A section of the flooring swung upward to reveal a dark passageway. Damp air wafted through the opening. It set some papers fluttering on the desk.

Artemis looked at her. "Are you ready?"

"Yes, but what about Mr. Pitney? We cannot leave him here."

"I will carry Pitney." He rose and thrust

the lantern into her hand. "You must lead the way."

She seized the lantern handle and plunged into the shadowy passage beneath the floor of the maze. Artemis scooped Pitney off the bloodstained carpet and slung him across one shoulder. He followed Madeline into the dank stone tunnel. He paused only long enough to pull the floor panel closed behind him.

Chapter Thirteen

"The wound is clean." Bernice finished tying the fresh bandage she had placed on Eaton Pitney's thin shoulder. "I saw no signs of infection, sir. You are extremely fortunate."

"You have my most profound thanks, madam." Eaton's rabbity features clenched in a grimace of pain, but he gave her a look of weary gratitude as he sank back onto the pillows. "I had some healing herbs in my desk drawer, which I managed to apply before I lost consciousness."

"You were fortunate to have them available," Madeline said from the foot of the bed.

"My study is fully stocked for just such emergencies," Pitney said. "Extra rounds for my pistol, food, water, that sort of thing. Always knew that I might have to take refuge in my maze one day. The Strangers were bound to make their move sooner or later."

The old man might be mad as a hatter, Artemis thought, but Pitney had been stouthearted and resourceful enough to elude whoever had shot him and chased him into that maze.

He glanced at Madeline. Speaking of stouthearted and resourceful, he thought. She appeared none the worse for the ordeal in the maze and the tunnel that had led them out of it. He felt a rush of admiration and pride.

She had bathed and changed into a pale gray muslin gown after they had returned from their venture. Her hair was once more neatly parted in the center and pinned into graceful waves on both sides of her head. Wispy little ringlets bounced in front of her ears. Had it not been for her concerned expression, one would have thought that she had done nothing more tiresome that afternoon than pay a call on an old friend.

It said a great deal about what she had been through in the past year that she could treat the day's events so coolly.

The hidden exit in the floor had led them through an ancient, moldering stone tunnel that had eventually emerged in an abandoned warehouse. Muddied and burdened with Pitney, they had had some difficulty hailing a hackney. But in the end they had arrived home.

In the midst of hurried, incomplete explanations, Bernice had taken charge of Pitney. Under her care he had finally awakened and become aware of his surroundings. He had recognized her immediately.

"Can you tell us what happened?" Artemis said.

"I fear that I am not quite as agile as I once was," Pitney said. "The Stranger took me by surprise. Wouldn't have happened in the old days."

Madeline gave a small sigh. Artemis did not blame her. Questioning Pitney was going to be difficult, he thought. The man apparently blamed everything on the illusionary beings he had invented.

Madeline looked at Pitney. "Do you know the identity of the, uh, Stranger who shot you, sir?"

"No. He had a cravat tied around his face in the shape of a mask, and he had a hat pulled down low over his eyes."

"Can you tell us anything at all about him?" Madeline persisted. "So that we can watch for him?"

Pitney furrowed his brow. "Moved like a man in his prime. Not bothered with rheumatism or stiff joints, I can tell you. Carried a walking stick with a gold handle."

Artemis saw Madeline's hands clench fiercely around the bedpost.

"A walking stick?" she repeated cautiously.

"Indeed. Remember thinking it rather odd. Not the kind of thing a Vanza-trained man would carry with him in that sort of situation." Pitney paused. "On the other hand, he had to approach the house from the street and no doubt he wished to effect a good disguise. A walking stick was appropriate to the rest of his attire, I suppose. Still, it struck me as unusual."

Madeline exchanged a glance with Artemis. Then she turned back to Pitney. "Can you tell us anything else about him, sir?"

"Don't think so. Didn't recognize his voice and I've got a good ear for voices. As I said, he was a Stranger."

Artemis took a step closer to the bed. "He spoke to you? What did he say, man?"

Pitney's eyes widened in alarm at the sharp tone of the questions. Madeline shot Artemis a warning frown, shook her head once, very slightly, and turned back to Eaton with a soothing smile.

"Mr. Hunt is quite eager to identify this particular Stranger, sir. There is no telling what he might have done to all of us if he had succeeded in rendering us unconscious with his incense. The smallest clue might help us find him."

Pitney nodded soberly. "Well, as to his

exact words, I can't recall precisely. Something about leading him to my secrets. Demanded the key to my desk or some such nonsense. Naturally, I knew immediately what he was after."

"What?" Artemis asked.

"Why, my notes, of course." Pitney peered suspiciously toward the door as if to make certain no one was eavesdropping in the hall. "Been working on them for years. Getting very close to the secrets, and *they* know it."

"Secrets?" Artemis glanced at Madeline. "Are you by any chance talking about the Vanzagarian *Book of Secrets*? The volume that was rumored to have been stolen from the Garden Temples last year?"

"No, no, no." Pitney's brows bristled in an expression of acute disgust. "The *Book of Secrets* is naught but a collection of ancient recipes for alchemical elixirs and potions. Complete rubbish. *My* researches go to the very heart of Vanza. I seek the great scientific secrets that the ancients discovered and which have been lost for centuries."

Artemis managed not to groan aloud. Questioning the man was hopeless.

Pitney looked at Madeline. "Pity about your marriage, my dear. I must admit I was quite relieved to hear that Deveridge had died in that fire. Excellent solution to a most unfortunate problem."

Artemis frowned. "Did you know Renwick Deveridge?"

"Never met the man, but not long before his death I began hearing certain rumors." Pitney nodded twice. "I have little doubt but that the man was a Stranger. They are very good at disguise, you know."

Artemis curbed his impatience with an effort of will. "What rumors did you hear, sir?"

Pitney glanced at Madeline. "Shortly before your father died, he sent word to some of his oldest acquaintances warning us that, if Deveridge came around asking questions about the ancient Vanza texts, we ought not to be taken in by his son-in-law's apparent charm. Knew right off Reed had discovered that he'd wed his daughter to a Stranger."

Artemis hesitated and then decided to take the plunge. "Linslade thinks that Deveridge's ghost paid him a visit in his library the other night."

Pitney snorted. "Bah, Linslade is forever talking to ghosts. Man's a crackbrain. Everyone knows it."

Artemis wondered if madness was any easier to recognize in others if you were yourself a candidate for Bedlam. "Do you think it's possible that Deveridge survived the fire and has come back in the, er, service of the Strangers to look for ancient secrets of Vanza?"

Pitney grunted. "Doubt it. Madeline here is her father's daughter. The lady is no fool."

"What is your point?" Artemis asked.

Pitney smiled benignly at Madeline. "Let's just say that I feel certain she would have had the great good sense to make sure that Deveridge was very dead before the fire consumed the house. Isn't that right, my dear?"

An expression of shock and dismay lit Madeline's eyes. "Really, sir, you surprise me. I would never have guessed that you gave heed to the dreadful gossip that maintains I murdered my husband."

Bernice made a brisk, disapproving sound. "Good heavens, Pitney, how on earth could you possibly believe such idle chatter?"

"Indeed, nothing but scandal-broth of the worst sort." Pitney winked broadly at Artemis. "Never pay any attention to that sort of talk myself. What about you, sir?"

Artemis realized that Madeline was watching him with an anxious expression.

He thought about the endless flow of rumors and snippets of information that arrived on his desk every morning, thanks to Zachary's Eyes and Ears.

"I find common gossip to be extremely boring," he said.

He was rewarded with the look of relief that flashed across Madeline's face.

He had told the truth, he assured himself silently. Only *uncommon* gossip was of interest to him.

Henry Leggett closed his notebook and prepared to take his leave. "It sounds as if the two of you had quite an adventure."

"That is certainly one way to describe it," Artemis said.

"Eaton Pitney is a very lucky man. He could easily have perished from his wound, even though he escaped the intruder."

"Pitney is tough."

"True. Nevertheless, it was a near thing. And if it had not been for her . . ." Henry paused. "Well, I must say, she is certainly a fine figure of a woman."

Artemis poured himself another cup of coffee and carried it to the window. He looked out into the garden and summoned up an image of Madeline. It was an easy task.

"Yes," he said. "Very fine."

"And possessed of a most impressive intellect."

"Indeed."

"A strong-minded woman, too. In fact, I found her conversation quite stimulating."

"Yes, she can be very . . . stimulating."

"Had a long chat with her today. I must say, a man doesn't encounter that sort of female very often."

"Very true."

Henry started toward the door. "I'll be off now. I regret that I have as yet been unable to turn up any further information on Renwick Deveridge, but I shall continue to make inquiries. I believe I shall go to some shops that make unusual walking sticks this afternoon. Perhaps I shall learn something about this gold-headed stick your villain carries."

"Thank you, Henry. If you learn anything at all, send word at once."

"Yes, of course." Henry opened the door.

Artemis turned slightly. "Henry?"

"Yes?"

"I am pleased to hear that you have begun to see Mrs. Deveridge in a more positive light. I know that you had some doubts about her because of the unfortunate rumors."

Henry gazed at him quite blankly for a few seconds. Then his expression cleared. "I was not speaking of Mrs. Deveridge. I was referring to her aunt, Miss Reed."

He went out the door and closed it firmly behind himself.

Artemis was still at work at his desk an hour later when Bernice entered the library. He took note of the resolute look in her eyes as he rose politely to greet her.

"Is there something I can do for you, madam?"

"Yes, I wish to speak with you on a somewhat delicate matter."

Artemis stifled a groan. "Please be seated."

She sat down on the other side of the desk and fixed him with a determined expression. "I'm sure you know what this is about, sir."

Instinctively he looked for a way to avoid a conversation that showed every indication of being quite unpleasant. He glanced at the door. "Where is Madeline?"

"Upstairs with Mr. Pitney. I believe she is seeking his opinion concerning an odd little book that was sent to her recently from one of Winton's old colleagues in Spain."

So much for hoping for rescue from that quarter.

"I see." Artemis sat down. "Speaking of Pitney, I must tell you that I am most impressed with your medical skills, Miss Reed. Madeline is right, you are extremely adept with herbs."

"Thank you. Several years ago Winton brought back some volumes of notes on the herbs and plants native to the Isle of Vanzagara. I have devoted a great deal of study to the subject. But that is not what I wish to discuss with you today."

"I feared as much." He picked up the watch fob seal on his desk and fingered it absently. "This is about Madeline, is it not?"

"Yes."

He studied the engraving on the seal for a few seconds. Then he looked up. "You are concerned about my intentions."

Bernice raised her brows. "You go straight to the heart of the matter, sir."

"I have spent a great deal of time pondering the subject myself."

Anger glinted in Bernice's vivid blue eyes. "I trust that is the case. After all, when a gentleman seduces a lady —"

He stilled. "She told you that I seduced her?"

Bernice brushed the question aside with a short, crisp movement of her hand. "There was no need. I knew something had happened as soon as I saw the pair of you together this morning at breakfast. I am well aware that some gentlemen regard widows as fair game, but I confess, sir, it never occurred to me that you would use my niece in such a way. You must know that in spite of her status, she has had very little experience of men."

"I am aware of that," he said through set teeth.

She gave him a very pointed look. "No doubt."

"Hold one moment here, madam." Artemis tossed aside the seal and sat forward. He folded his hands on the desk. "I am not the one you should be pressing so strongly. It is your niece who refuses to take a properly serious view of the situation that now exists. I tried to discuss the matter with her this very afternoon before we went into Pitney's house, and she would have none of it."

"If your intentions are honorable, it is your duty to take the lead."

"*My* intentions?" Exasperated, he glared at her. "She is the one who claims *nothing has changed* because of what occurred between us. She took great pains to point that out."

"Rubbish, everything has changed. The two of you are involved in an affair."

"She maintains that doesn't alter the case. She feels that she is still the Wicked Widow in the eyes of the world today, just as she was yesterday."

"Yes, yes, she fed me that nonsense, too, but it is ridiculous. In my family we do not concern ourselves with the world's opinion. We pay attention to the facts." Bernice gave him a grim look. "And the plain fact here, sir, is that yesterday my niece was an innocent young woman. Today she is not so innocent and that is your fault entirely."

"I suggest you tell her that, Miss Reed. She certainly will not listen to me on the subject." He narrowed his eyes. "In fact, it is beginning to appear to me that she is using me for her own ends."

Bernice's eyes widened. "Using you?"

"Precisely. To find that damned ghost who is plaguing her. She treats me like an employee, not a lover."

"Oh, I see what you mean." Bernice pursed her lips. "Yes, there is the matter of Renwick's ghost, isn't there?"

He waited for a moment but Bernice did not attempt to disabuse him of his conclusion. He got to his feet and stalked to the window. "I do not think she will acknowledge any warm feelings for me."

"Have you made inquiries in that direction?"

"There was no need to ask a direct question," he said quietly. "Your niece has made it plain that she is deeply wary of any gentleman connected to Vanza. There is no getting around the fact that I am Vanza."

There was a short, taut silence. After a moment he turned and looked at Bernice. He was surprised to see that she was studying him with a meditative air. She started to tap one finger on the arm of the chair.

He silently ground his teeth.

"I believe you do not entirely comprehend the situation, sir," Bernice said eventually.

"Indeed? And just what the bloody hell do I fail to comprehend, madam?"

"It is not the gentlemen of Vanza who worry Madeline."

"On the contrary, she takes every opportunity to point out the shortcomings of those who are connected with the philosophy. As far as she is concerned, men of the Vanzagarian Society are, at best, eccentric crackpots such as Linslade and Pitney, and at worst, dangerous villains."

"Hear me out, sir. Madeline blames herself for being taken in so completely by Renwick Deveridge. She thinks that if she had not fallen for his seductive ways and married him, her father would be alive today."

Artemis stilled.

"It is not the gentlemen of Vanza she feels she cannot trust." Bernice paused. "It is her own intuition and female sensibilities."

Chapter Fourteen

Oswynn walked unsteadily out of the smoky gaming hell with his new companion. He tried to focus on the hackney that waited in the street. For some reason it was difficult to make out the vehicle, although he heard the stomp of a hoof and the rattle of a harness. He concentrated, but the outline of the carriage wavered ever so slightly. He'd had a fair amount to drink that evening, but no more than usual. In any event, he'd never suffered this peculiar problem with his vision even when he was thoroughly foxed, and he'd had a lot of experience in being drunk. Perhaps it was the light fog that blurred the scene.

He shook his head once to clear it and clapped his new acquaintance on the shoulder. The golden-haired man called himself a poet. He certainly had the languid physical grace and the handsome face to go with the claim.

The poet was also a man of fashion. His cravat was tied in a unique and extremely intricate style. His dark coat was elegantly cut. His walking stick was most unusual. The gold knob had been sculpted into the head of a fierce-looking bird.

The poet, exuding a world-weary ennui and an amused disdain for others, was not the type to waste time on those who bored him. The fact that the golden-haired man had taken an interest in him, Oswynn thought, meant that the poet considered him one of the worldly elite, a man who savored only the most exotic pleasures.

"I've had my fill of wine and cards tonight," Oswynn announced. "I believe I shall repair to a certain establishment in Rose Lane. Care to accompany me?" He winked broadly. "Word has it that the old bawd who operates the house there has some new wares in from the country to auction off tonight."

The poet gave him a brief glance that held unutterable boredom. "A gaggle of whey-faced milkmaids, I presume."

Oswynn shrugged. "And a milkboy or two, no doubt." He chuckled richly at his clever play on words. "Mrs. Bird prides herself on catering to a variety of tastes."

The poet came to a halt on the pavement. A golden brow rose in amused derision. "I'm surprised that a man of your experience would be so easily satisfied with such offerings. What sport is there in bedding a dull-witted farmer's daughter who has been rendered nearly unconscious by a dose of laudanum?"

"Well . . ."

"And as for the boys, I know for a fact that Mrs. Bird gets them out of the stews, where they have been well trained to pick your pocket while you're recovering from your exercise."

His new companion's condescending attitude was irksome, but Oswynn acknowledged that the poet was a gentleman of infinitely refined sensibilities. Everyone knew that his sort indulged themselves in the most exquisite excesses. Something to do with being an author, he supposed. The rumors of Byron's escapades in the stews were legendary.

Oswynn found himself struggling to defend his own particular enthusiasms. "Thing is, I prefer the young ones, and Mrs. Bird generally has the most tender morsels."

"Personally, I prefer my morsels awake and well schooled."

Oswynn blinked again, trying to clear his vision. "Schooled?"

The poet went down the steps. "I assure you, there is an amazing difference between a girl who has been properly instructed in the erotic arts and your typical milkmaid who arrived in town in the back of a vegetable cart."

Oswynn watched his fair-haired companion walk toward the waiting hackney. "Instructed, you say."

"Indeed. I generally choose one who has been trained in the Chinese methods. But occasionally, when I am in the mood for a variation, I select a girl who has been taught the Egyptian techniques."

Oswynn hurried down the steps. "These girls you mention. They are all suitably young?"

"Of course." The poet opened the carriage door and smiled an invitation to enter. "For a price, one can purchase a lively, entertaining lass who is not only well versed in the most exotic arts but also guaranteed to be virgin. In my considered opinion, there is nothing like a well-schooled innocent."

Deeply intrigued now, Oswynn put one hand on the edge of the carriage door. "They train *virgins* in these foreign practices?"

The poet's eyes gleamed in the amber light of the vehicle's lamps. "Do not tell me that you have never sampled the delights of the Temple of Eros?"

"Can't say that I have."

"You are welcome to join me tonight."

The poet vaulted lightly up into the carriage and sat down on the midnight blue squabs. "I shall be happy to introduce you to the proprietor. She accepts new clients only upon the recommendation of those who already patronize her establishment."

"Very kind of you, sir." Oswynn clambered awkwardly into the carriage and sat down too suddenly. For a few seconds the interior of the carriage whirled gently around him.

The poet watched him from the opposite seat. "Are you feeling ill, man?"

"No, no." Oswynn rubbed his forehead. "Must have drunk a bit more than I usually do. Just need some fresh air and I'll be as good as new."

"Excellent. I would not want you to miss out on the very special entertainment I plan to show you this evening. So few men have the ability to appreciate the exotic and the rare."

"I've always had a taste for those things."

"Indeed?" The poet sounded politely doubtful.

Oswynn leaned his head back against the cushion and closed his eyes to shut out the spinning carriage. He tried to think of some escapade in his past that might impress the poet, but it was difficult to concentrate.

Though the night was young, he was very tired for some reason. "A few years back some associates and I founded a club dedicated to experiencing the most unusual erotic pleasures."

"I have heard rumors of such a club. In addition to yourself, the members included Glenthorpe and Flood, did they not? You called yourselves the Three Horsemen, I believe."

A whisper of dread roused Oswynn briefly. He managed to get his eyes open. "How d'ye come to hear of the Horsemen?" He heard himself slur the *s* in the last word.

"One picks up these little tidbits of gossip here and there." The poet smiled. "Why did you disband your club?"

Another trickle of unease went through Oswynn. He already regretted mentioning the damned club. After the events of that night five years ago, they had all solemnly vowed never again to speak of it. The actress's death had thrown a scare into them.

He had thought himself free of the memory of the woman's vow that her lover would someday return to destroy them. It was true that for a year following the incident, he had been troubled by sudden attacks of fear in the middle of the night that had left him soaked with sweat. But his nerves had eventually quieted.

He had assured himself that he was safe. But three months ago he had received a letter with an all too familiar gold seal inside. The nightly attacks of fear had returned. For weeks he had looked over his shoulder constantly.

But nothing had happened and he had concluded that the message with the seal inside had been a bizarre joke perpetrated by Flood or Glenthorpe. It defied common sense to believe that the mysterious lover had come for his revenge. She had been an actress, after all, a low creature with no family. The lover, if indeed he ever existed, had no doubt been a careless rakehell who had probably long since forgotten her name. No gentleman would waste a second thought on a foolish little lightskirt who had come to a bad end.

"The Three Horsemen Club became a dead bore." Oswynn tried to make a gesture of casual dismissal with his hand, but he couldn't seem to get his fingers to move properly. "I went on to more interesting pursuits. You know how it is."

"I do indeed." The poet smiled. "It is the curse of those of us who possess the heightened sensibilities required to savor the rare and the exotic. We must forever seek out fresh stimulation."

"Yeth . . . I mean, *yes*." It was becoming increasingly difficult to collect his thoughts, Oswynn realized. The sway of the carriage seemed to have a mesmerizing effect on him. He just wanted to go to sleep. He gazed at the poet through shuttered lids. "Where did you thay . . . *say* we were headed?"

The poet seemed to find the question vastly amusing. His laugh echoed in the night. The fiery light of the carriage lamp turned his hair to gold.

"Why, to another hell, of course," he said.

The audience held its collective breath when the tall, thin, silver-haired man on stage addressed the young lady seated in the chair.

"When will you awaken, Lucinda?" he said in authoritative tones.

"When the bell rings." Lucinda spoke in a curiously flat voice.

Standing at the back of the room, one shoulder propped against the wall, Zachary leaned close to Beth and whispered in her ear. "This is the best part. Watch what happens now."

Beth was riveted by the performance but she flashed Zachary a coy smile.

Onstage the mesmerist moved his hands in a weaving motion in front of the blank-faced Lucinda. "Will you remember that you quoted the speech from *Hamlet* while you were in a state of trance?"

"No."

The mesmerist picked up a small bell. He rang it gently. Lucinda gave a start and opened her eyes. She looked around with an air of bemusement.

"What am I doing on this stage?" she asked. She appeared genuinely surprised to find herself facing the audience in which she herself had been sitting a short while earlier.

The audience gasped in amazement and clapped loudly.

Lucinda blushed and looked helplessly at the mesmerist.

The mesmerist smiled reassuringly. "Tell us, Lucinda, do you read a great deal of Shakespeare?"

"No, sir, not now that I'm out of the schoolroom. I prefer Lord Byron's poetry."

The audience laughed appreciatively. A girl after his own heart, Zachary thought. He was halfway through the copy of *The Corsair* that Mr. Hunt had given him. It was just the sort of thing he liked, plenty of exciting action and daring adventure.

"Have you ever memorized any of the

speeches from *Hamlet*, Lucinda?" the mesmerist asked.

"My governness made me learn some passages, but that was a long time ago. I don't remember any of them."

Murmurs and exclamations rippled across the audience.

"That is very interesting, because you have just given us an excellent recitation of a passage from the first scene of the second act of that particular play," the mesmerist announced.

Lucinda's eyes widened. "Never say so. That's impossible. I don't recall a word of it, I swear."

The audience erupted in applause and exclamations of amazement. The mesmerist took a deep bow.

"That was astonishing," Beth whispered to Zachary.

He grinned, pleased with her reaction. "If you liked that, I've got something even more amazing to show you." He took her arm and guided her out of the Silver Pavilion.

The night was cool and the hour was late. The crowds that had filled the pleasure gardens all evening had begun to drift toward the gates. It was nearing closing time.

"I suppose you must walk me home,"

Beth said. "It's been such a lovely evening."

"Would you like to see the Haunted Mansion before we leave?"

Beth peeked at him from beneath the brim of her clever little hat. "I thought you said that particular attraction is not yet opened to the public."

Zachary chuckled. "I've got connections here. I can arrange for us to go inside." He paused meaningfully. "But I better warn ye that ye might see some very strange and terrifying sights."

Beth's eyes widened. "Is the mansion truly haunted?"

"No need to be afraid," he assured her. "I'll take care of ye."

She giggled. Zachary held her arm a little more tightly. He liked it when she giggled. Her perky straw hat made a nice frame for her blue eyes, he thought. Beth always seemed to have the prettiest hats and caps. A side benefit of her job in a milliner's shop, no doubt.

He knew she liked him. This was the third time he had invited her out for an evening in the Dream Pavilions and she had accepted quite readily. One of the benefits of *his* job was that he could get his friends into the gardens at no cost.

He was feeling optimistic tonight. With a

bit of luck and some careful planning, he hoped to surprise Beth into a kiss. His scheme depended on the effectiveness of the ghost he had arranged in the Haunted Mansion that afternoon. If the plan worked properly, Beth would scream very nicely and throw herself into his arms.

"I quite enjoyed the demonstration of mesmerism," Beth said as she watched him open the gate that blocked access to the closed section of the gardens. "Would you volunteer to let him put you into a trance?"

"No mesmerist could put me into a trance." Zachary released her arm for a moment to close the gate and light a lantern. "My mind is too strong."

"Too strong? Really?"

"Aye." He held the lantern aloft to light the gloomy path. "I am studying a secret philosophy that gives a man's mind great powers of concentration."

"A secret philosophy. How exciting."

He was gratified by her response. "There's physical exercises, too. I'm learning all sorts of clever tricks to protect myself and you from footpads and villains."

"That is all very interesting and I'm sure you're much too strong-minded to be put into a trance. Nevertheless, you must admit that the demonstration tonight was most impressive. Just imagine reciting an entire speech from a play and not remembering that you did so afterward."

"It was amazing," he agreed. In his opinion, the mesmerist had very likely paid Lucinda a handsome sum to memorize the passage from *Hamlet*. But far be it from him to question the authenticity of the trance. No one admired a clever scheme more than himself, and he knew that Mr. Hunt was quite pleased with the crowds that flocked to the pleasure gardens to see the demonstrations of mesmerism.

He guided Beth around a corner and brought her to a halt. He raised the lantern so that she could get the full effect of the Haunted Mansion looming in the fog.

Her eyes widened with excited dread. "My, it is a terrifying place. Looks just like the castle in Mrs. York's new book."

"*The Ruin?*"

"Yes. It's a wonderful story. Have you read it?"

"I prefer Byron myself."

He urged her up the steps and stopped to open the heavy door. There was a suitably eerie groan from the hinges. The opening enlarged gradually, revealing the interior with ominous slowness.

Beth hesitated on the threshold, peering

into the thick darkness. "Are you sure it's safe to go inside?"

"There's nothing to worry about." He angled the lantern so that it cast a thin wedge of light into the room. "I'm with you."

"Thank goodness." Beth stepped daintily into the room.

Zachary readied himself for her shrieks. He would be right behind her, ready to catch her in his arms when she saw the ghost.

Beth came to a halt. Her mouth fell open in shock. But she did not give a ladylike shriek; she screamed bloody murder. The high, shrill screech of terror reverberated through the mansion. Zachary set down the lantern and covered his ears.

"What the bloody hell?" He winced. "It's not a real ghost."

Beth was not listening. She whirled around. In the dim light he saw the stark fear in her eyes. She did not throw herself into his arms as he had imagined she would. She shoved him quite forcibly out of her path and hurled herself toward the door. He seized her arm to restrain her.

"Beth, wait! It's just an old sheet."

"Get out of my way!"

"It can't hurt you." He tried to hold her still as she clawed at him.

"It's horrible! How could you do this? Let

me out of here!" She struggled desperately to free herself. *"Let me out!"*

Not knowing what else to do, Zachary released her. "Beth, for God's sake, there's no need to carry on like this. I swear, it really is just a sheet."

But Beth was already outside, plunging down the steps toward the path. She vanished around a curve of the dark walk that led back toward the main grounds of the Dream Pavilions.

So much for his grand scheme, Zachary thought glumly. He wondered if it would pay to consult with Mr. Hunt on the subject of women. He was obviously in need of advice, and during the past three years he had come to respect Mr. Hunt's opinion on a variety of important matters.

He turned around to see why his ghost had failed to have the proper effect. That was when he finally saw what Beth had seen a moment earlier.

The ghost he had rigged from the rafters fluttered eerily enough in the draft from the doorway. But it was not the empty eyeholes cut into the old sheet that stared sightlessly back at him from the alcove in the stone staircase. The blood was a very effective touch. But he certainly had not thought to soak his fake specter in the stuff.

Chapter Fifteen

The glow of the flames in the rear hall was brighter now. A terrible crackling and snapping accompanied the approach of the fire, the sounds of a great beast feasting on its fresh kill. She had almost no time left. She picked up the bloody key and fumbled it into the lock of the bedchamber door.

She saw the glint of gold. She glanced toward it and noticed that Renwick's walking stick lay on the carpet beside his body. She forced herself to concentrate on getting the blood-slick key into the lock.

To her horror it slipped from her shaking fingers. She thought she heard Renwick laugh at her as she bent down to retrieve it, but when she looked at him he was still dead. She seized the key and once again tried to insert it into the lock.

It fell from her grasp a second time. She stared down at it, aware of an overpowering sense of terror and frustration. She had to open the locked door.

Out of the corner of her eye, she saw Renwick's hand move. As she watched in horror his dead fingers reached for the key. . . .

Madeline came awake as she always did after she'd had the dream, very suddenly and in a cold sweat. The familiar sense of disorientation enveloped her. She shoved aside the covers, lit a candle, and looked at the clock. It was a quarter past one in the morning. For the second time since moving into Artemis's house, she had actually slept for two whole hours before the dream had exploded in her mind. If nothing else, she was catching up on some badly needed rest here.

But she knew herself well enough to realize that there was no point in trying to go back to sleep. She would likely stay awake until dawn. Her gaze fell on the little book on her escritoire as she reached for her wrapper. Frustration flickered through her. She had shown it to Eaton Pitney just to ease her mind. He had examined it with considerable interest, but he had professed himself mystified.

He had, however, reassured her concerning a nagging question that had begun to trouble her.

"I know you will be amused by my conjecture, sir," she had said, "but you are an expert on the scholarly aspects of Vanza, so I must ask your opinion. Is there any possibility that this little book is the *Book of Se-*

crets? The volume that is rumored to have been stolen and destroyed in a fire several months ago?"

"None whatsoever," he had answered her with absolute conviction. "The *Book of Secrets*, assuming it ever existed, is said to have been written entirely in the ancient language of Vanzagara, not some mishmash of Greek and Egyptian hieroglyphs as this book is. And rumor has it that it was a sizable tome, not a small volume such as this one."

She had been greatly relieved to hear Pitney's verdict, but for some reason it had not completely satisfied her.

She slid her feet into a pair of slippers, picked up the candle, and turned resolutely toward the door. If she was going to be awake for some time, she might as well fetch a bite to eat from the kitchens. A bit of cheese or some leftover muffins might help dispel the images left behind by the dream.

Her fingers brushed against the key in the lock as she turned the doorknob. She hesitated at the touch of the cold iron, seeing again the bloody key on the floor in her dream.

She pushed aside the vision, drew a deep breath, and hurried out the door into the hall. She descended the stairs with only a couple of squeaks and made her way to the darkened kitchens. Setting the candle down on a table, she began her quest.

She felt his presence in the doorway behind her just as she located the remains of an apple pie. Startled, she dropped the pie plate on the table and whirled around.

Artemis stood in the shadowy opening, his hands thrust deep in the pockets of a black silk dressing gown. His dark hair was mussed in a most interesting manner.

"Is there enough for two?" he asked.

It was clear that he had just risen from his bed. There was a warm, lazy gleam in his eyes that told her he was making precisely the same observation about her. Memories of the passionate interlude in his library flooded through her. This man knew her as no other man did. The sensual intimacy of the moment threatened to freeze her in place.

She cleared her throat. "Yes, of course." She had to summon an inordinate amount of willpower in order to pick up the knife.

"Were you unable to sleep because of our venture into Pitney's maze?" he asked casually as he sat down at the table.

"No. I was awakened by a dream. One I have had many times since —" She broke off. "One I have frequently."

He studied her intently as she cut two slices of pie and positioned them on plates. "Your aunt felt it necessary to corner me in my library this afternoon."

"Good heavens." She scowled as she sat down on the other side of the table and handed him a fork. "Why on earth would she do such a thing?"

Artemis plunged the tines of the fork into a plump chunk of apple. "She made it clear that she is aware of the fact that I have preyed upon your innocence."

Madeline gasped for air and promptly choked on the mouthful of pie she had just taken.

"Preyed on my innocence?" she wheezed.

"Yes. I pointed out to her that you were of the opinion that nothing had changed. Gave her your logic concerning your status as the Wicked Widow, et cetera, et cetera. But she did not seem to be inclined to go along with that line of reasoning."

"Good heavens." Madeline coughed again, breathed deeply, and then stared at Artemis, unable to think of anything intelligent or clever to say. "Good heavens."

"She is naturally concerned that I took advantage of you."

"You did no such thing, sir." She stabbed her fork into the pie. "It is not as though I am some green girl fresh out of the school-room. In the eyes of the world, nothing —"

He stopped her by holding up one hand, palm out. "I would be greatly obliged if you would not say it. I have heard the words too many times already today."

"But it is nothing less than the truth, as you and I are both well aware. *Nothing has changed.*"

His eyes glittered enigmatically. "You may speak for yourself, madam. But do not presume to speak for me."

She glared at him. "You are teasing me, sir."

"No, Madeline, I am not teasing you." He took another bite of his pie. "Things have changed for me."

"Dear heaven." Her eyes widened. "This is about your being wracked with guilt, is it not? You feel honor-bound to make amends because you discovered that I was a virgin. I assure you, sir, you need not concern your-self."

"It is not your place to dictate the fine points of my honor."

"Bloody hell, sir, if you are thinking of doing something so outlandish as to pro-pose marriage simply because of that . . . that *incident* on the settee, you can forget it." She was horrified to hear her voice rising to the shrill pitch of a fishwife's, but she could not seem to stop it. "I was married once because a man thought to use me for his own ends. I will most certainly not be married a second time for a similar reason."

Very slowly he put down his fork. He looked at her with dangerously enigmatic eyes. "You think that marriage to me would bear a striking resemblance to your first marriage? One Vanza husband would be very much like another? Is that what you believe?"

She would have given anything to simply disappear. Instead she flushed furiously as she realized how he had misinterpreted her words. "Good Lord, no, of course not. There is no resemblance between you and Renwick Deveridge. I did not mean to imply as much and I think you know that quite well."

"Then what precisely did you mean, madam?"

She clamped her hand around the handle of her fork and attacked the pie again. "I meant that I do not intend to be wed so that you can satisfy some ridiculous point of honor."

"You do not consider honor an adequate reason for marriage?"

"Under certain circumstances it is indeed

a sufficient reason," she said brusquely. "But not in our case. At the risk of repeating myself, nothing has —"

"If you say it, I will not be responsible for my actions."

She glowered at him.

His gaze softened. "Perhaps we had best change the subject. Tell me about your dream, the one that awakened you tonight."

A chill went through her. The last thing she wanted to discuss was the recurring nightmare. On the other hand, it was an alternative to the even more unnerving topic of marriage.

"I tried once or twice to describe it to Bernice, but I discovered that talking about it somehow makes it all the more vivid," she said slowly.

"How long have you suffered from these dreams?"

She hesitated and then decided there was no great harm in telling him part of the truth. "Since shortly after my father died."

"I see. Is your father in your dream?"

The question took her by surprise. She looked up quickly. "No, it is my . . ."

"Your husband," he concluded for her.

"Yes."

"You say that you have had this dream frequently during the past year. Has it grown any less vivid with the passing of time?"

She put down her fork and met his eyes across the table. "No."

"Then what do you have to risk by describing it to me?"

"Why do you want to hear the details of a particularly unpleasant nightmare?"

"Because we are trying to solve a mystery and your dream may contain some clues."

She stared at him, astonished. "I do not see how that is possible."

"Dreams can often convey messages," he said calmly. "Perhaps there is something we can learn from yours. After all, we are searching for a man who may be posing as the ghost of Renwick Deveridge, and Deveridge, I gather, is featured in your dream. It may pay us to examine some of the details."

She hesitated. "I am aware that Vanza teaches that dreams can be important, but in my opinion, the things that happen in dreams cannot be properly explained."

He shrugged. "Do not try to explain anything. Just describe it. Walk me through your dream as it comes to you."

She pushed aside the pie and folded her arms on the table in front of her. Were there any clues hidden in her nightmares? It was true that she had not explored them closely. Her only goal had been to forget them, not to recall the dreadful details.

"It always starts in the same place," she said slowly. "I am crouched in front of the door of a bedchamber. I am aware that there is a fire in the house. I know I must get into the room, but the door is locked. I do not have the key, so I try to use a hairpin."

"Go on," he said softly.

She drew a deep breath. "I see Renwick's body on the carpet. The key to the bedchamber lies beside him. I pick up the key and I try to open the door with it. But the key is wet. It slips from my fingers."

"Why is the key wet?"

She looked at him. "It is covered in blood."

He was silent for a moment but his gaze did not waver. "Continue."

"Every time I try to insert the key into the lock, I hear Renwick laugh."

"Good God."

"It is . . . very unsettling. The key falls from my hand. I turn to look at Renwick but he is still quite dead. I reach down, pick up the key, and go back to work trying to unlock the door."

"Is that the end of it?"

"Yes. It is always the same." It occurred

to her that that was not quite true about the most recent version of the nightmare. Renwick's dead fingers had reached for the key in that night's dream. That was new.

"Tell me everything you can about what you see in the hallway." Artemis moved his plate out of the way and reached across the table to take her hands in his. "Every detail."

"I told you, I see Renwick's body."

"What is he wearing?"

She frowned. "I don't . . . no, wait, I think I do remember some things. He has on a white shirt, which is stained with blood. Trousers. Boots. The shirt must be partially unbuttoned because I can see the Flower of Vanza tattoo on his chest."

"What else do you see?"

She forced herself to examine the scenes of her dream. "His walking stick. It is lying on the floor beside him. I notice the gold handle."

"Is he wearing a waistcoat or cravat?"

"No."

"No coat or hat or cravat, yet he has his walking stick."

"I told you, it was important to him because his father had given it to him."

"Yes." Artemis looked very thoughtful. "Do you see any furnishings in the hall?"

"Furnishings?"

"A table or chair or candleholder, perhaps? Wall sconces?"

Why on earth did he want that sort of detail? she wondered. "There is a side table with the pair of silver candlesticks on it that Bernice gave me on my wedding day."

"Interesting. Do you see any — ?"

He broke off abruptly at the sound of loud knocking on the kitchen door.

Madeline flinched at the unexpected noise. She turned her head very quickly toward the locked door.

"A milkmaid or a fishmonger," Artemis said gently.

"It is too early," she whispered. "It is nowhere near dawn."

"An intruder or a thief who got past the guard and the dog would hardly bother to knock." Artemis got to his feet and went to the door. He paused, his hand on the lock. "Who is there?"

"It's Zachary, sir." The muffled voice was harsh with urgency. "Got a report for ye. Very important."

Madeline watched Artemis unlock and unbolt the heavy wooden door. Zachary stood on the step, his face pale and grim.

"Thank God yer home, sir. I was afraid ye might be out at one o' yer clubs and I'd be obliged to waste time tracking you down."

"What's wrong?" Artemis asked.

"There's a body, sir. In the Haunted Mansion."

"Zachary, if this is another one of your elaborate jests, I had better warn you that I am not in the mood."

"This is no jest, sir." Zachary wiped sweat off his brow with the back of his sleeve. "On me oath, sir, there's a dead body in the mansion. And there's something else."

"What else?"

"A note sir. It's addressed to you."

The Dream Pavilions had closed shortly after midnight, the customary hour on weeknights when no special event or masquerade ball was scheduled. Artemis checked his watch as he walked through the darkened grounds toward the Haunted Mansion. In the light of the lantern that Zachary carried, he could see that it was now close to two in the morning.

"You're certain the man is dead? Not drunk or ill?"

Zachary gave a visible shudder. "Believe me, sir, he's dead right enough. Gave me a start, I can tell ye. Like to give up the ghost meself when I first saw him."

"And the note? Where was it?"

"Pinned to his coat. I didn't touch it."

The pleasure garden was another world after closing time. Without the sparkling lights of the hundreds of colorful lanterns that normally lit the paths, the grounds were steeped in shadows. The light fog added to the gloom tonight. The pavilions loomed, their windows dark and impenetrable.

Artemis paused at the barrier that had been erected to keep visitors away from the incomplete mansion. Zachary held the lantern higher so that he could see to unlatch the gate.

Once on the other side, they went swiftly down the winding path that led to the attraction. When they reached the door, Zachary hesitated.

"Give me the lantern." Artemis took it from him. "There is no need for both of us to go inside."

"I'm not scared of no dead man," Zachary insisted. "I've already seen him."

"I know, but I would rather you stay out here and keep watch."

Zachary looked relieved. "Right ye are, sir. I'll do that."

Artemis paused. "What do you think Beth will say about this?"

"Beth got a great fright and she blames me for it, but she thinks it was all part of the new attraction. I didn't tell her that the body was real."

"Excellent." Artemis opened the door and walked into the front hall. The veils of some artificial cobwebs drifted over his arm. The skull on the pedestal grinned.

He walked toward the alcove where Zachary had wanted to hang an imitation skeleton. He saw the body. It was sprawled on the floor, face turned toward the wall. The light revealed a pair of expensive-looking trousers and a dark coat.

There was a great deal of blood on the front of the white shirt but none on the floor. The man had not been shot here, Artemis thought. He had been murdered somewhere else but the killer had gone to a great deal of trouble to carry the body here.

He stood over the dead man and let the lantern light fall on the too white face.

Oswynn.

A cold rage swept through Artemis. His hand tightened into a fist around the lantern handle.

The bloodstained note was right where Zachary had said it would be, pinned to Oswynn's coat. Lying next to it was a watch fob seal engraved with the head of a stallion.

Taking care to avoid touching the dried blood, Artemis picked up the note and opened it. He read the message quickly.

You may take this as both a favor and a warning, sir. Stay out of my affairs and I will stay out of yours. By the bye, be so kind as to give my regards to my wife.

Chapter Sixteen

She heard him come back into the house sometime before dawn. There was an unusual scurrying on the staircase. She caught the muted voices of two footmen and then silence fell.

She waited as long as she could stand the suspense before letting herself out into the hall. There she paused a moment, listening. The faint sounds of the usual early morning routine had not yet begun to drift up from the region of the kitchens. The servants were still abed, except for the two footmen who had disappeared belowstairs.

She went cautiously down the hall to the far end and knocked gently on Artemis's door. There was no response. The man had a right to some sleep, she told herself. He must surely be exhausted.

Disappointed, she started to turn away. She would have to wait until morning to get her answers.

The door opened with no warning. Artemis stood there, his hair gleaming damply from a recent bath. He had changed out of the trousers and shirt that he had worn when he left the house with Zachary and was once again in his black dressing gown. She realized that the rushing about she had heard earlier had been footmen carrying hot water.

Artemis had been called out to deal with a dead man, she reminded herself. Under such circumstances she would have felt the need of a bath, too.

"I thought it might be you, Madeline."

In spite of her overwhelming curiosity, she paused long enough to glance back along the hall. This was an unusual household but that did not mean the servants would not gossip if they were to see her entering Artemis's bedchamber.

Satisfied there was no one in the corridor, she slipped into the room. The tub he had recently used sat in front of the fire, partially concealed by a screen. Damp towels hung over the edge. A tray containing a pot of tea, a cup and saucer, and a plate of bread and cheese was on a table. None of the food appeared to have been touched.

She stopped short when she saw the single amber-colored taper burning on the low table. She recognized it immediately as a Vanza candle. The melting wax gave off a faint, complex, distinctive scent, the product of a unique blend of Vanzagarian herbs. Artemis was a full master of Vanza. Every master created his own personal blend of herbs that forever distinguished his candles from those of other masters.

She heard the door close behind her. She turned quickly. The unease she had been feeling grew more unsettling.

Artemis's face was shuttered and drawn, all hard angles and grim planes. She knew at once that the dead man, whoever he was, had not been a stranger to him. But there was no grief in his eyes, only a controlled fury.

She had never seen him look more dangerous than at that moment. She was forcibly reminded that in spite of the intimacy that had passed between them, there was a great deal she did not know about this man.

"I am sorry to disturb you at your meditations, sir." She edged toward the door. "I will leave you in peace. We can talk later."

"Stay." It was a command. "Whether or not you wished to do so, you involved yourself in my affairs when we made our pact. There are things you must be told."

"But your meditations —"

"A futile exercise, to say the least."

He crossed the bedchamber to the low table, reached down, and snuffed out the taper.

She clasped her hands together and faced him. "Who was he, Artemis?"

"His name was Charles Oswynn." Artemis contemplated the thin trail of smoky vapor that marked the death of the small flame. "He was one of three men who destroyed a woman named Catherine Jensen. They kidnapped her for a lark one night. They raped her. She fell to her death attempting to flee. Her body was found three days later by a farmer in search of some of his sheep."

The lack of inflection in his words only heightened their impact.

Madeline did not move. "She was a friend of yours?"

"More than a friend. We had much in common, you see. We were both alone in the world. Catherine's mother had died when she was young. She was raised by distant relatives who used her as an unpaid servant. She ran off to become an actress. I met her one night after a performance in Bath. We dreamed our dreams together for a while."

"You were lovers?"

"For a time." He did not take his eyes off the unlit candle. "But in those days I was penniless. I could not give her the security she craved."

"What happened?"

"I made the acquaintance of a master of Vanza. I was fortunate. He took an interest in me. Arranged for me to study in the Garden Temples. I made plans to sail for Vanzagara. Before I left, I promised Catherine that when I concluded my studies, I would make my fortune and we would be wed. I sailed back to England every summer to see her. But when I returned the last time, I learned that she was dead."

"How did you discover the names of the men responsible for her death?"

"I went to see the farmer who had found her body. He helped me search the area. I discovered the cave where they had taken her." He stopped talking and went to a small desk. He opened a drawer and removed an object. "I found this on the floor of the cave. I believe Catherine seized it during her battle with the three men. I traced it to a shop off Bond Street."

Madeline walked to where he stood. She took the watch fob and seal from him and examined the stallion head engraved on it. "The shopkeeper who made this told you who had purchased it?"

"He told me that he had been commissioned to craft identical seals for three gentlemen of the ton, Glenthorpe, Oswynn, and Flood. I made some more inquiries and learned that the three were close friends and had formed a small club devoted to, as they described it, the exquisite pleasures of debauchery."

She looked up from the seal. "You vowed revenge."

"At first I simply planned to kill them."

She swallowed. "All three men?"

"Yes. But I concluded that would have been too easy. I determined to destroy each of them, socially and financially, instead. I wanted to savor the *exquisite pleasures* of their descent into poverty. I wanted them to know what it was like to be an outcast from the Social World, to have no protection because of their low status and lack of resources. I wanted them to understand to some extent what it was like to be in Catherine's position."

"And when you had achieved your goal? What did you plan to do then, Artemis?"

He said nothing. There was no need for him to speak. She knew the answer.

A terrible fear arced through her. Very carefully she put the watch fob and seal down on the table beside the unlit candle.

"That is why you have endeavored to keep your ownership of the Dream Pavilions secret. It is not because you fear Society's censure if it should discover that you are in trade. You are not hunting for a wife."

"No."

"You kept your secrets because you needed access to the world in which Oswynn and the others moved in order to carry out your revenge."

"The scheme worked quite well until now. My income from the gardens made it possible for me to meet Oswynn and the others on their own ground. It took me months to set up the snare that was designed to ruin them." Artemis picked up the empty teacup and turned it gently between his hands. "I was so close. So very, very close. And now *he* has deprived me of one of my targets."

She took a step forward, reaching out with her hand. "Artemis —"

"The bloody *bastard*. How does he *dare* to interfere in my affairs?" Without warning, Artemis hurled the cup against the wall. "Five years I worked to put it all together. Five damned years."

Madeline froze as the dainty china shattered into dozens of jagged pieces. It was not the small explosion that stunned her. It was the shock of seeing Artemis in the grip of such fierce emotion.

In all the time she had known him, he had been so controlled, so unshakably in command of himself. Even when he had made love to her, his self-mastery had been complete.

He looked down at the shards as if he were looking into the mouth of hell. "Five years."

She could not bear his pain any longer. It was too much a reflection of her own inner anguish. She ran to him, threw her arms around his waist, and pressed her face against his shoulder.

"You blame yourself for her death," she whispered.

"I left her alone." He stood unyielding in her embrace, as cold as stone. "She had no one to protect her while I was away. She told me that she was a woman of the world. Said she could take care of herself. But in the end . . ."

"I understand." She hugged him with all of her strength, trying to impart some of her own warmth into his chilled body. "I know how it feels to live with the knowledge that your decisions brought about another's death. Dear God, I understand."

"Madeline." He turned abruptly. His hands closed convulsively around her head.

"At times I thought I would go mad." She

buried her face against his black silk dressing gown. "Indeed, if it had not been for Bernice, I would have long since been consigned to a house for the insane."

"What a pair we make," he muttered into her hair. "I have lived for revenge and you have cursed yourself for your father's death."

"Now I have brought some malign force into your life that threatens the thing you care about most, your vengeance." She fought to squeeze back the tears. "I am so very sorry, Artemis."

"Do not say that." He cradled her face and raised her head so that she had to meet his eyes. "I vow, I will not have you bearing the blame for what happened tonight."

"But it is my fault. If I had not sought your help, none of this would have happened."

"I made my own decision in the matter."

"That's not true. It all started that night when I virtually blackmailed you into helping me find Nellie."

"Enough." He covered her mouth, silencing her with a heavy, drugging kiss.

The need she sensed in him tore at her heart. Instinctively she wanted to offer comfort, but his desire was sudden and overwhelming. She was lost beneath the crashing wave.

He dragged her down onto the bed. She sank into the quilts and clung to him as his mouth moved on hers. Then he shifted to kiss her throat. Her wrapper parted beneath the onslaught. His hands closed over her breasts.

The desperate urgency in him ignited a response deep within her. She pushed her hands beneath his dressing gown and sought the sleek, hard contours of his body. He muttered something unintelligible when she stroked his muscled back and arched herself into his fierce heat. She felt him slide his hand up along the inside of her thigh beneath her nightgown. She gasped when he cupped her with his palm.

She opened herself to him and he claimed what she offered. She felt herself grow damp and warm and full. Lost in the spiraling need, she touched every part of him that she could reach. He pushed his thick, hard shaft into her fingers. She stroked him gently, learning the feel of him.

He groaned and then he rolled onto his back and pulled her down on top of him. The edges of her wrapper fluttered. She gripped him with her knees and cried out when his hands moved between her legs.

She looked down at him. He was watching her with an intensity that left no room for words. At that moment the only thing that mattered in the whole world was satisfying the dark hunger that she could see in his eyes.

She felt his hands close around her hips, guiding her as she struggled to fit herself to his heavily aroused body. When he started to enter her, she felt herself tighten against the intrusion. She was still tender from their last encounter.

"Slowly," he promised, his voice low and husky. "We'll take it slowly this time."

He eased himself gently, deliberately, and carefully into her. He stilled, allowing her to adjust to the feel of him buried so deeply inside her. She breathed in cautiously and allowed herself to relax. She still felt too full but there was no pain this time, only a growing anticipation.

He found the sensitive bud with his thumb. She sucked in her breath. His fingers glided against her, slick and warm and unbearably thrilling.

"Artemis." She sank her nails into his shoulders.

"Yes." His eyes gleamed in the shadows. "Just like that."

He began to move within her. A great tension seized her. She tossed her head and grappled with him, seeking some inexplicable release from the heady demands of her body.

He refused to increase the pace. She wanted to scream with frustration. He continued to move slowly, unpredictably within her.

She seized his shoulders and took control, establishing her own rhythm. She did not know what it was she sought so desperately, but she sensed that the magic was out there, waiting for her to find it.

Artemis laughed silently up at her and in that moment she knew that he had plotted all along to bring her to this point. She did not care. An end to the coiled need was the only thing that mattered now.

Without warning, the dam inside her burst. Wave after wave of pleasure pulsed through her. Artemis pulled her head down, covering her mouth with his own when she would have cried out.

For a few dizzying seconds he seemed to savor the tiny shivers of her release. Then he gave a hoarse, muffled groan and pumped himself into her until they were both exhausted.

He roused himself reluctantly from the sweet lethargy a few minutes later. The cold rage that had flowed through his veins for the past few hours had dissipated, at least for a while. Madeline's doing, he thought. Her passion had served as a poultice to the old wound that had opened within him. He knew now that it had never healed.

Beside him she stirred, sat up quickly, and blinked, as though dazed. Then her eyes cleared. She looked at him steadily.

"You must have loved her very much," she whispered.

"I cared for her. I felt responsible for her. We were lovers. I do not know if it was love. I do not know how love feels. But I do know that what I felt for her was important."

"Yes," she said.

He held her gaze and struggled to find the words to explain. "Whatever Catherine and I had between us has faded in the five years since her death. I am not haunted by her memory, only by the knowledge that I failed her. I promised her ghost that I would avenge her. It was the only thing left that I could do for her."

Madeline smiled wistfully. "I understand. You have lived for your revenge, and now, in helping me, you have put your vengeance at risk. I'm sorry, Artemis."

"Madeline —"

"Good heavens, look at the time." She stirred and groped for the sash of her wrapper. "I must get back to my bed-chamber. Someone might come in here at any moment."

"No one will enter this room without my permission."

"One of the maids, perhaps." She got to her feet and hastily tied the sash. "It would be very awkward for both of us."

"Madeline, we must talk."

"Yes, I know. Perhaps after breakfast." She took a step back and came up hard against the dressing table.

She put out a hand to steady herself. He saw her fingers brush against the note he had found pinned to Oswynn's coat. She glanced at it.

"You may as well read it." He sat up slowly on the edge of the bed.

She looked at him. "It is addressed to you."

"The killer left it."

Fresh alarm sparked in her gaze. "The villain wrote a note to you?"

"A warning to keep out of this business." He stood and went to the dressing table to pick up the bloodstained message. Without a word he opened it and handed it to her.

She read it quickly and he knew precisely when she came to the last line. Her fingers shook slightly as she read it aloud.

" 'By the bye, be so kind as to give my regards to my wife.' " She raised her head. Dread filled her eyes. "Dear God, it's true. Renwick is alive."

"No." He ripped the note out of her fingers and pulled her close against him. "We don't know that."

"But he mentions me." A thin veil of barely concealed horror underscored her words. " 'Give my regards to my wife.' "

"Madeline, think. It is far more likely that someone wants us to believe he is alive," Artemis said.

"But why?"

"Because it suits his purpose."

"None of this makes any sense." She put her hands to her temples. "What is happening? What is this all about?"

"I don't know yet, but I promise you that we will discover the truth."

She shook her head once. Determination settled on her like a dark cloak. "I regret everything I have done to involve you in this affair, sir. Bernice and I must leave this house today."

He raised his brows. "I trust you will not put me to the effort of posting a guard to keep the pair of you here. It would be extremely inconvenient."

"This has gone too far, Artemis. The note

is a warning. Who knows what he will do next?"

"I doubt that he will take it upon himself to dispatch two more gentlemen of the ton in short order."

"But he has already killed one of them."

"Oswynn was an easy target because he has little in the way of family who will be concerned by his death. Given his reputation, it will not surprise anyone to learn that he got himself killed by a footpad on the way home from one of the hells. But murdering Flood and Glenthorpe will involve far more risk. I believe our mysterious villain is smart enough to know that."

"But Oswynn's body was found on the grounds of the Dream Pavilions. That will surely involve you in a great scandal."

"No," Artemis said evenly. "Oswynn's body, when it is eventually discovered, will turn up floating in the Thames. Zachary and I took care of the matter an hour ago."

"I see." She absorbed the implications of that statement and frowned. "But that does not solve our problem. The villain obviously knows about your connection to the Dream Pavilions. That is why he left Oswynn's body there for you to discover."

"Yes."

"He also knows about your plans for revenge."

"Yes."

She looked at him with a troubled expression. "He can cause you a great deal of mischief."

"If he does, I will deal with it."

"But, Artemis —"

He closed his hands around her shoulders. "Listen to me, Madeline. Regardless of what happens, we are in this together. It is too late for either of us to change our course."

She watched him for several taut seconds. Then, without a word, she put her arms around him and rested her head on his shoulder.

He held her tightly. Outside the window the first gloomy light of a fog-shrouded dawn appeared.

Chapter Seventeen

"I vow, I believe I would have gone mad if we had not escaped from Hunt's house for a while this morning." Bernice studied the street through the carriage window. "Do not mistake me, I appreciate his concern for your safety, but I confess I had begun to feel quite trapped."

"Our freedom this morning is little more than an illusion," Madeline said wryly.

Latimer was on the box but he was not alone. Zachary sat beside him, armed with a pistol. He had been at the house when Madeline and Bernice summoned the carriage. He had insisted upon accompanying them.

"Yes, it is rather as if we are traveling under armed guard, is it not?" Bernice said. "Nevertheless, it is good to be outside again, even in this fog."

"Yes."

"A pity Mr. Leggett was not around when we left the house," Bernice said casually. "I would have suggested that he accompany us."

Madeline blinked. "You would have liked

for Mr. Leggett to join us?"

"We had a very interesting conversation while you and Mr. Hunt were out having your adventure in Pitney's maze. Got to know each other better, as it were. He is a well-traveled gentleman."

"Is he?"

"He spent some time on the Continent during the war, you know."

Madeline was nonplussed by this turn in the conversation. "No, I did not know that. What was he doing there?"

"He was quite circumspect about it, but I gained the impression that he brought back some reports on the system Napoleon used to keep his troops supplied. His notes were of great help to Wellington."

"Good heavens. Mr. Leggett was involved in the war in some clandestine fashion?"

"Well, he did not come right out and say it, of course, but then he wouldn't, would he? He is a gentleman, after all. Gentlemen do not speak of such things. He is really quite charming, don't you think?"

It occurred to Madeline that although she had known Bernice all of her life, she had never before noticed this particular sparkle in her aunt's eye. She coughed discreetly to cover her astonishment. "Very charming indeed."

"And quite fit for a man of his age."

Madeline grinned. "Mature yet still agile, would you say?"

To her amazement, Bernice turned a rosy shade of pink. Then she smiled ruefully. "Indeed."

The carriage came to a halt, saving Madeline a further discussion of Mr. Leggett's many charms and accomplishments. The door opened. Zachary handed first Bernice and then Madeline down to the pavement. There was a troubled expression on his lean face.

Reluctantly he walked them to the front door of the small shop.

"We will not be long," Bernice told him. "You may wait out here."

"Aye, ma'am. I'll be right here if ye need me."

Madeline followed Bernice into the shadowy interior of Moss's Apothecary.

The shop had changed little in all the years she had known it. The exotic scents of incense and strange spices brought back memories of her childhood. Her father had been a frequent patron of Moss's, as had many of the gentlemen of Vanza. Augusta Moss was one of a very small number of apothecaries who carried Vanzagarian herbs.

"Miss Reed, Mrs. Deveridge, how kind of

you to stop by today." Augusta Moss, large and dignified looking in the flowing apron that covered much of her gown, emerged from the fragrant regions at the rear of the shop. "So good to see you both. It has been a while, has it not?"

"Indeed," Bernice said cheerfully. "But I am in need of several types of herbs, so Madeline and I thought we would pay a call on you today."

Mrs. Moss inclined her head. "Excellent. What herbs do you need?"

"Madeline has not been sleeping well of late."

"A pity." Mrs. Moss made a small clucking noise that conveyed sympathy and understanding. "A sound night's sleep is so vital to good health and strong nerves."

"It certainly is." Bernice warmed to her favorite topic with relish. "I have supplied her with my usual remedies, but they have failed. I thought to try some Vanzagarian herbs that I experimented with once or twice several years ago. One burns them to form a soothing vapor that induces sleep. Do you happen to have any in stock?"

"I know the type you mean. Quite rare. I am able to get them only two or three times a year. However, I do not have any in stock at the moment."

"Oh dear," Bernice murmured. "I am sorry to hear that. There are so few apothecaries in town who stock herbs from Vanzagara. We have already been to the others, and none of them have had a shipment for months."

"It is very unfortunate that you did not stop by a fortnight ago. I had a large supply at that time." Mrs. Moss's eyes went regretfully to an empty jar at the end of the shelf. "A gentleman who is a member of the Vanzagarian Society purchased all that I had on hand."

Madeline held her breath and was careful not to exchange a glance with Bernice.

Bernice raised her brows. "You say your new client purchased your entire supply? Whoever he is, he must have great difficulty with his sleep."

Mrs. Moss shook her head. "I don't think that sleep was a problem for him. I believe he intended to use them in some experiments. He has developed an interest in the production of visions and hallucinations, you see."

"I wonder if this gentleman would be willing to let me have some," Bernice said thoughtfully. "Perhaps if he knew how much Madeline needs them, he would be good enough to part with a portion of the supply he purchased from you."

Mrs. Moss shrugged. "No harm in asking him, I suppose. I sold the herbs to Lord Clay."

Madeline rushed through the door behind her aunt. She looked at the house-keeper. "Has Mr. Hunt returned home yet? It is urgent that I speak with him immediately."

"There is no need to look for me." Artemis said from halfway up the stairs. "I am right here. It's about time you returned. Where the devil have you been?"

His voice was the distant drumroll of thunder that heralds the oncoming storm: close enough to gain your immediate attention but not yet a dire threat.

Madeline looked up sharply. She saw at once that while his tone was still under full control, strong emotions already darkened his eyes.

"How fortunate that you are here, sir."

Bernice gave him a bright-eyed look. "We have had quite an eventful day. Madeline has much to tell you, sir."

"Does she indeed?" Artemis did not take his eyes off Madeline as he came down the staircase. "You will join me in the library, Mrs. Deveridge. I am extremely eager to hear all about your *eventful* day."

Mrs. Deveridge. No doubt about it, Madeline thought as she preceded him into the library. He was not in a good mood.

"There is no need to snap at me, sir." She turned to look at him as the door closed, leaving them alone in the library. "I do not appreciate it. If the strain of recent events has begun to take its toll, I suggest that you try one of my aunt's tonics."

"I believe I shall stick with my brandy." He walked around the corner of his desk.

"Sir, I can explain —"

"Everything?" His brows rose. "I certainly hope so, because I have a great many questions. Let us begin with the most pressing matter. How dare you leave the house without telling me where you were going?"

She stood her ground. "Sir, your tone of voice is quite annoying. I am prepared to be patient and understanding because, as I just mentioned, recent events have put a strain on everyone's nerves. However, if you continue to carry on as though you were . . ." She stopped.

"As though I were what, madam? As though I were concerned?" He flattened his hands on the top of the desk. His eyes were hard. "As though I had every cause to be alarmed? As though you had behaved in a willful, headstrong, utterly thoughtless manner?"

It was too much on top of everything else. Her temper flared. "I was about to say, *as though you were my husband.*"

A stunning silence descended. Even the clock seemed to stop. Madeline would have given anything to recall the words, but it was far too late.

"Your husband," Artemis repeated in a perfectly uninflected tone.

She stiffened and concentrated on loosening the fingertips of her gloves. "Forgive me, sir. I got a bit carried away in my analogy. It is just that I have discovered some very important clues today. We cannot waste time with arguments."

He ignored her words to inquire with icy curiosity, "Am I truly acting like your husband? I believe you have described him as a murderous villain of the first order."

She felt light-headed with remorse. "Don't be ridiculous, sir. Of course I was not comparing you to Renwick. He was a complete bastard, totally lacking in honor. Quite the opposite of yourself."

"Thank you for that much, at least," he said through set teeth.

She concentrated fiercely on peeling off her right glove. "As you know, my memories of my marriage are not happy ones. It is possible that I overreacted a moment ago when you began to shout at me."

"I did not shout."

"No." She went to work on the left glove. "You are quite correct. I misspoke. You did not shout. I doubt that you ever raise your voice, do you, Artemis? It is probably quite unnecessary. You are perfectly capable of freezing a person in his or her tracks with only a word."

"I do not know about freezing a person in his tracks, but I can assure you that when I arrived home a short while ago and discovered that you had left the house, the news froze me to the bone."

She frowned. "Didn't the housekeeper inform you that we took Latimer and Zachary with us?"

"Yes, and that is the only thing that kept me from sending the Eyes and Ears out to search for you."

She dropped one of the gloves. For a few seconds the only thing she could do was stare at it where it lay on the carpet. Then she raised her eyes slowly to look at Artemis. She tried to read the emotions that glittered in the depths of his gaze.

It was not easy. He was a man who had long ago learned to close himself to the world. He lived far inside himself, hidden behind locked gates, shuttered windows, and high stone walls. But he had a core founded upon honor and integrity. Unlike Renwick, he was not a beautiful, hollow statue who cared only about himself. Artemis understood the demands of responsibility. All she had to do was look at Zachary and Henry Leggett and the others who served him with such obvious loyalty and affection to know the truth about him.

Above all, he knew the pangs of guilt and failure, just as she did.

"Please accept my apologies, Artemis." Forgetting about the glove at her feet, she took an impulsive step closer to the desk. "I lost my temper. Husbands are a sore point with me."

"You have made that very clear."

"Latimer and Zachary were both armed, and I had my pistol and my knife. I am not a fool."

He watched her steadily for a long while. "No, of course you are not a fool. You are an intelligent, resourceful woman who is accustomed to making her own decisions." He straightened abruptly and turned toward the window. "Obviously, I am the one who is overreacting."

"Artemis —"

"Pursuing this argument will gain us nothing." He clasped his hands behind his back and gazed fixedly out into the garden. "Let us move on to a more useful subject. Tell me what was of such great interest to you that it drew you out of this house today."

He had to be one of the most stubborn men on the face of the earth. She raised her eyes toward the ceiling, but there was no divine inspiration to be had from that source.

"Yes, indeed, sir," she said briskly. "By all means let us move on to a less inflamed subject. Nothing like a little pleasant conversation about murder and dark plots to lighten the mood, I always say."

He glanced at her over his shoulder. "A word of advice, madam. Do not press your luck. You may be accustomed to making your own decisions, but I assure you that I am equally accustomed to being master in my own house." He paused to raise one brow in a meaningful manner. "And at the moment, you are living in that house."

She cleared her throat. "You make an excellent point, sir. You have every right to give the orders here. You have my word that I will not go out again without making certain that you are aware of my destination."

"I suppose I must be content with that. Now then, tell me about your adventures today."

"Yes, well, to be brief, it occurred to me that there are very few apothecaries in London who stock Vanzagarian herbs, and of those, only a small number keep a large quantity on hand. Whoever burned the incense in Pitney's maze in an attempt to render us unconscious must have had a rather sizable amount."

He was silent for a few seconds as he absorbed the implications of her logic. "So you set out to see if you could discover where the herbs had been purchased?"

She was pleased to see that he had grasped the import of her plan so quickly. "Actually, I had a fair notion of where to begin. This morning my aunt and I visited those apothecaries we thought most likely to have sold the sleeping herbs."

He turned around fully to face her. She realized she had finally got his interest.

"Go on," he said.

"As I said, there are very few apothecaries who stock the herbs. Several months ago one of them was slain in his own shop."

"I heard about that murder." Artemis narrowed his eyes. "There was a rumor that it was connected to the *Book of Secrets*."

"Yes. But most of the gossip evaporated after Ignatius Lorring took his own life."

"I wondered at the time if there might have been a link between Lorring's suicide and the rumors about the *Book of Secrets*," Artemis said thoughtfully. "He was one of the few men in all of Europe who might have been able to decipher it."

She shrugged. "If Lord Linslade is to be believed, we are once more dealing with rumors of that wretched book. In any event, Bernice and I decided to call at Mrs. Moss's shop to inquire about the sleeping herbs."

He rubbed the back of his neck absently. "I know of Moss's Apothecary. When I crafted my own meditation candles, I purchased the herbs I needed from her."

"Many Vanza scholars have patronized her establishment over the years. Indeed, she once mentioned that Lorring himself bought herbs from her. Be that as it may, she told me that although she stocked the sleeping herbs, she was temporarily out of them because she had recently sold her entire supply to a gentleman who was a member of the Vanzagarian Society."

Artemis definitely looked intrigued now. He left the window and crossed the room to face her across the desk. "Who is he?"

"Lord Clay."

Artemis appeared briefly startled. Then he scowled. "I have met the man once or twice. He is pleasant enough, but somewhat vague. In your terms, he is merely another crackbrain member of the Society. As far as I am aware, he has no great interest in the old tongue of Vanzagara. I find it difficult to believe that he would pursue something as arcane as the *Book of Secrets*."

"Nevertheless, it appears he is in possession of the only large amount of Vanzagarian sleeping herbs available in London at the moment."

Artemis picked up the letter opener and absently tapped the end of it against the blotter. "Not much to be going on with."

"Can you offer anything more helpful?" she asked bluntly.

He tossed aside the letter opener. "No. Very well, we shall pursue your clue."

"How? We can hardly search his house. It is not empty as Pitney's was. It will be filled with servants at every hour of the day and night."

Artemis smiled slowly. "There is an old bit of Vanza wisdom that holds that an overcrowded fortress is as vulnerable as an empty one."

She frowned. "I have never heard that saying."

"Probably because I just made it up on the spot."

She gazed steadily into the flame until it expanded to fill her entire field of vision. The scent of the candle, delicate and complex, infused the air of her bedchamber.

A few minutes ago she had closed the heavy curtains and locked the door to ensure privacy. The bedchamber lay in deep shadows. The muffled noises of the household and the street below her window faded into the distance.

Her father had taught her the art of Vanza meditation many years ago, but it was Bernice who had selected the herbs to blend into the special tapers. The fragrance was gentle and soothing to the senses. Like the scents in Mrs. Moss's shop, it brought back memories that linked her to the past. Fleeting images drifted through her mind: her father bending toward her as he explained how to decipher a particularly difficult passage in an old text.

There were no images of her mother, who had died a year after giving birth to her, but there were many of Bernice.

It was Bernice who had moved into the Reed home to take care of her grieving older brother and his little daughter. It was

Bernice, buoyant and cheerful and warm and loving, who had proved to be the steady anchor the household had needed in the wake of Elizabeth Reed's death.

Bernice had taken Madeline into her heart and given her the love and affection of a mother. She had supplied the chaotic household with firm direction. She had forced her devastated brother to emerge from the abyss into which his wife's death had plunged him.

In the end it had not been her father's life-long study of Vanza that had saved the family in its time of crisis, Madeline thought. It had been Bernice.

Gently she eased aside the images from the past and let the scenes from the hellish landscape of her recurring nightmare drift, ghostlike, through her mind. She did not want to examine her dream again, but she had no choice. There had been something different about the last one, something she knew she needed to comprehend.

Time passed. She sank deeper into the visions in her head; so deep that she was once more aware of the crackle of the beast of flame; deep enough to feel the iron of the key in her hand. She caught the glint of gold on the carpet.

She felt herself grow cold, just as she did

when she dreamed the images in her sleep. Her fingers trembled but she did not turn away from the images.

It had been Artemis's questioning that had given her the notion of looking at the scenes of the nightmare while in a meditative state. Last night her description had been interrupted by Zachary's appearance at the kitchen door. All day long she'd had the uneasy sensation that she had failed to tell Artemis something important about the slightly altered version of the dream.

He had been most curious about Renwick's walking stick, but that was a common feature in the nightmare and she had no interest in taking a closer look at it. The elegant stick was not important. It was simply a manifestation of Deveridge's vanity.

It was the key that bothered her today. She had dreamed the dreadful nightmare many times in the months since the fire. There were occasional variations in the images, all of them saturated with her growing fear that she would not be able to unlock the bedchamber door.

But she did not recall any version of the dream in which Renwick's dead hand had reached for the key, which kept falling from her grasp.

She did not try to force the scenes. With the aid of the candle and deliberate concentration, they appeared readily enough. The flames, Renwick's harrowing laughter, the smell of smoke; they were all there in her head.

The key fell from her hand. She bent to retrieve it. Renwick laughed. She turned her head to look at him.

He reached for the key with dead fingers. . . .

A scream reverberated in the bedchamber. The candle flame flickered and vanished. The room was abruptly overwhelmed by deep shadows.

She barely had time to realize that she was the one who had cried out and knocked over the candle before she heard the thud of boots pounding on the stairs. A moment later a fist slammed against wooden panels.

"Madeline! Open this door at once!"

Breathless and drenched with a cold sweat, she scrambled to her feet and hurried to unlock the door. She threw it open and was nearly run down by Artemis as he came through the opening.

"What the bloody hell — ?" He halted just inside the bedchamber and swept the room in a single glance.

"It's all right," she said quickly. "I'm sorry about the scream."

He glanced at her and then he crossed to the window in three long strides. He yanked aside the curtain and checked the locks. He swung around and looked at the extinguished candle.

"I was meditating," she explained. "Trying to recall images from the dream."

Bernice appeared in the doorway. Her face clouded with concern. "What in heaven's name is going on here?"

"I say, something amiss?" Eaton Pitney, arm in a crisp white sling, arrived behind Bernice. His bushy brows snarled in a thicket of alarm. "Was it the Stranger?"

"No, no, no," Madeline said. She groaned when she saw that Nellie and the housekeeper had also materialized in the hall. "I was meditating. Something startled me. Please, there is no reason to be concerned."

"I will deal with this, Mrs. Jones," Artemis said to the housekeeper. "Kindly inform the staff that all is well."

"Aye, sir." Mrs. Jones turned briskly away with an expression of relief and disappeared with Nellie in tow.

Artemis waited until they had retreated

down the back stairs. Then he looked at Madeline. "What the devil happened?"

"My dream." She glanced at Eaton Pitney. "It is a long story, sir, but suffice it to say that I have had a recurring nightmare. Last night there was something different about it. There is a key, you see."

"A key?" Pitney cocked his head to the side. "To a door, do you mean?"

Artemis looked at her. "What of the key?"

"It is always in my dream, but last night I dropped it and instead of picking it up, as I generally do —" She broke off and turned back to Pitney. "Sir, yesterday you told me you did not believe that little volume I showed you could be the *Book of Secrets*."

"Quite impossible. The thing is not even written in the correct language."

"But you and I discussed the possibility that it might be some sort of code."

"What of it?"

She drew a breath. "Lord Linslade had a conversation with an intruder he took to be the ghost of my dead husband. Linslade said he and the phantom discussed the *Book of Secrets*. Renwick's ghost apparently mentioned the fact that even if the book was found, one would need some means of translating it because there were so few scholars who could read the ancient tongue."

352

"Quite right," Pitney said.

"And you yourself said that the Stranger who surprised you in your maze demanded a key."

"What are you getting at here, Madeline?" Artemis asked.

"What if the *Book of Secrets* was not consumed in the flames?" Madeline said very steadily. "What if someone has it and now seeks the code he needs to unlock its secrets? What if that strange little book I have been studying is the key to the *Book of Secrets*?"

Chapter Eighteen

He waited in the pooling shadows behind the screen and watched through the small openings that had been embroidered into the design. The two men entered the elegantly appointed dining room one by one. Each was startled to see the other, although they quickly covered their mutual surprise with the usual pleasantries. Neither was entirely successful at concealing his unease, however. They did not meet each other's eyes as they surveyed the firelit chamber.

The table had been laid for four. Candlelight sparkled on the crystal and silver. Thick velvet drapes shut out the view of the fog-swathed pleasure gardens outside the tall window. The sounds of music and the noise of the crowds were muffled and distant. The gentlemen's footsteps were hushed by the heavy carpet. There were no servants about.

Silence cloaked the private dining parlor.

Glenthorpe broke the conversational ice first. "Wasn't expecting to see you here tonight. I take it you're a shareholder in this enterprise, too?"

"The mining project, d'ye mean?" Flood helped himself to the bottle of claret that stood on the table. He poured a generous serving into one glass but did not offer to pour any for Glenthorpe. "Got into it right at the start. Going to take my profits early."

"I was told that the opportunity to invest at the beginning was limited to only a handful of gentlemen."

"Yes, I know. By invitation only." Flood downed half the claret in his glass and regarded Glenthorpe over the rim. "So you were one of those who got in at the start of the venture?"

"You know me, Flood." Glenthorpe's laugh rang hollow in the small room. "I've always been one to take advantage of a good thing when it comes my way."

"Yes, I know you," Flood said quietly. "And you know me. And we both knew Oswynn. Rather interesting, is it not?"

Glenthorpe jerked in response to that question. "You heard the news?"

"That they pulled his body out of the river this morning? I heard."

"Footpad got him," Glenthorpe said. He sounded both eager and desperate. "You recall his temperament. Wild and reckless. He was always one to take chances. Spent too much time in the most dangerous parts of town. It was a wonder he didn't break his neck or get himself shot by a villain in the stews years ago."

"Yes," Flood said. "A wonder. But now he's gone, isn't he? And there are only two members of our little club left."

"For God's sake, Flood, will you stop carrying on about Oswynn?"

"Two of us left, and by a strange coincidence we are both here tonight to meet the master of our enterprise and to be told of our profits."

Glenthorpe went to warm himself at the fire. "You're well and truly foxed. Mayhap you should avoid the wine until after we've completed our business."

"Our business," Flood repeated thoughtfully. "Ah, yes, our business. Tell me, do you not find it curious that no one else has arrived?"

Glenthorpe scowled. Then he jerked his watch out of his pocket and flipped open the cover. "It's only a quarter past ten."

"The invitation was for ten o'clock."

"What of it?" Glenthorpe dropped the watch back into his pocket. "The grounds are crowded tonight. The other investors have no doubt been delayed."

Flood eyed the four places at the table.

"There cannot be many of them."

Glenthorpe followed his gaze. His hands worked nervously. "At least two more."

Flood continued to study the four dishes on the table. "If we assume that one of the places is set for the master of this venture, that leaves only a single investor left to account for, other than ourselves. Apparently just three of us were invited to make our fortunes in this affair."

"Don't understand it." Glenthorpe fiddled with the fobs on his watch. "What man would be late to learn of his profits?"

Artemis walked out from behind the screen.

"A dead man," he said quietly.

Flood and Glenthorpe whirled to face him.

"Hunt," Flood muttered.

"What the devil is this all about?" Glenthorpe's expression of wide-eyed fear transformed into blank confusion. "Why did you conceal yourself behind that screen? Should have announced yourself when we arrived. This is no night for games."

"I agree with you," Artemis said. "There will be no more games."

"What did you mean with that remark about a dead man?" Glenthorpe demanded brusquely.

"You're a fool, Glenthorpe." Flood did not take his eyes off Artemis. "You always were a fool."

Glenthorpe bristled furiously. "Damnation, how dare you call me a fool, sir? You've got no call to insult me."

"Hunt is not the third investor," Flood said wearily. "He is the master of the mining venture. Is that not right, sir?"

Artemis inclined his head. "You are correct."

"Master of it?" Glenthorpe looked at the four place settings and then switched his gaze back to Artemis. "Then who is the third investor?"

Flood's mouth twisted. "I suspect that Oswynn was the third man induced to stake his entire fortune on this project."

Artemis did not move out of the shadows. "Again you are correct in your conclusion. But then, you always were the cleverest of the three, were you not?"

Flood's jaw tightened. "Tell me, just out of curiosity, precisely how much of our total investment have we lost?"

Artemis went to the table, picked up the claret bottle, and poured a glass. He looked at the two men.

"You have both lost everything," he said.

"Bloody bastard," Flood whispered.

Glenthorpe gaped. "Everything? But that's not possible. What of our profits? We were going to make vast fortunes in the venture."

"I fear your profits, as well as all of the money you invested, have disappeared down the shaft of that imaginary gold mine in the South Seas," Artemis said.

"Are you saying there is no mine?"

"Yes, Glenthorpe. That is precisely what I am saying."

"But . . . but I mortgaged my estates to raise the funds to put into that mining venture." Glenthorpe gripped the back of a chair to steady himself. "I will be ruined."

"All three of us wagered far more than we could afford." Flood pinned Artemis with venomous eyes. "We allowed ourselves to be dazzled. We were deceived by an illusion. Hunt here was the magician behind the scenes."

Glenthorpe staggered. His face pinched in an expression of anguish. He put a hand to his chest. He took a few shallow breaths and then slowly straightened. "Why? What is this all about?"

Artemis looked at him. "It's about Catherine Jensen."

Glenthorpe paled. He pulled himself to a chair and sat down hard. "Damnation. It was you who sent the seal a few months ago, was it not?"

"I wanted you to have time to contemplate the past before I took the next step," Artemis said.

"You're a cold-blooded devil, Hunt," Flood said almost casually. "I should have reasoned it out long before tonight."

"No." Glenthorpe rubbed his nose with the back of his hand. "No, this is impossible. How can it be? It all ended five years ago."

Artemis spared him only the briefest of glances. Flood was the dangerous one. "There is no time limit on revenge."

"It was an accident." Glenthorpe's voice rose. "She made a fuss. Who'd have thought the little lightskirt would fight like that? She got away from us. We tried to catch her but she ran off. It was so dark that night. No moon. Couldn't see your bloody hand in front of your face without a lantern. It's not our fault she fell from that cliff."

"But I do consider it your fault," Artemis said softly. "Yours and Oswynn's and Flood's."

"Well then," Flood said quietly, "are you going to murder us the way you murdered Oswynn?"

Glenthorpe's jaw dropped. "You killed

360

Oswynn?" He twitched violently and clutched at the table to steady himself. "It wasn't a footpad?"

"Of course it was Hunt who killed Oswynn," Flood said. "Who else could it have been?"

"As it happens," Artemis said, "I did not kill Oswynn."

"I don't believe you," Flood said.

"What you choose to believe is up to you, of course, but if you spend your time watching for me over your shoulder, you may not notice the real killer standing in front of you."

"Just as we failed to notice that we were being lured to our financial ruin?" Flood snarled.

Artemis smiled. "Precisely. My advice is to be wary of all new acquaintances."

"No." Glenthorpe's breath was shallow and uneven. "No, this cannot be happening."

Flood's jaw tightened. "If you didn't murder Oswynn, Hunt, who did?"

"An excellent question." Absently, Artemis sipped his claret. "One I hope to answer soon. In the meantime I think we must assume the killer may go after each of you next. It is quite possible that he will dispatch you both. That is why I summoned you here tonight. Before you die, I wanted you to know that Catherine Jensen was indeed avenged."

Glenthorpe shook his head in helpless agitation. "But why would this villain try to kill us?"

"For the same reason that he murdered Oswynn. He hopes to distract me from another project in which I am deeply involved," Artemis said. "I must admit that he has succeeded in dividing my attention. I cannot allow that situation to continue."

Flood looked at him. "What is your other project?"

"My other venture is none of your affair," Artemis said. "Suffice it to say that my association with you and Glenthorpe is finished for the time being. Events have forced me to play my hand sooner than I had planned. For now I shall have to be satisfied with the knowledge that you will both find your creditors on your doorstep in the morning."

"I am destroyed," Glenthorpe wheezed. "Utterly destroyed."

"Yes." Artemis walked toward the door. "It does not begin to compensate for what you did five years ago, of course, but it will give you something to think about on long, cold nights. Always assuming that the man who killed Oswynn does not get to you first."

"Damn you to hell, you bloody bastard," Flood snarled. "You won't get away with this."

"If you feel I have in any way impugned your honor," Artemis said very softly, "feel free to have your seconds call upon mine."

Flood went red with rage but he said nothing.

Artemis went out into the hall and shut the door. He heard something crash against the wood panels. The claret bottle, perhaps.

He went down the back stairs and let himself out into the foggy night. The mist had not affected the enthusiasm of the crowds, but most visitors chose indoor attractions tonight. The lights of the Crystal Pavilion glowed. He made his way along a path that wound through a lantern-lit grove. He had the graveled walk to himself.

It was over at last. Five long years of biding his time, all the planning and the endless plotting of strategy; all ended tonight. Oswynn was dead, Flood and Glenthorpe were ruined and might very well die at the hands of the mysterious villain who had adopted the guise of Renwick Deveridge's ghost. Surely it was enough.

He realized that he was waiting for something, but he felt nothing. Where was the satisfaction? The sense of justice done? A bit of peace?

He listened to the applause spilling out of the Silver Pavilion. The demonstration of mesmerism had just ended.

It occurred to him that he had been in a trance himself for the past five years. Perhaps Madeline was right. Mayhap he was eccentric in the extreme. What sane, clear-headed man spent *five years* plotting revenge?

He knew the answer to that question: A man who had nothing more important to live for than a cold vengeance.

The oppressive knowledge settled on him, as gray and featureless as the fog but far heavier on his soul. He walked out the west gate and started toward the first in the row of hackneys that loomed in the shadows.

He stopped when he saw the small black carriage waiting in the street. The exterior lamps glowed with ghostly radiance in the mist. The interior of the cab was cloaked in darkness.

"Bloody hell."

The emptiness inside him was suddenly eclipsed by anger. *She was not supposed to be here.*

He went toward the carriage. Atop the

box, the lump that was Latimer greeted him as he drew near.

"Sorry about this, Mr. Hunt, sir. Tried to talk her out of following ye tonight, but she would 'ave none of it."

"We will discuss the issue of who gives you your orders later, Latimer."

He yanked open the door and vaulted up into the unlit cab.

"Artemis." Madeline's voice was choked with some emotion that he could not immediately identify. "You met with those two men tonight. Flood and Glenthorpe. Do not bother to deny it."

He sat down across from her. She was heavily veiled as she had been that first night. Her gloved fingers were tightly clenched in her lap. He could not see anything of her expression, but he felt the tension that shimmered through her.

"I have no intention of denying it," he said.

"How dare you, sir?"

Her rage stopped him cold for a few seconds. "What the devil is this?"

"You did not even have the courtesy to inform me of your plans for this evening. If Zachary had not happened to mention that you sent messages to two gentlemen with whom you had business dealings, I would not have known what you were about. How could you do such a thing without telling me?"

Her anger baffled him. "My business with Flood and Glenthorpe tonight was none of your affair."

"You told them of their impending ruin, did you not?"

"Yes."

"Damnation, sir, you could have been killed."

"Highly unlikely. I had the matter completely in hand."

"Good God, Artemis, you orchestrated a showdown with your two greatest enemies and you did not even take Zachary along to guard your back?"

"I assure you, there was no need for Zachary to be there."

"You had no right to take such a risk. What if something had gone wrong?" Her voice rose. "What if Flood or Glenthorpe had challenged you to a duel?"

Her fury was unsettling and somewhat intriguing. She was, he realized, quite overwrought on his behalf. "Flood and Glenthorpe are not the sort who risk their necks in duels. If they were, I would have challenged them long ago. Madeline, calm yourself."

"Calm myself? How can you even suggest such a thing? What if one of them had pulled out a pistol and shot you dead on the spot?"

"I was not entirely unprepared," he said soothingly. "I hesitate to remind you of my deficiencies, but I am Vanza, after all. I am not an easy man to kill."

"Your bloody Vanza training is not proof against lead, sir. Renwick Deveridge was Vanza, yet I took a pistol and shot him dead in his own upstairs hall."

The carriage was in motion but the silence inside was so loud that it masked the clatter of wheels and hooves. Madeline listened to the echo of her own confession of murder and wondered if she truly had gone mad. After all the months of keeping her great secret — a secret that could get her hanged or transported — she had blurted it out in the course of a flaming row.

Artemis looked thoughtful. "So the rumors and speculation are right. You did shoot him."

She tightened her hands in her lap. "Yes."

"And your recurring nightmare, I take it that it is a fairly accurate account of events that evening?"

"Yes. I did not tell you the first part."

"The part where you shoot Deveridge."

"Yes."

He did not take his gaze off her. "Nor did you tell me why you were so desperate to unlock the bedchamber door even though the house was burning down around your ears."

"Bernice was inside the bedchamber."

There was a beat of grim silence.

"Bloody hell." Artemis contemplated that for a moment. "How did she come to be locked in the room?" he finally asked.

"Renwick kidnapped her that night after he poisoned my father." Her fingers ached. She glanced down and saw that she had clenched her hands into a single fist. "He brought her to his own house, bound and gagged her, and left her to die in the blaze."

"How did you find her?"

"Papa was still alive when I discovered him. He told me that Renwick had taken Bernice and that eventually he would come for me. He told me that swift, decisive action was my only hope. He bid me remember all that he had taught me of Vanza."

"What did you do?"

"I followed Renwick to the house. By the time I arrived, he had already set the fire in the laboratory. He was preparing to ignite another blaze downstairs in the kitchens. I entered the garden, looked up, and saw Bernice's face in the window of the bedchamber. She had managed to drag herself that far, but her hands were still bound. She could not open the window. I had no means of climbing up to it."

"So you went into the house?"

"Yes. There was no other choice." She closed her eyes as the memories rushed back with chilling speed. "Renwick was still in the kitchens. He did not hear me. I went up the stairs and down the hall to the bedchamber. It was quite dark except for the glow of the fire on the rear stairs."

"You found the bedchamber locked."

She nodded. "I tried to use a hairpin. I could hear the crackle of the flames. I knew I didn't have much time. Then, quite suddenly, *he* was there in the hall. He must have seen me on the stairs."

"What did he say to you?"

"He laughed when he saw me crouched in front of the lock. He held up the key. And he laughed. 'Is this what you need?' he asked."

"What did you say?"

"Nothing." She looked at him through the veil. "The pistol was on the floor beside me, hidden by the folds of my cloak. He did not see it. Papa had told me that I must not hesitate, because Renwick was Vanza. So I said nothing. I reached down, picked up the pistol, and shot him dead in a single motion. He was no more than two yards away, you see. Striding toward me. Laughing like the demon he was. I could not miss. I dared not miss."

Artemis watched her with gleaming eyes. "And then you picked up the key, unlocked the door, and rescued your aunt."

"Yes."

"You are really quite incredible, my dear."

She stared at him. "I had never been so terrified in my life."

"Yes, of course," he said. "That is what makes it all so amazing, you see. I do not wish to make you dwell on the subject any longer than necessary, but I must ask you again, since you and your aunt were the last to see Renwick alive, are you quite positive that he died that night?"

She shuddered. "Yes. Bernice made us stop long enough for her to make certain. She said we could not make any mistakes, because he was such a mad and dangerous man."

"He was also a very cunning man."

She collected herself and fixed him with a determined look. "Almost as clever and cunning as you, sir. Nevertheless, he was not clever or cunning enough to evade a bullet."

"I take your point and I thank you for your concern."

"Damnation, Artemis, do not treat me as though I were a featherbrained idiot. I know what a bullet fired at very close range can do to a man's chest."

"Indeed. Why did you choose this moment to tell me the truth about what happened that night?"

She stiffened. "I assure you I did not intend to confess to murder."

"Self-defense."

"Yes, well, not everyone would believe that, Artemis."

"I believe it."

"Forgive me, sir, but you are taking the news that I am a murderess somewhat casually, to say the least."

He smiled slightly. "No doubt because it is not exactly news. I have been quite certain for some time that either you or your aunt shot Deveridge. Of the two, I was inclined to put my money on you. Bernice would have done the deed with poison, not a pistol."

"I see." She looked down at her tightly clasped hands. "I'm not sure what to say to that."

"There is no need to say anything." He paused. "But concerning the manner in which you flung the truth . . ."

"I cannot imagine what came over me. I must have lost my mind." She frowned. "No, not my mind, my temper. How *dare* you risk your neck the way you did this evening?"

"Why are you so angry with me?" he asked evenly. "Is it because you fear that if I get myself killed by Glenthorpe or Flood, you will be deprived of my services?"

A pure, cleansing rage swept through her. "Bloody hell, Artemis, you know that is not true. I am furious because I cannot bear the thought of anything happening to you."

"You mean that you have grown fond of me, in spite of my Vanza past? You feel you can overlook my connections to trade?"

She gave him a fulminating look. "I am in no mood for jesting, sir."

"Nor am I." Without warning, he reached for her. His hands closed around her shoulders. "Tell me precisely why you cannot bear the thought that I might get myself killed."

"Don't be an ass, sir," she said through her teeth. "You know perfectly well why I don't want you injured or worse."

"If it is not because you dislike the notion

of being put to the trouble of finding your-self another Vanza expert, is it because you cannot stand the thought of shouldering still more guilt? Is that the reason you are so worried about me?"

"Damnation, Artemis."

"You fear that if something happens to me while I am in your service, you would be obliged to accept the responsibility, just as you do for what happened to your father, don't you?"

She suddenly realized that he, too, was seething. "Yes, that is part of it. I do not need any more guilt, thank you very much."

"You will not take responsibility for me, madam." His voice was as cold and sharp as a blade. "Is that understood?"

"I will take whatever I bloody well please."

"No, you will not." He removed his right hand from her shoulder, seized the trailing edge of her veil, and tossed the gauzy net-ting back over her head. "We are both in this affair together and we will see it through together."

"Artemis, if anything happens to you, I believe that I truly will go mad," she whis-pered starkly.

He caught her face between his hands. "Listen closely. I make my own decisions. It is not your place nor your right to assume the blame for whatever happens because of those decisions. Devil take it, Madeline, I am not your *responsibility*."

"What are you, then, sir?"

"By God, madam, I am your *lover*. Do not ever forget that fact."

He crushed her mouth beneath his own and then he pushed her back and down onto the cushions. The weight of his body pinned her to the seat. His leg crumpled the folds of her gown.

"Artemis."

"A few minutes ago as I walked out of the Dream Pavilions, I felt as if I were moving out of a trance." He framed her face between his hands. "A trance that lasted for five long years. My plans for vengeance were all that had kept me going during those years. Tonight I realized for the first time that there is now something infinitely more important in my life."

"What is that, Artemis?"

"You."

He bent his head and sealed her mouth with fierce, demanding kisses. Near-violent sensations, his as well as her own, scalded her senses. She clung to him, kissing him back with the same raging passion that he showered on her.

His mouth traced a trail of heat down her throat. "I am your lover," he said again.

"Yes. *Yes.*"

He shoved her skirts up to her waist. She felt his hands, warm and possessive, on her bare skin just above her garters.

He found her with his fingers first, working her to a fever pitch of desire with only a few swift strokes.

"You respond to me as though you were made for me." There was awe in his husky voice.

She felt the full crown of his erect manhood pressing against her and realized that he had somehow managed to unfasten his trousers. He grasped one of her ankles and then the other. He tugged both over his shoulders. Between the enveloping folds of her gown and cloak and the thick shadows, she knew that he could not possibly see her, but she nevertheless felt utterly exposed. She had never experienced such intense vulnerability. Instead of alarming her, it only served to heighten her excitement.

And then he entered her with a single long stroke that filled her completely. She drew a shuddering breath but he began to move before she could adjust herself to him. His thrusts were quick, urgent, unrelenting.

The insistent tension in her lower belly

was suddenly released in dozens upon dozens of sweet, pulsing shivers that seemed to flow through her whole body.

She heard Artemis's muffled exclamation of satisfaction and release, felt the muscles of his back grow rigid beneath her hands. She held him close as he spent himself within her.

An hour after he went to bed, Artemis finally gave up the attempt to sleep. He tossed back the covers, got to his feet, and reached for his black dressing gown.

He crossed the room to the low table, sank down on the rug, and lit the meditation candle. Closing his eyes, he allowed the tang of the herbs to calm his restless thoughts.

After a time he reviewed every plan, every precaution, every move he had made thus far, searching for flaws and weak points.

But when he had satisfied himself that he had done all he could for the moment, his thoughts were once more roiled by the image of Madeline.

He had to keep her safe. She was the one who had brought him out of his long trance.

Chapter Nineteen

The glittering chandeliers lit the long ball-room with a brilliant glow. Everyone who was anyone had come to be entertained at the home of Lord Clay and his lady, a noted hostess. In spite of knowing the real reason she was here tonight, Madeline could not help but be slightly dazzled. She had spent very little time in Society before her marriage and none at all afterward. It truly was another world, a realm as filled with sparkling illusions as the Dream Pavilions.

She stood with Bernice near the open French windows and watched as women in weightless gowns swam the waltz in the arms of elegantly garbed gentlemen. Liveried footmen circulated through the crowd with silver trays laden with champagne and lemonade. Brittle conversation and artificial laughter did battle with the music.

Bernice eyed her from head to toe and beamed with satisfaction. "You can hold your own with any woman here tonight, my dear."

Madeline glanced down at her pale yellow satin skirts and wrinkled her nose. "Thanks to you."

"Humph. The thanks go to Hunt. He was the one who stood his ground and insisted that you not wear black tonight. I must say, it is about time that you started dressing in a manner befitting the young woman you are."

The yellow satin gown had materialized as if by magic that afternoon, together with a skilled seamstress who had fitted it carefully to Madeline's figure. Matching gloves and kid dancing slippers had also appeared out of thin air.

Bernice had been so pleased with herself that Madeline knew she had been in on the scheme. But it was the glinting look of masculine pleasure in Artemis's eyes that had convinced her that perhaps it was time to put her mourning for her father behind her.

It had been Artemis's idea to take advantage of the fact that the Clay mansion would be filled to overflowing tonight. A perfect opportunity to search his lordship's study, Artemis had explained. They needed to know what Clay had done with the large quantity of sleeping herbs he had purchased at Moss's Apothecary.

Madeline glanced uneasily toward the grand staircase. Artemis had disappeared half an hour ago to conduct his clandestine search. There had been no sign of him since.

"He has been gone a long time," she muttered to Bernice.

"I'm sure there is no cause for concern. Hunt is far too clever to get caught in the act of searching Clay's study."

"I am not worried about him getting caught. I am annoyed because he got the easy part of this night's business. He left me to handle the difficult end of things."

"What on earth are you talking about?"

"Isn't it obvious? I am the one who must deal with all these stares and sly comments. Didn't you notice the stir that went through the crowd when we entered the ballroom? I vow, it is as if all of these people have nothing better to do than gossip about the fact that Artemis Hunt is with the Wicked Widow tonight."

Bernice chuckled. "You are quite correct, my dear. None of these people has anything better to do than discuss that fact. Your connection with Hunt is obviously the latest topic of interest in the ton."

"It is rather like being part of an attraction at the Dream Pavilions. I ought to make these people purchase a ticket."

"Come now, it is not that bad."

"Yes, it is. I would much rather be the one searching Clay's study. It would serve Artemis right to be down here on the receiving end of all these curious glances."

"The Polite World grows weary of gossip quite rapidly," Bernice assured her. "The news that you are involved with Hunt will soon cease to be titillating."

"I certainly hope you are correct."

"Bernice." The unfamiliar voice was sharp with feigned surprise. "So good to see you again. It's been such a long time."

Madeline turned to see a middle-aged woman in rose colored silk bearing down on them. The lady regarded her through a quizzing glass.

"You are Mrs. Deveridge, are you not?"

Madeline decided on the spot that she did not like the woman. "Have we been introduced, madam?"

"Your aunt can deal with the niceties. She and I are acquainted."

"Lady Standish," Bernice murmured. "Allow me to present my niece, Madeline."

"The Wicked Widow." Lady Standish gave Madeline a chilling smile. "One must admire Hunt's fortitude. Not every gentleman would be so brave as to take a lady with your reputation into his house."

Madeline was dumbstruck by the outright rudeness. Bernice, however, rose immediately to the occasion.

"Artemis Hunt is not your typical, timid

sort of gentleman," Bernice said easily. "Unlike your son, Endicott, who seems to prefer more tepid company, Hunt has a taste for intelligence and style."

Lady Standish's eyes gleamed with outrage. "And a taste for dangerous wagers, too, from all accounts."

Madeline frowned. "What on earth are you talking about, madam?"

Lady Standish's smile turned thin and nasty. "Why, my dear Mrs. Deveridge, didn't you know that your name is in the betting books of every gentlemen's club in town? There is a standing offer of a thousand pounds to any man who survives a night with you. I assume Hunt has already collected his winnings."

Madeline's jaw dropped.

"Never fear," Lady Standish continued. "Perhaps you can persuade him to split the profits with you."

Madeline was speechless.

Bernice was not. She eyed Lady Standish with the cool disdain of a battlefield general sizing up an opponent. "Obviously you have not heard that our host issued a challenge in his club the other night. He made it clear that any gentleman who mentions my niece's name in a manner that Hunt considers the least bit offensive will be invited to a dawn appointment. You might want to caution young Endicott. As I recall, he is your one and only heir. Be a pity to lose him in a duel over my niece's honor, would it not?"

It was Lady Standish's turn to gape. Shock appeared in her frosty eyes. "Well, I never —"

She whirled around and sailed off into the crowd without another word.

Madeline finally managed to collect herself. She turned on Bernice. "What was that about? Never say that Hunt has actually issued a challenge to any man who insults me?"

"Nothing to worry about, my dear. No one will be so foolish as to take him up on it."

"That is not the point." Madeline could scarcely contain her panic and fury. "Good God, I cannot allow Hunt to risk his neck in such a ridiculous manner. And why didn't anyone tell me about the wager in the betting books?"

"I knew it would only upset you, my dear." Bernice patted her hand. "You have had quite enough on your mind lately."

"But how did you come to hear of these things?"

"I believe Mr. Leggett may have mentioned them," Bernice said, cheerfully vague.

"I vow, I shall have a few words to say to him about this," Madeline seethed.

"To Mr. Leggett?"

"No." Madeline narrowed her eyes. "To Artemis."

Artemis heard the key rattle in the door lock just as he finished searching the last drawer of Clay's desk. Swiftly he put out the candle and stepped behind the heavy velvet drapery that cascaded down the side of the tall window.

He heard the door open. Someone entered the library. Artemis caught the glint of a candle, but he could not see who carried it.

"There ye are, Alfred," a voice said from the hall. "They're lookin' for ye in the kitchens."

"Tell 'em I'll be along directly. I've got to make me rounds first. Ye know how anxious the master's been about keeping an eye on his valuables since the robbery the other evening. He told me I was to be especially alert tonight on account of the house being filled with people."

"Huh. I'd hardly call it a robbery. The only thing that went missing was that jar of herbs he brought home from the apothecary last month. Good riddance, if ye ask me."

"No one's askin' ye, George."

That certainly answered the most pressing question of the evening, Artemis thought as he listened to the door close behind the retreating footmen. The sleeping herbs had been stolen. Another midnight visit from the mysterious ghost, no doubt. Lord Clay was evidently not involved in this affair.

Artemis stepped from behind the curtain. He let himself out of the library and went down the hall to the stairs. A few minutes later he made his way through the crowded ballroom to where Madeline stood with Bernice.

Some of the frustration that had resulted from his failure to gain any useful information in Clay's library faded at the sight of Madeline. She looked glorious, he thought. She put every other woman in the shade, not because she was the most beautiful lady present, but because, as far as he was concerned, she was the most riveting of them all.

He could not take his eyes off her as he walked toward her. He had been right about that particular shade of yellow, he thought. Sunlight was definitely her color.

"Good evening, ladies," he said easily as he came to a halt at Madeline's shoulder. "Enjoying yourselves?"

Madeline spun around. He was startled to see that her eyes were ablaze with anger.

"How dare you do something so idiotic?" she demanded without preamble. "What on earth were you thinking? Have you no sense at all? What made you do such a stupid thing?"

Mystified, Artemis glanced at Bernice for guidance. She merely raised her brows, gave a tiny shrug, and turned back to watch the dancers. He was on his own, he realized.

He looked into Madeline's irate eyes. "Uh —"

"Did you think I wouldn't discover the truth?"

"Well —"

"I cannot believe it."

"Believe what?" he asked warily. "If this is about my search of Clay's study, you were aware that I intended —"

"It is not about that and well you know it," she snapped.

He glanced around, taking note of the small group of ladies standing nearby. He reached for Madeline's arm. "I suggest we repair to the gardens for a breath of fresh air."

"Do not think you will get out of this by changing the subject, sir."

"First I must discover what the subject is," he said as he hauled her out through the French doors. "Then I will worry about changing it."

"Hah. Do not pretend ignorance."

"It is no pretense, I assure you." He brought her to a halt in the shadows at the edge of the terrace. "Now then, what is this all about, Madeline?"

"It is about what I am told occurred in your club."

He groaned. "Someone mentioned the wager."

"I do not give a bloody damn about the thousand-pound wager. One can only expect that sort of nonsense from rakehells who have nothing better to do than place bets on everything from flies on a wall to boxing matches."

He was truly bemused now. "If it is not the wager that has put you out of countenance, what the devil is it?"

"I have just been informed that you have issued a challenge to every gentleman in your club. Is it true?"

He frowned. "Who told you that?"

"Is it true?"

"Madeline —"

"I would remind you, sir, that we made a pact not to lie to each another. Is it true that you intend to challenge to a duel any man who insults me?"

"I think it highly unlikely that anyone will insult you in my hearing," he said as soothingly as possible. "So there is nothing to be concerned about."

She took a step closer to him. "Artemis, if you risk your neck in something so foolish as a duel over my honor, I swear I will never, ever forgive you."

He smiled slightly. "Never, ever?"

"I mean it."

He was aware of warmth unfolding inside him. "Do you love me a little, then, Madeline? In spite of my Vanza training and my connections to trade?"

"I love you more than I have ever loved anyone in my life, you crackbrained idiot. And I will not tolerate any more of this sort of foolishness from you. Is that quite clear?"

"Perfectly clear." He pulled her close and kissed her hard before she could realize just what she had said.

Chapter Twenty

Short John pulled the warm woolen scarf Mr. Hunt had given him more snugly around his neck and watched the two men emerge from the tavern. The cove on the left was the one he'd been following all day. Zachary had told him that his name was Glenthorpe.

"Devil take it, I feel a bit odd." Glenthorpe staggered on the steps. "Didn't think I'd had that much to drink tonight."

"You likely lost track, my friend." The man with the golden hair laughed. "But don't worry, I'll see you safely home."

"Kind of you, sir. Most kind."

Short John watched Glenthorpe stumble again as he went down the steps. The gent would have fallen on his face if the other cove, the one with the walking stick, hadn't reached out to steady him.

Short John felt a rush of anticipation. Visions of a nice profit danced in his head. Zachary had told him to pay particular attention to any gentleman who accompanied Glenthorpe.

The man with the walking stick had entered the tavern several minutes after

Glenthorpe, but they were definitely close companions now. Short John did not take his eyes off his quarry as he finished the meat pie he had snatched a short time earlier. He had been thinking of making his way back to the snug room above a stable that he shared with five other lads, but now he was glad he'd stuck to business.

The man who had come out of the tavern with Glenthorpe paused to put on his hat. Short John marveled at the way the cove's hair glowed in the lamplight. It looked as if it had been spun from the finest gold floss. But it was the walking stick that drew his professional attention. Red Jack, the receiver, would give him a nice bit of blunt for it.

Unfortunately, it did not look as if it would be a simple matter to make off with the stick. Glenthorpe might be foxed but the man with the golden hair looked fit and alert. Short John knew that his sort often carried a pistol.

Not worth the risk, he decided. In any event, Mr. Hunt would give him just as much for sound information as he could get from Red Jack for the stick. Furthermore, unlike the receiver, Mr. Hunt always paid promptly and well for services rendered. Short John believed in maintaining good relationships with customers who paid their bills in a timely manner.

The man with the golden hair raised his walking stick to hail a passing hackney. He bundled Glenthorpe into the carriage and then went forward to have a word with the coachman.

Short John inched out of his doorway and strained to listen as the golden-haired man gave instructions.

"Crooktree Lane, my good man." The rich, elegant voice echoed strangely in the fog.

"Aye, sir."

Short John did not wait to hear any more. He knew Crooktree Lane well. It was near the river. At this hour of the night it would be a dark, dangerous place inhabited by the nastiest sort of rats: the kind that went about on two legs.

Madeline was awake in her bedchamber, bent over the strange little book, but she could not focus on the gibberish on the page in front of her. All she could think about was the reckless manner in which she had blurted out her love to Artemis.

Thank heavens he had been too much of a gentleman to mention the subject again. Or perhaps he had been as shocked as she had been by the wild words. Perhaps they were the very last words he had wanted to hear from her.

He called himself her lover, but he had never claimed to love her.

There was a knock on the door. Madeline looked up, relieved by the interruption. She glanced at the clock. It was after midnight. "Enter."

The door opened to reveal Nellie, dressed in her nightgown and cap. "Beggin' yer pardon, ma'am, but there's a lad at the kitchen door. Demands to speak with Zachary or Mr. Hunt, but neither of 'em's returned yet."

Artemis had gone out earlier to make the rounds of his clubs in another attempt to pick up rumors and information. Zachary had accompanied him in the guise of coachman.

"A lad, you say?"

"Aye, ma'am. One of them boys what runs errands for Zachary and Mr. Hunt. He says it's important. Says he must speak to someone about a man he's been watching for two days."

"Glenthorpe." Madeline leaped to her feet. "Tell the lad to wait in the kitchens. I'll get dressed and come down at once."

"Yes, ma'am." Nellie started to retreat.

"Wait," Madeline called from the wardrobe. "Rouse Latimer. Tell him to hail a hackney. There should be some in the street at this hour. Hurry, Nellie."

Nellie paused. "Ye don't want him to horse yer own carriage, ma'am?"

"No, it might be recognized."

Nellie's eyes widened. "Is there some danger afoot, ma'am?"

"It's quite possible. Hurry, Nellie."

"Yes, ma'am." Nellie disappeared.

Madeline dressed swiftly, stepped into a pair of half boots, and bolted for the door. Halfway across the room she stopped and rushed back to the chest that sat beneath the window. She flung open the lid and seized the box containing the pistol and balls that lay inside. Then she grabbed the ankle sheath and knife her father had given her.

When she was ready, she let herself out into the upstairs hall, ran down the stairs, and arrived, breathless, in the kitchens. She recognized the scruffy boy with the eyes that were far too old for his face.

"Short John. Are you all right?"

" 'Course I'm all right." The words were indistinct because he had half a muffin crammed into his mouth, but there was no mistaking the note of disgust. "Came to make me report to Zachary or Mr. Hunt."

"They're both out. They are likely at one of Mr. Hunt's clubs. Tell me quickly what you saw tonight."

He looked dubious. "What about me fee?"

"I will make certain that you receive it."

He wrinkled his nose as he pondered that. Then he made his decision. "Saw Glenthorpe gettin' into a carriage with a man. Glenthorpe was drunk as a lord but the other cove was right sober. Heard him tell Glenthorpe he'd see 'im 'ome but then 'e told the coachman to take 'em to Crooktree Lane."

"Where's that?"

"Near the river. Not far from the south gate of the Dream Pavilions. I've been keepin' me eye on Glenthorpe fer two days now and I can tell ye that's not where 'e lives."

Latimer loomed in the doorway, struggling into a jacket. "What's this all about, ma'am?"

Madeline whirled around. "Have you got us a hackney?"

"Aye, but what's the hurry?"

"We must try to find Mr. Hunt at one of his clubs and go to Crooktree Lane at once. Glenthorpe has been taken there by a man who may be a —" She stopped short of uttering the word *killer.* She did not want to frighten Short John, although she doubted there was much that could alarm the street-wise lad. "He has been taken there by a man who may be quite dangerous."

Short John rolled his eyes. "She means the man what done in that gentry cove they pulled out o' the river. Zachary told me all about it." He reached for another muffin and took a healthy bite.

"Mr. Hunt said something like this might happen," Madeline explained. "He said it would give him a chance to catch the villain. But we must get word to him." She turned to Short John. "You may stay here with Nellie until we return."

"Don't worry about me," Short John said, reaching for another muffin. "I ain't goin' nowheres until I get me fee."

Artemis shrugged into his greatcoat as he walked swiftly toward his carriage. It occurred to him that this was not the first time he had been summoned from his club by Madeline. It was getting to be something of a habit.

He opened the door and vaulted inside while Zachary scrambled up onto the box to join Latimer. The hackney Madeline had used to drive to St. James disappeared into the fog, the coachman in search of another fare.

"Artemis." Madeline looked at him as he sat down across from her. "Thank heavens we found you so quickly."

"What is this all about?" he asked as the carriage clattered into motion.

"Short John saw Glenthorpe go off with a gentleman, just as you suggested might happen. Their destination is Crooktree Lane. I gather it is a disreputable neighborhood near the river."

"It is certainly not a fashionable part of town," he allowed. He studied the busy street through the window. "It is also conveniently close to the south gate of the Dream Pavilions."

"Convenient?"

"Close enough to drag a man after one has shot him dead. I wouldn't be surprised to learn that Oswynn was killed in Crooktree Lane before his body was left in the Haunted Mansion."

"First Oswynn and now Glenthorpe. I don't understand, Artemis. Why is the villain doing this? It makes no sense."

He looked at her in the shadows, surprised by her comment. "Don't you comprehend? He is determined to remove me from this affair. Apparently I am proving to be an obstacle."

"But how will killing your enemies get

you out of the way?"

"After his one rash attempt to dispatch me failed, he obviously concluded it was too risky to confront me again, so he has come up with another approach to the problem."

"What do you mean?"

"I believe that Oswynn's death was meant as a warning. But tonight our ghost no doubt intends a more direct threat. Perhaps he has concluded that if he can involve the Dream Pavilions in a murder scandal, he will cause me enough trouble to divert my attention."

"Yes, of course. Your business could well be ruined if the public were to learn that a dead body was found in one of the garden's attractions."

"Perhaps. Perhaps not." Artemis looked grimly amused. "It has been my experience that the public is inevitably lured by the most bizarre attractions. One can only speculate on the drawing power of a pleasure garden that was the scene of a prominent murder or two."

"What a ghastly notion. There really is no accounting for taste, is there?"

"I suspect that the threat to my business is the least of his goals."

"But what else could he hope to accomplish?"

He hesitated and then decided he might as well tell her the rest. "It's possible that his real aim is to implicate me in the murders."

"*You?*" Her eyes widened. "Good God, Artemis, do you really believe that if a body is discovered on the grounds of the Dream Pavilions, you, as the proprietor, might be viewed as a suspect in the murder? Surely that is highly unlikely."

"Not so unlikely if it gets out that I consider the dead man to have been my mortal enemy and that I had been involved in a scheme to destroy him," he said quietly.

"Yes, I see what you mean." She gave a visible shudder. "This villain obviously knows your deepest secrets. It is as if he really is a ghost who can walk through walls."

"He is trying to force me out of this affair so he can get to you," Artemis said. "He must suspect now that you possess the key."

Latimer's expertise with the reins and Zachary's knowledge of the less reputable areas of the city enabled the carriage to make excellent progress. Artemis instructed Latimer to halt the vehicle two blocks away from the locked gates at the south entrance.

"Why are we stopping here?" Madeline demanded.

"To cover all eventualities." He cracked open the door and jumped down to the ground. "Listen closely, my friends. Latimer, you and Madeline will stay with the carriage. Find a place from which you can watch the south gate without being seen."

Madeline stuck her head out the window. "Why must we stay here?"

"Because if Zachary and I are too late to prevent Glenthorpe from being killed, the villain will likely bring the body into the Dream Pavilions through this gate."

"I understand." Madeline fumbled in her reticule and produced her small pistol. "Latimer and I are to stop the villain if he gets past you and Zachary."

"No, you will not try to stop him." Artemis took a step that brought him very close to the window. "Listen to me and listen well, madam. You and Latimer are to watch him to see which direction he goes after he enters the park, but you are not to make any attempt to accost him. Is that clear?"

"But, Artemis —"

"The man is deadly, Madeline. You will not risk your neck or Latimer's. Just observe his movements. Nothing more."

"What will you and Zachary do?"

"We are going to try to catch the bastard before he does me any more favors." He looked at Zachary. "Ready?"

"Aye, sir." Eagerness and excitement hummed in Zachary's voice. He jumped down from the box.

Madeline leaned out of the carriage. "Artemis, you and Zachary must promise me that you will both be very, very careful."

"Yes, of course," he said.

He smiled slightly to himself as he turned away. Neither of them had brought up her fierce declaration of love last night. He had the impression that she wished to pretend it had not occurred, and he was content for the moment to play out the charade. She needed time to adjust to the notion of loving him, he thought. It had no doubt come as a great shock. She could not know how it had warmed his soul.

He motioned to Zachary. "Let us be off."

He led the way down a nearby alley that would take them to Crooktree Lane. Zachary followed quickly, a silent shadow at his side.

The glow of moonlight in the fog and the occasional lamp-lit window provided enough light to guide the way. Here and there a prostitute turned up her lantern and called to them from a doorway.

They passed through the web of narrow streets and alleys that bordered their destination without incident and emerged into a narrow, sharply angled passage.

"This is Crooktree Lane, sir," Zachary said. "I used to come here often enough in my former career. A lot of the lads know it because Red Jack has a shop nearby. A fine receiver he is, but very particular. Only accepts the best wares."

"I'll take your word for it." Artemis surveyed the street from the mouth of the tiny lane in which they stood. "I had hoped to get here before the hackney dropped off our quarry, but it appears we are too late. I do not see a carriage —"

He was interrupted by the rumble of hooves and wheels.

"There," Zachary whispered.

A hackney rounded the twist in Crooktree Lane with great caution. The lamps glared weakly. The coachman wielded the whip briskly, exhorting his horse to a trot, but the nag showed no enthusiasm for the effort.

"Faster, old gel." The coachman's voice was a rough, urgent growl. "This ain't the sort o' neighborhood either of us wants to 'ang about in on a night like this."

Artemis stepped out into the street as though he wished to hail the vehicle. "A moment of your time, sir."

"What's this?" Startled, the coachman reined in his horse and peered uneasily at Artemis. He relaxed a little when he saw the expensive greatcoat and gleaming boots. "Are ye needin' a coach, sir?"

"What I need is information and I need it quickly." Artemis tossed the man a coin. "Did you just set down some passengers?"

"Aye, sir." The coachman plucked the coin out of the air and pocketed it with professional dexterity. "Two coves, one of 'em so drunk 'e could 'ardly stand. The other tipped me quite 'andsomely, 'e did."

"Where did they leave your coach?"

"Just around the corner at number twelve."

Artemis tossed another coin to the coachman. "For your trouble."

"No trouble at all, sir. Will you be wantin' transportation?"

"Not tonight."

Artemis moved back into the shadows. The coachman sighed and jiggled the reins. The hackney lumbered off down the street.

"We may be in time after all." Artemis removed his pistol from the pocket of his greatcoat. "But we must move quickly."

"Aye." Zachary checked his own pistol.

Artemis led the way, hugging the deepest

shadows. He felt a peculiar flash of almost paternal pride when he realized that Zachary was making as little noise as himself. The younger man was taking to his Vanza lessons with alacrity.

For some reason, that made him think fleetingly of what it might be like to have a son of his own. Or perhaps a headstrong daughter with her mother's eyes. Madeline's eyes . . .

He pushed the wistful feeling aside. He had other, more pressing matters to deal with tonight.

"Why in bloody blazes d'ye want to go into that foul alley, sir?"

Artemis stilled. Glenthorpe. There was a response — a man's voice. Very low. It was impossible to make out the actual words, but the impression of growing impatience was clear.

Zachary halted and looked at Artemis, awaiting instructions. The sound of stumbling footsteps echoed in the night.

Glenthorpe whined again. "I don't want to go in there. You said we were going to a tavern. But there aren't any lights. Shouldn't there be lights?"

Artemis raised his pistol and flattened himself against the stone wall at the mouth of the alley. He peered around the corner.

In the dim glare of the lantern that Glenthorpe's companion carried, he could make out the dark figures of the two men. Both wore greatcoats and hats.

"Yes, Glenthorpe," Artemis said coldly, "there should most assuredly be some lights."

The man with the lantern whirled around. At this distance and in the poor light, it was impossible to see his face clearly, but Artemis got the impression of narrow, fine-boned features and glittering eyes.

"What's this?" Glenthorpe, struggling to maintain his balance, grabbed hold of his companion's shoulder. "Who goes there?"

With remarkable speed the other man dropped the lantern, disengaged himself from Glenthorpe, and fled toward the far end of the alley.

"Bloody hell." Artemis bolted after him.

"Watch out, he'll have a pistol," Zachary called.

At the same instant, Artemis saw the movement of his quarry's arm. The weak illumination glinted on the barrel of the gun. Light flashed as the spark struck the powder. The shot crashed loudly in the darkness.

Artemis had already moved, flinging himself to the greasy paving stones. He fired his own pistol simultaneously but he knew the shot would probably go wild, just as the villain's had. Pistols were not accurate at this distance.

He rolled to his feet immediately and started down the alley again. But the fleeing man was already halfway up the wall at the end of the street. The folds of his greatcoat flared out like huge, dark wings.

The bastard was climbing a rope ladder. Artemis realized that the villain must have left it handy for himself long before he brought Glenthorpe into the alley. He had planned to commit cold-blooded murder tonight, and naturally, he'd had his escape route readied well in advance.

The wings of the black greatcoat flapped once more and then vanished through a window.

Artemis seized the trailing end of the rope, but the villain had loosened it from its moorings above. It fell to the pavement at his feet. The small anchor hooks rattled on the stone.

Artemis knew that his quarry would be long gone before he could secure the ladder again.

"Bastard."

He had not even gotten a close look at

the man who had fled.

But Glenthorpe had seen him, he reminded himself. And so had Short John. Before dawn he would have a good description of the ghost. For the first time they would have some solid, firsthand information about the villain. Progress at last.

He turned and went swiftly back toward the alley entrance, where Zachary waited with the slumped Glenthorpe.

"Flood claimed that you were trying to frighten us." Glenthorpe sat limply in the chair in Artemis's library, hands dangling between his knees, and stared at the carpet. "He said there was no mysterious villain. Said Oswynn had got himself murdered by a footpad, just as the newspapers had it. He said that you wouldn't kill us outright because you wanted us to savor our ruin."

Bernice had given him a vast quantity of tea to drink, but it had taken over an hour for Glenthorpe to come to his senses. Now he appeared despondent but he had finally begun to speak in coherent sentences.

"Flood was right about my own goal," Artemis said. "But he was wrong about the killer. You met him yourself tonight. He is no ordinary footpad. I want to know precisely how that meeting came about. Tell me every word you can recall of his conversation."

Glenthorpe grimaced and rubbed his temples with one hand. "Can't remember much of it. Had a lot to drink, y'see. Trying to forget the state of my finances. He must have joined me at the table at some point. I remember he said something about an investment he was considering."

"What sort of investment?" Madeline asked quietly.

"Something to do with building a canal for barges. Can't recall the details. We had a glass or two while he explained things. He made it sound like a fine opportunity, a way for me to recover from my losses in the gold mine venture."

"What did he tell you to make you go with him?" Artemis asked.

"Can't recall exactly. Something about finding a place to discuss our business in private. I must have told him that I was interested in the canal shares. The next thing I knew, we were in a carriage. Then that alley." Glenthorpe raised his head to peer blearily at Artemis. "I realized that something was very wrong then, but I couldn't think of what to do about it. My mind was in a fog."

"He fed you some sort of drug," Bernice said.

"Yes, I suppose that must have been the case," Glenthorpe muttered.

"But he told you nothing about where he lived?" Artemis prodded. "What coffeehouses he patronized? Did he name a brothel or a tavern?"

"I don't recall —" Glenthorpe broke off, scowling intently. "Wait, I believe he said something when we passed a tavern."

Artemis moved to stand in front of him. "What did he say?"

Glenthorpe shrank back in the chair. He swallowed a couple of times. "I . . . I think I had just told him that I was bloody glad to have made his acquaintance because I was anxious for a good investment. He said he knew I was in bad straits. I asked him how he'd discovered that."

"What explanation did he give?" Artemis asked.

"He looked out the window. Saw the lights of the tavern. Said it was amazing what a man could learn if he frequented the lowest sorts of establishments in London."

"Did he say anything else? Did he mention which taverns he prefers? Did he give any indication of where he has his lodgings?"

Glenthorpe screwed up his face in intense concentration. "No. Didn't mention his address. Why would he? But when we drove through a little park, he said something about having been brought up in that part of town."

Madeline caught Artemis's eye. Then she looked at Glenthorpe. "What did he say about his past?"

Glenthorpe went back to staring at the pattern on the carpet. "Very little. Just something about how he and his half brother had once played games in that particular park."

"Golden hair. Blue eyes. Features perfectly suited to one of the romantical poets." Madeline shivered as she came to a halt in front of the fire. "He and his *half brother* once played games in a park."

"That explains the family resemblance that allowed Linslade to mistake him for Renwick." Artemis paused in the act of pouring a brandy. He glanced at her. "It also tells us why he has not allowed you to get a close view of him. He may look a little like Renwick, but they were not twins. You say Renwick never mentioned that he had a half brother?"

"No." She shook her head in exasperation. "I told you, Renwick lied to me from the day we were introduced. He told us he had been raised in Italy and that he was an orphan."

"Deveridge was obviously deep into the Strategy of Deception. He invented a whole new past for himself. He must have been a very skilled liar in order to deceive your father." Artemis paused. "And you."

"It was my own fault." She clenched one hand into a fist. "If I had not abandoned myself so quickly to a rash impulse, to what I took for lasting affection, I would have known soon enough that he was a charlatan."

"Indeed. Those rash impulses cause trouble every time."

She flashed him an irritated glance. "My foolishness amuses you, sir?"

He smiled slightly. "You are too hard on yourself, Madeline. You were a naive, inexperienced woman who was swept away by the excitement of her first serious romance. Everyone of us has, at one time or another, given in to the same rash impulses."

"Few have paid such a price," she whispered.

"I will not deny that. But then, few young ladies are confronted with such a clever viper as Deveridge."

She looked into the fire. "They must count themselves fortunate."

He set down his glass and came to stand behind her. He put his hands on her shoulders and turned her around so that she was obliged to meet his eyes.

"The important thing is that you did not allow yourself to continue to be deceived by Deveridge. Nor did you allow him to intimidate you. You took action to free yourself from the serpent's coils. You fought back with courage and determination."

She searched his face. "As your Catherine did?"

"Yes." He pulled her tightly into his arms. "In the end, you slew the dragon, Madeline. That is what matters."

She pressed her face into his shirt. "I am so sorry that your Catherine died in the course of her battle."

"I give thanks that you survived," he said into her hair.

For a moment she stood quietly in his arms. Then she blinked back the tears that threatened to soak his shirt, straightened, and wiped her eyes on the long sleeve of her gown. She attempted a somewhat tremulous smile.

"One thing is certain about our ghost," she said. "He shares Renwick's penchant for melodrama."

"Indeed."

She put her hand on the end of the mantel. "We cannot go on like this, Artemis. We must act. He has already killed one man. Tonight he tried to kill another and then he shot at you because you had cornered him. There is no telling what he will do next."

"I agree. We are getting closer to him each time he makes a move, and he knows it. He is very likely feeling unnerved now, perhaps even desperate after nearly getting caught tonight."

"My father was very fond of an old Vanza saying, 'Desperation breeds haste; haste sires mistakes.' "

"We must strike while he is still rattled from tonight's near miss," Artemis said quietly. "We have our bait."

"The key?"

"Yes. Now we must set our snare."

She gripped the mantel. "You have a plan?"

He raised one brow. "That is why you employed me, was it not? To craft a Vanza plan to catch a Vanza ghost?"

"Artemis, this is no time to dredge up old quarrels."

"Agreed." He held up a hand. "My scheme is only half formed, but if our ghost is as unsettled and enraged at this moment

411

as I suspect, it stands a chance."

She brightened. "Tell me about it."

"Its success will depend on two factors. The first is that the villain told Glenthorpe the truth tonight when he implied that he collected information in the taverns."

"And the second factor?"

Artemis smiled coldly. "Whether or not the villain shares his half brother's fatal flaw."

"What flaw is that?"

"A tendency to underestimate the female of the species."

Short John took the unusual step of paying for the meat pie. The temptation to pocket the coin he had been given and steal his evening meal, as was his custom, was almost overpowering. But in the end, far-sighted business thinking won out. Mr. Hunt had been very precise in his instructions, and Short John was determined to satisfy the client.

So he paid for the meat pie and then, relishing the luxury of not having to rush off down the street, he hung around the vendor's cart to exchange a bit of gossip.

The lad who operated the meat pie cart was only a few years older than Short John. He had a circle of acquaintances of his own, most of whom were not averse to sharing the occasional rumor during the slow hours of a long evening on the streets.

Short John was not the only one who had been given a coin and a promise of another if instructions were followed. Throughout the night, Zachary's Eyes and Ears drifted through the lanes and alleys of London. Some chatted with cooks and scullery boys taking a break from the hot fires of tavern kitchens. A few hailed hackneys for drunken gentlemen. Others paused to gossip with match girls and pickpockets.

At every point along the way, the rumor that was spread involved a sweet little old lady who was terrified of a ghost and desperate to get rid of a dangerous volume written in a strange foreign language.

"It's cursed," Short John explained somberly to several more pie vendors, pickpockets, receivers, and other business associates. "It's worth a lot of money but there's a ghost after it, y'see. Scared to death, the old lady is. Wants to find a way to give the book to the specter before it kills someone in her household."

Paul, who made his living holding horses for gentlemen while they patronized some of the more disreputable brothels, was skeptical. "How's the old lady gonna let the ghost know she wants to give him the book afore he murders her in her bed?"

"Don't know," Short John admitted. "But she says her nerves won't take any more haunting. She's taking tonics every few hours for 'em as it is."

Chapter Twenty-One

The message was delivered to Bernice the following day. An urchin contrived to collide with her outside the bookshop where she had just purchased Mrs. York's newest horrid novel. When she brushed off her skirts after the grimy encounter, she discovered the note that had been jammed into her reticule.

The excitement that burst within her threatened to wreak havoc with her nerves, but she reminded herself that she had a fresh bottle of tonic waiting for her at Hunt's house. She went straight back to the carriage and urged Latimer to drive home with all possible speed.

Once inside the front door, she flung her bonnet in the general direction of the hapless housekeeper.

"Where is my niece?" she demanded.

"Mrs. Deveridge is in the library with Mr. Hunt and Mr. Leggett," Mrs. Jones said.

Bernice waved the note in her hand as she dashed through the open door. "The plan worked. The villain has given me a message."

Artemis, seated at his desk, looked up

with the cool satisfaction of the hunter who knows that his prey is at last within reach. Madeline's reaction was just as satisfying. She looked first amazed and then euphoric.

But it was the expression of pride on Henry's face that warmed Bernice to the very center of her being.

"Congratulations, Miss Reed," he said. "Your acting these past two days has been nothing short of superb. If I did not know how strong-minded you are, I myself would have believed that you were a woman whose nerves have been strained to the breaking point."

"I like to think that I brought a degree of conviction to my role," Bernice said modestly.

"You were brilliant," Henry assured her with a fond look. "Absolutely brilliant."

"Actually, it was Artemis's plan that was brilliant," Bernice felt obliged to point out.

"It could not have been carried out so effectively without you, madam," Henry insisted.

Artemis exchanged a glance with Madeline.

She cleared her throat. "We can discuss the brilliance of all involved later. Read the note, Aunt Bernice."

"Yes, of course, dear." Aware that this

was her moment of glory, Bernice unfolded the note with a snap. "It is quite short," she warned. "But I believe it conveys precisely what Artemis anticipated.

"Madam:

If you wish to exchange the book for the life of one who is close to you, I suggest you make an excuse to attend the theater tonight. Bring the volume with you in your reticule. Say nothing to Hunt or your niece. Contrive to be alone in the crowd at some point. I will find you.

If you fail to follow these instructions precisely, my dear wife's life will be the forfeit."

"Interesting." Artemis leaned back in his chair, stretched out his legs, and crossed his ankles. "He wants a large crowd around to give him cover when he takes the book from you, Bernice. A combination of the Strategy of Diversion and the Strategy of Confusion."

Madeline frowned. "If he uses a disguise and is sufficiently clever, it will be difficult to spot him, let alone catch him in the throng outside the theater."

"He will make his move when I go to fetch the carriage after the performance," Artemis said with impressive confidence.

Bernice raised her brows. "How do you know that?"

"Because it is the only opportunity that I shall allow him," Artemis said with deadly softness. "I will not leave you or Madeline alone until that moment. This time we will play the game according to my rules."

Artemis had planned for every eventuality except the one that proved to be the most unsettling, Madeline concluded as the performance drew to a close that night. She had been so involved in the details of the scheme that she had not realized she would be the object of so many interested stares. It was worse than the night she had attended the Clay ball. Between acts the lights glinted on any number of opera glasses aimed in the direction of the box she shared with Artemis and Bernice.

For his part, she noted with some irritation, Artemis appeared sublimely oblivious of the speculative gazes. She had a suspicion that, unlike her, he had anticipated the attention they would draw. It did not seem to concern him in the least. He lounged in his seat with casual grace, commenting on the delivery of the actors and arranging for glasses of lemonade to be brought into the box. Unlike many of the other well-dressed gentlemen present, he did not make any excuses to pay calls on the inhabitants of the other boxes. He remained with his guests, the perfect host in every respect.

"Well, what did you expect?" Bernice murmured a few minutes later as they waited in the crowded lobby while Artemis went to fetch the carriage. "You are the Wicked Widow, after all. What is more, you have taken up residence in the man's home. It is all quite a delicious scandal."

"You told me that the news of my connection with Artemis would soon cease to amuse the ton."

"Yes, well, apparently it will take a bit more than an appearance at one ball and a night at the theater to render the topic boring."

"I vow, Aunt Bernice, I could almost believe that you are enjoying yourself."

"I have news for you, my dear, I am having an absolutely splendid time. My only regret is that Henry could not join us tonight."

"Artemis said that he needed Henry positioned outside the theater to watch for the villain. Zachary could not do the job alone."

"Yes, I know. Such a fearless gentleman."

"Artemis? Yes, he is, isn't he?" Madeline pursed her lips. "A bit too fearless, for my taste. I really wish that he did not have such a taste for —"

"I was referring to Mr. Leggett, dear."

Madeline hid a smile. "Yes, of course."

She started violently when someone jostled her elbow. But when she turned her head, she saw only an elderly matron in a pink turban. The woman moved on without paying her any notice.

The plan was a simple one. Artemis assumed that the villain would arrange to snatch Bernice's reticule just outside the lobby and escape into the streets, which were choked with carriages. But Zachary and Henry had been strategically stationed to keep watch. When the villain made his move, they would track him through the crowd while Artemis closed in on him. It was an ancient Vanza maneuver.

"I wonder if —" Madeline broke off as something hard and sharp jabbed the small of her back.

"Silence, my dear sister-in-law." The voice was low and masculine. It carried the underlying accents that had flavored Renwick's speech, but this was not Renwick. "You will do precisely as you are told, Mrs. Deveridge. My companion has an annoying little street urchin named Short John in one of those carriages outside. If you and I do not get into that vehicle together quite soon, he has instructions to slit the lad's throat."

Horror shot through her. The only thing she could think to do was to stall. "Who are you?"

"I beg your pardon, we have not been properly introduced, have we? Renwick died before you got around to meeting the rest of the family. We are not a closely knit clan, you see. Nor is our name Deveridge, as Renwick led you to believe. The name is Keston. Graydon Keston."

"Madeline?" Bernice turned to look at her. "Is something wrong?" Her eyes went past Madeline to the man who stood behind her. "Dear God."

"Give the key to your niece, madam."

Bernice stiffened and clutched her reticule with both hands.

"Do it, Aunt Bernice," Madeline whispered. "He has Short John."

"I also have a knife," Keston drawled. "In this crush, I can sink it between Mrs. Deveridge's ribs and be gone before anyone even sees her fall to the floor."

Bernice's shocked eyes flashed to Madeline's face. All of the cheerful excitement that had animated her a moment ago had vanished.

"Madeline," she whispered in a voice that quavered with fear. "No."

"I will be all right." She reached out and took the reticule from Bernice.

"Very good." Keston used the blade to prod her toward the door. "Now let us be off. You have caused me enough trouble, Mrs. Deveridge."

Madeline started forward and then stopped short as Zachary loomed in front of her. His grim gaze was on Keston.

"You must be the bodyguard," Keston said calmly. "I expected as much. Move aside or I will kill her right before your eyes."

"Please, Zachary, you must do as he says," Madeline whispered tightly. "He has Short John."

Zachary hesitated. There was a desperate expression on his face.

"Tell him about the knife I have in your ribs, my dear sister-in-law."

Zachary's jaw tightened at the words. He stepped back and disappeared almost immediately into the crowd.

"Gone to tell his master that the plans for the evening have been altered, I expect." Keston urged Madeline out into the fogbound night. "Did Hunt really think I would be so easily manipulated? He is not the only one who has studied the ancient arts of strategy."

He pushed her swiftly to the fringes of the noisy crowd that had formed near the carriages. Madeline felt his hand on her shoulder. He shoved her between several hackneys that were parked closely together. Drivers shouted. Horses flattened their ears.

She hesitated and promptly felt the point of Keston's knife in her back. She gasped, stumbled, and brushed up against the shoulder of a massive coach horse. Already made nervous by the congestion and the loud voices, the great creature took exception. Its ears went back and it half reared. The huge hooves came within inches of Keston's leg. A whip cracked loudly in the darkness.

"Have a care, you little fool," Keston snarled.

Yanking Madeline past the restive horse, he moved her quickly through the dense, chaotic maze of carriages and teams, dodging footmen and the flocks of young boys trying to earn coins by securing hackneys for those who had not arrived in private vehicles.

Halfway along the street, Keston pulled her to a halt. A carriage door flew open.

"Got her, I see." A large hand reached out to haul her into the unlit interior of the vehicle. "Hunt's mistress, ye say. Now, that presents some interesting possibilities."

Madeline smelled brandy fumes on the man's breath. His fingers were rough on her arm as he pulled her down onto the seat beside him. Her foot brushed up against a solid bundle on the floor. She looked down. There was just enough light from the outside carriage lamp to see a familiar face.

"Short John. Are you all right?"

He looked up at her with wide, frightened eyes and bravely nodded his head. She realized that he was bound and gagged.

Keston paused halfway into the carriage to call orders to the coachman. "Let's be off, man. There's extra blunt in it if you get us to our destination quickly."

The whip cracked ominously in the night, and the horses plunged forward.

"I believe we have an enthusiastic man on the box," Keston noted with satisfaction as he dropped into the seat across from Madeline. He lifted the edge of his cloak and deftly slipped his knife into a sheath strapped to his leg. Then he straightened and removed a pistol from his coat pocket.

He trained the weapon on Madeline. "We should arrive at our destination in short order."

"If you had any sense, you would free Short John and me and try to flee the country before Hunt tracks you down," Madeline said fiercely. "If you harm either of us, he won't stop until he finds you."

The man beside her stirred uneasily. "She's right about one thing. Bloody bastard never lets go. Who'd have thought that after all these years —"

"Shut up, Flood," Keston said.

Madeline whirled partway around in the seat to stare at the big man who loomed next to her. "You're Flood?"

"At your service." Flood's teeth gleamed in a brief, brutal grin. "On second thought, it will be you who will soon be at my service."

She turned back to Keston. "Flood was your source of information?"

Keston shrugged. "One of them. And only in recent days. Most of my information came from the taverns and from the odd bits and pieces I managed to acquire from my half brother's notes."

She glanced at Flood with disgust. "So you allowed him to use you. Don't you think that was a somewhat risky move on your part?"

"He didn't use me," Flood said loudly. "I'm his partner in this venture."

Keston smiled. "Flood has been most helpful. I have promised to reward him well, and, as it happens, thanks to Hunt, he is quite desperate for the money."

"It isn't only money I'll be collecting when this night is over." Flood leered at Madeline. "You're part of my reward."

"What are you talking about, you dolt?" Madeline demanded.

"Keston here has agreed to give you to me when he's done with tonight's scheme," Flood said. "I'm going to get a bit of my own back for what Hunt did to me. I'm going to use you well, my sweet. The way I used his little actress."

"How very odd," Madeline said. "And to think that Hunt always considered you the most intelligent of his three enemies. Obviously he was mistaken."

For an instant she thought he was unaware that he had just been insulted. Then Flood's face worked furiously. He reached out and slapped her hard. Her head snapped to the side. She sucked in a deep breath.

"We'll see how mouthy you are after I'm done with ye. Maybe you'll jump off a cliff the way his other whore did, eh? That should prove amusing."

"Enough," Keston said. "We do not have time for these games. Open the reticule she has in her hand. There should be a book in it. A small, slender volume bound in red calf."

Flood snatched Bernice's large reticule from Madeline's grasp and yanked it open. He reached inside, fumbled around, and brought out a package wrapped in cloth.

"Still don't understand why you've gone to all this trouble for a bloody damn book," Flood muttered.

"My aims in this matter need not concern you," Keston said tersely. "Unwrap the volume and give it to me. I want to make certain that I have not been duped."

Madeline heard fabric rip in the shadows.

"Here's your damned book." Flood handed the volume to Keston. Then he reached back into the reticule and removed another object. "Aha, what have we here?"

Madeline glanced at the small flask he held. "That belongs to my aunt. She always carries a bit of brandy with her. She uses it for a tonic in emergencies. She has very weak nerves."

"Brandy, eh?" Flood removed the top of the bottle and sniffed the contents with great interest. "Some of Hunt's best, I'll wager."

He downed the contents in a single swallow.

Keston looked disgusted. "No wonder Hunt's scheme to ruin your finances worked so well, Flood. You have no control over your own urges, do you?"

Flood glared at him as he wiped his mouth with his sleeve. "You think you're so bloody clever, but where would your plans be without me, eh?" He hurled the little bottle out the window. "You'd have got nowhere without me and don't you forget it, sir."

Madeline ignored Flood. The carriage was flying along at a great speed, making things most uncomfortable inside the vehicle. After a particularly violent lurch, she felt Short John bump onto his side, facing her foot. She prodded him with her toe, willing him to search for the small blade sheathed just beneath the hem of her gown.

"So this is what all the fuss is about, eh?" Keston spoke to himself as he held up the book.

Madeline sensed his excitement. "That is the key you seek." She thrust her ankle into Short John's fingers. "Although I cannot imagine it will do you any good without the *Book of Secrets*. Surely one is of no use without the other."

"So you know about the rumors concerning the old volume, do you?" Keston asked. "Not surprising, I suppose. They have been floating around since before Lorring's death."

"Only the most eccentric members of the Vanzagarian Society believe the *Book of Secrets* actually exists," she said.

"Eccentric or not," Keston said easily, "there are some extremely wealthy members of the Society who will pay a fortune for this little volume. Many are convinced the *Book of Secrets* survived the fire in Italy. The fools will waste their lives searching for it. But in the meantime they will pay dearly for the key because they will believe that it will bring them one step closer to the ultimate secrets of Vanza."

She searched his face in the shadows. "Do you not seek those secrets for yourself?"

Keston uttered a crack of humorless laughter. "I'm not the madman that my half brother was, Mrs. Deveridge. Nor am I a complete crackpot, like so many of the doddering old fools in the Vanzagarian Society."

"For you, this has been about money right from the beginning, has it not? You did not come to London to avenge Renwick."

Keston's chuckle held the echo of a

demon's amusement. "My dear Mrs. Deveridge. Don't you know Vanza teaches that all strong emotions are dangerous? Vengeance requires a degree of passion that can cloud the mind and cause one to do irrational things. Unlike Renwick, I do not allow myself to be guided by my passions. I certainly would not go out of my way to avenge the fool."

"But he was your brother."

"My half brother. We shared a father but not a mother." Keston stopped laughing very suddenly. His eyes glittered in the shadows. "The last time I saw Renwick, it had become obvious he was falling victim to the same insanity that infected our sire."

"But you both studied Vanza."

"That was because our father was deeply involved in the philosophy." Keston studied the gold handle of his walking stick. "Looking back on it now, I realize that dear Papa was quite mad early on. He was convinced that the great secrets of the world were to be found in the alchemical notions that lie at the heart of the shadow side of Vanza. As we grew older, Renwick became obsessed with the same beliefs. In the end, his fascination with the occult destroyed him."

The coach bounced and swayed.

Madeline felt Short John's fingers close around her ankle at last. He had discovered the sheath. Neither man was paying attention to their smaller victim, but just to be on the safe side, she casually shook out the folds of her cloak so that the hem covered Short John's movements.

A thought struck her. "It was you who kidnapped my maid that night, was it not?"

Keston smiled approvingly. "Very good, my dear. Your logic is really quite astounding for a woman. Yes, I thought I would question the girl to see if she was aware of any books having been added to your father's library recently. But when the effort failed, I decided to concentrate my efforts elsewhere for a while. It took me some time to decide that the key must indeed be in your possession."

Flood burped and reached out to steady himself. He shook his head as if to clear it.

Madeline struggled to keep the conversation going. She had to hold Keston's attention at all costs. "I cannot help but notice that you carry a walking stick identical to the one Renwick used."

"Ah, yes." Keston smiled as he closed his hand more tightly around the golden knob. "A gift from our mad parent. Tell me, Mrs.

Deveridge, what did happen the night Renwick died? I confess I am somewhat curious. I find it difficult to believe that a common housebreaker managed to get the best of him."

"It was Renwick's insanity that got the best of him," she said quietly.

"Damnation." There was a note of astonishment in Keston's voice. "The rumors are true. You *did* kill him, didn't you?"

The carriage lurched and shuddered wildly as the team thundered around a corner. Madeline felt Short John slide the knife out from the ankle sheath. *Clever lad.*

"Bloody coachman," Flood mumbled as he seized the strap to steady himself. "He'll overturn us if he's not careful."

"The man is determined to earn his tip." Keston braced one hand on the edge of the door. The pistol in his fingers did not waver, however.

Flood lost his grip on the strap and toppled forward against the opposite seat.

"Bloody fool on the box," he grumbled as he pushed himself back into his corner. His words sounded slurred. "Driving too fast. What's the matter with the bastard? Tell 'im to slow down, Keston."

Keston gave him a thoughtful look. "How much claret did you drink this evening?"

"I had only a couple of glasses to steady myself."

"I have no use for a drunken assistant."

Flood rubbed his forehead. "Don't worry. I'll finish the job. Nothing I want more than to get my own back. Hunt's going to pay. By the devil, he'll pay."

"You'll soon have your chance for revenge, provided you do as you are told." Keston peered out through the window. "We are very near to our destination."

"What do you intend to do?" Madeline could no longer feel Short John's hands. She prayed that he was working on the ropes that bound his feet.

Keston's smile was feral. "We shall stop first near the south gate of the Dream Pavilions. I want to leave a last message on the grounds for Hunt."

"I see," she said coldly. "You're going to murder Mr. Flood and leave his body for Hunt to find just as you did with Oswynn."

Flood jerked around, mouth gaping. "What's this about murdering me?"

"Calm yourself, Flood." Keston sounded amused. "It is not your body I intend to leave inside the Dream Pavilions. It is the boy's body Hunt will find on the grounds."

Madeline felt cold sweat trickle down her back. "You cannot kill the boy. Please, there is no reason to hurt him, and you know it. He cannot harm you."

"It will teach Hunt a lesson."

Madeline glanced uneasily at Flood, who was swaying in his seat. She had to create a distraction. The only thing she could think of was to try to pit Flood against Keston.

"Why don't you tell Mr. Flood the truth? He is the one you intend to murder."

"Huh?" Flood squinted as though he could not focus clearly. "Why d'ye keep talking about murder, you silly bitch? I'm his partner in this venture. We made a pact."

She felt the carriage slow. "Don't you understand, sir? He no longer needs you."

"He can't kill me." Flood tried to steady himself as the carriage came to a shuddering halt. But he fell forward once more. This time he landed facedown on the opposite seat, partially covering Short John's legs. "We're partners," he mumbled into the cushions.

Making no move to right himself, Flood lay crumpled awkwardly in the middle of the carriage. As he let out a belch, his big frame rolled farther onto Short John's much smaller one. Madeline prayed that the boy could still breathe. A couple of twitches of his arm reassured her.

"My congratulations, Mrs. Deveridge." Keston surveyed Flood with raised brows. "What exactly was in that little flask he took from your aunt's reticule?"

"My aunt is very skilled with herbal tonics." She looked at him, trying to hold his gaze, willing him not to glance down at Short John. "It occurred to her that whoever snatched her reticule tonight might decide to help himself to the brandy."

"So she poisoned it. Well, well, well. A talent for deviousness must run in your family, my dear. First you managed to kill Renwick, no mean feat, and now your aunt has done in my so-called partner. The two of you are a surprisingly efficient pair of females."

"Flood is only asleep, not dead."

"Pity. I thought perhaps she had saved me the trouble of getting rid of him. Now I shall have to take care of the business myself." He motioned with the nose of the pistol. "Open the door, my dear. Quickly now, I do not want to waste any more time. Hunt will reason out soon enough that I intend to leave him another message in his precious gardens."

She hesitated and then slowly opened the carriage door.

"I will get out first," Keston said. "You

will follow and drag the boy out behind you. You needn't bother calling out to the coachman. He knows full well that I am the one who will be paying his fee tonight. He will not want to get involved in this affair."

Keston kept the pistol trained on Madeline as he moved toward the open door. He jumped down lightly onto the pavement, then turned to face her and reached into the carriage for an unlit lantern.

"Now come out slowly, Mrs. Deveridge." Keston lit the lantern as he spoke.

She reached down to touch Short John. He nodded his head once. She caught a glimpse of his unbound ankles, but he was pinned beneath Flood. He could run if she found a way to gain him the opportunity to escape.

"Tell me, Mr. Keston," she said as she prepared to alight. "How long do you think you will be able to elude Hunt? A day or two, perhaps?"

"I will allow the bastard to find me when and where I choose. And when we do meet again, I shall kill him. But first I want him to know that I have bested him in this affair. He may be a master of Vanza, but he is no match —"

The dark cloud swirled out of the night

sky without warning. The many-caped greatcoat dropped straight down on Keston, enveloping him in folds of heavy wool.

"What — ?" Keston's shout of surprise and rage was muffled by the coat, which covered his head and shoulders. He struggled wildly to throw it off.

"Get down, Madeline!" Artemis shouted as he followed his greatcoat to land on top of Keston.

Both men hit the ground with a sickening thud. The pistol roared as Keston blindly pulled the trigger. The shot went wild but the horses reared and lunged in panic.

"Short John!" Madeline whirled around to grab the boy.

Apparently sensing what was about to happen, he was trying desperately to scramble out of the carriage. But his movements were severely hampered by his bound hands and the dead weight of the heavy Flood.

Madeline felt the carriage lurch as the frightened horses heaved against their harnesses. In a few seconds they would plunge forward in tandem.

She managed to catch hold of one of Short John's shoulders. She tried to haul him toward the door, but she could not free him from underneath Flood.

Short John stared at her with helpless, terrified eyes. He knew as well as she did what could happen to passengers caught in a runaway carriage. Broken necks were common.

Frantic now, Madeline ignored the two men writhing on the ground and climbed back into the vehicle. A shudder went through it as the horses fought the harness. She knew the animals were on the verge of bolting.

She wedged herself against the seat and used it to gain leverage. She planted the sole of her half boot against Flood's ribs and shoved as hard as she could.

The carriage rolled forward.

She pushed harder. Flood's heavy frame finally shifted. Short John managed to wriggle out from under it. She seized him in a more secure grip. Together they leaped from the carriage and tumbled out onto the hard pavement.

The coach thundered off down the narrow street. At the corner the horses dashed to the left. The heavy coach swayed violently and overturned with great force. The horses broke free. Thoroughly maddened now, they pounded away into the darkness, leaving the carriage on its side, wheels spinning aimlessly.

Clutching Short John's arm, Madeline got to her feet and turned around in time to see that Keston had got free of Artemis. She expected him to try to flee into the night. Instead, with a shout of raw fury, he groped for his walking stick where it lay in the gutter.

Madeline thought that perhaps he would try to strike at Artemis with the stick. Instead he twisted the knob with a savage movement of his hand. In the light of the lantern, she saw a long, wicked blade emerge.

"Artemis!"

But he was already in motion. Half lying on the pavement, he swung his booted foot in a short arc that caught Keston hard on the thigh. With a scream of pain Keston fell back onto the hard stones.

Artemis was on him before Madeline could blink.

"Oh God, the knife," she whispered.

Short John wrapped his arms around her waist and buried his face against her cloak.

The combat ended with horrifying suddenness. Both men went still. Artemis lay beneath Keston.

"Artemis!" Madeline shouted. *"Artemis!"*

"Bloody hell." Short John raised his face and stared at the two men in shock. "Bloody hell."

After what seemed an eternity, Artemis heaved himself upward and rolled free of the unmoving Keston. Blood gleamed in the glare of the lantern.

Madeline threw the edge of her cloak around Short John, instinctively trying to shield him from the sight.

Artemis got to his feet and looked at her. He seemed unaware of the blood that dripped from the knife in his hand.

"Are you all right?" he asked harshly.

"Yes." She stared at the knife. "Artemis, are you — ?"

He looked down at the knife. Then he glanced at Keston. "I'm fine," he said quietly.

Short John shoved aside Madeline's cloak and demanded, "Is he dead?"

"Yes." Artemis flung the knife aside, which clanged loudly on the pavement.

Madeline ran to him.

Chapter Twenty-Two

"Who would have dreamed that Flood was involved?" Bernice shuddered. "And here I thought I was being so clever by putting that sleeping potion into my reticule. I intended Keston to drink it, not Mr. Flood."

"What matters is that Flood did drink it." Artemis eyed the glass of brandy he had just poured for himself. "And I, for one, will never look at brandy in quite the same manner again. I must thank you again, madam. Just as I thank you, Madeline, for rescuing Short John from the runaway carriage. All in all, there was very little left for me to do."

Madeline glared at him. "Do not make light of the events, sir. You could have been killed."

"Speaking of which," Bernice murmured, "I trust you are not too annoyed by Flood's untimely death in the carriage accident. I realize you had wanted him to suffer through his recent reversal of fortunes."

"I am done with elaborate schemes of extended revenge." Artemis glanced at Henry. "I have discovered that they tend to entail far too many complications and unforeseen consequences."

"A wise decision, sir," Henry murmured. "You have better things to do these days."

"Yes." Artemis looked at Madeline, who was curled on the sofa. "Most definitely."

Madeline looked up from the key she had been studying. "What of the sleeping herbs?"

"I found what remained of the supply that Keston had stolen from Lord Clay when I searched his rooms this morning," Artemis said. "I also discovered small quantities of other herbs that he must have used to drug his victims."

"Did you find anything else of interest?" Madeline asked.

"Yes. Keston's journal. The long and the short of the matter is that he has been on the trail of the key since he first learned of its existence several months ago. It took him some time to track it to London. After he got here, he narrowed his search to those gentlemen in the Society he deemed most likely to be capable of translating it. Then he systematically searched their libraries."

"It must have given him quite a shock the night Linslade discovered him," Madeline said.

"Yes. But it also gave him the idea of pretending to be his half brother returned from the dead. He determined to use the charade to terrify you after he realized you might be the one who had the key."

Henry swirled the brandy in his glass. "But by that time, Madeline was safely installed here in your house."

"Yes. He made one quick bid to get rid of me early on."

Madeline frowned. "The night he attacked you on the street."

Artemis took a swallow of the brandy and nodded. "When that failed, he realized I was going to be a bit of a problem."

"And that," Madeline said smugly, "was the understatement of the year."

"So he tried to encourage me to remove myself from the affair by interfering with my plans for Oswynn, Flood, and Glenthorpe, threatening to leave bodies lying about on the grounds of the Dream Pavilions."

"Which would have led to the discovery that you owned the pleasure gardens," Bernice noted.

Artemis smiled. "He was quite certain that I would do anything to conceal my connection to trade, you see. He assumed I put a great value on my position in the ton."

"When the truth of the matter was that the only thing you cared about was your vengeance," Madeline concluded.

Artemis met her eyes. "He could not have known I was rapidly losing my taste for that."

She smiled. "You really are an extraordinary man, Artemis."

"Even if I am Vanza?" he asked politely.

"Not every gentleman of the Vanzagarian Society is a complete crackbrain," she said magnanimously.

"Thank you, my dear. It is very reassuring to know that I have at last risen above the level of a crackbrain in your opinion."

Henry chuckled. Bernice looked amused.

Madeline turned pink. She waved the small book in her hand. "About the key, sir."

"What of it?"

"We really must decide what to do with it."

"Yes." His answer was unequivocal. "It is of no practical use without the *Book of Secrets*, but it will likely attract more trouble."

"I agree with you, but it is knowledge and it goes against everything my father taught me to willfully destroy knowledge. Who knows what value it may hold for those who come after us?"

"What would you suggest that we do with it?"

"The *Book of Secrets*, if it is ever found, belongs to the Garden Temples of Vanzagara," she said slowly. "I believe the key to the text belongs there, too."

Artemis thought about that for a while. "You may be right."

"A certain logic to that," Henry agreed.

"As far as I am concerned, the farther away it is from England, the better," Bernice put in with great depth of feeling.

"The question, of course, is how can it be safely conveyed back to Vanzagara?" Madeline mused.

Artemis smiled. "I can think of no safer way to transport it than as cargo on one of Edison Stokes's vessels. His ships call regularly in Vanzagara. Let him take the responsibility for protecting it en route. Whatever happens, we shall be free of the bloody book."

Chapter Twenty-Three

He promised himself that he would not put it off another day. He had to have the answer or he truly would become as crazed as any crackpot in the Vanzagarian Society.

But he could not ask the question inside the house. Perhaps it was his Vanza nature, but he craved the cover of darkness.

Madeline frowned when he asked her to accompany him on a walk in the garden.

"Are you mad?" she asked. "It's cold out there tonight. The fog is quite thick, too. We might very well take a chill."

He set his teeth. "I promise you that we will not stay outside long."

She opened her mouth. He could see the next objection forming on her lips. He braced himself for another round of arguments. Then she gave him a strange look. Without a word, she put down the book she had been reading and got to her feet.

"Give me a moment to fetch my cloak," she said. She brushed past him and went out into the hall.

He collected his greatcoat while he waited for her. When she joined him, they walked

446

down the rear hall together, opened the door, and stepped out into the night.

The fog pooled in the garden but the night was not as cold as Artemis had anticipated. Perhaps he was distracted by what lay ahead.

"I trust my aunt and Mr. Leggett are enjoying themselves at the theater tonight," Madeline said in a bright, conversational tone that sounded oddly brittle. "They make a charming couple, don't you agree? Who would have guessed?"

"Mmm." The last thing Artemis wanted to discuss was the rapidly blooming romance that had developed between Bernice and Henry. He had his own romance to worry about.

"I expect this is about getting rid of your houseguests, is it not, sir?" Madeline pulled the hood of her cloak up over her head. "I realize we have been a nuisance. I assure you, Aunt Bernice and I can be packed by morning."

"There is no hurry. My household appears to have adjusted rather nicely to your presence."

"It is all right, Artemis, I assure you. We will be gone by noon."

"I did not bring you out here to discuss your departure. I want to —"

447

"We are both very grateful to you, sir. Indeed, I do not know what we would have done without your assistance. I hope that you are satisfied with your payment."

"I am content with your father's journal, thank you," he growled. "I don't want your bloody gratitude."

She clasped her hands behind her back. "Before I take my leave, I wish to apologize for several occasions on which I may have inferred that you were a trifle eccentric."

"I *am* eccentric. Probably a good deal more than just a trifle."

"I certainly never considered you a complete crackbrain." In the deep shadows her eyes were very earnest. "I want to make that clear. Indeed, it has been brought very forcibly to my attention lately that there is a strong strain of eccentricity in my own family from which I am not entirely exempt."

"Mmm. Well, there is that. Thank you for reminding me."

"You need not agree with such alacrity, Artemis."

"Early on in our association, you mentioned that you were quite taken with the logic that one must fight fire with fire, catch thieves with thieves, et cetera, et cetera. What do you think of the notion that it takes an eccentric to deal with an eccentric?"

She slanted him a distinctly wary look. "What do you mean?"

"If one follows your line of reasoning, one might conclude that the marriage of two noted eccentrics might prove quite satisfactory to both parties."

She cleared her throat. "Marriage?"

"Provided, of course, that the various eccentricities of the individuals involved proved complementary and compatible."

"Of course." Her words came hesitantly.

"I am of the opinion that you and I exhibit some mutually compatible eccentricities," he plowed on determinedly. "From time to time you have given me reason to believe that you might be in accord with that opinion."

She froze in the deep shadows of the high wall. Beneath the hood of her cloak her eyes were unfathomable. He realized that he was holding his breath.

"Good heavens, Artemis, are you by any chance asking me to marry you?"

"As you have noted, I have some serious drawbacks as a husband. I am Vanza, I am eccentric, I am in trade —"

"Yes, yes, I know all that." She cleared her throat. "I never felt that your being in trade was a serious barrier, sir. And as for your Vanza connections and eccentricities, well, I have my own, do I not? I can hardly complain."

"Nevertheless, you did complain."

"Really, Artemis, if you are going to hold every casual little remark that I might have made in passing against me —"

"Your feelings about Vanza aside, there are a few other problems, as well. I have spent far too long living alone and nursing a vengeance that I should have dealt with years ago. I expect those things have left their marks on me."

"We all carry the marks of our pasts, Artemis."

"I am no longer a young man with a young man's lightness of spirit." He paused. "I am not certain that I ever knew what anyone would call a lightness of spirit."

"You are hardly an old man, sir." She coughed slightly. "Indeed, I find you to be an excellent combination of maturity and agility."

"Maturity and agility?"

"Yes. And as it happens, I am not exactly endowed with what would be termed a young woman's lightness of spirit. So you see, we are quite well matched in that respect."

"Will you marry me, Madeline?"

She said nothing.

Despair lanced through him. "Madeline?"

She did not respond.

"For God's sake, Madeline, will you marry me?"

She groaned. "You are supposed to tell me that you love me first."

"I'm supposed to — ?" He caught her by the shoulders and said, "Devil take it, woman, is that why you hesitated and thereby nearly caused my heart to fail? Because I forgot to tell you that I loved you?"

"It is no small oversight, Artemis."

He stared at her. "How could you not know that I love you as I have never loved another?"

She smiled. "Probably because you failed to mention it."

"Well, I am bloody well mentioning it now." He hauled her close and kissed her soundly.

When she was breathless in his arms, he raised his head. "Will you marry me?"

"Of course I will marry you." She twined her arms around his neck and gave him a glowing smile. "Mature yet still agile gentlemen are not so thick on the ground that a woman in my position can afford to be choosy."

He looked into her loving eyes and felt happiness shimmer through him. "How fortunate for me."

She framed his face between her palms and kissed him in a manner that made his heart sing and his blood run hot in his veins.

"I do love you, Artemis."

He tightened his arms around her and savored the dizzying excitement and the joy that fountained within him.

"There is just one small thing," she began firmly.

"Anything, my sweet."

"There must be no duels. Is that understood?"

"I told you, it is highly unlikely that anyone would risk —"

She shook her head violently. "No, you must promise me, Artemis. Absolutely no duels."

Ah well, there were other ways to handle that sort of problem if it arose, Artemis told himself. He could be subtle when necessary. "Very well, no duels."

She laughed. The glorious sound floated up out of the high-walled garden, as light as happiness and as real as love.

The employees of Thorndike Press hope you have enjoyed this Large Print book. All our Large Print titles are designed for easy reading, and all our books are made to last. Other Thorndike Press Large Print books are available at your library, through selected bookstores, or directly from the publishers.

For more information about titles, please call:

(800) 257-5157

To share your comments, please write:

Publisher
Thorndike Press
P.O. Box 159
Thorndike, Maine 04986